PRAISE
FOR
THE MISSING

"A taut, incisive look at two lives as they slowly implode."
—*Kirkus Reviews*

"Ben Tanzer's latest novel, *The Missing*, combines master storytelling with an impeccable understanding of the human condition. It's an unflinching look at the way our frailties and failings cause ripples that reach out through space and time, and harm the ones we love most. Tanzer, in his own inimitable way, shows us that learning how something happened is the only way to fix what's broken, and heal the parts of ourselves that are not whole."
—**Giano Cromley, author of *American Mythology* and *The Last Good Halloween***

"*The Missing* is a hold-your-breath story exploring the many layers of love in a life, in a marriage, in a family. Vices and regret frozen in thin ice, nostalgia comforts and chokes. Ben Tanzer has written a book like a cigarette—smoke blurring out and swirling around what it means to be married, what it means to be a parent, what it means to be human... sinking, sinking into the mystery of what's truly missing. How and where to find it?"
—**Leesa Cross-Smith, author of *Goodbye Earl, Half-Blown Rose,* and *This Close to Okay***

"In this heady story of unwilling empty nesters, Ben Tanzer surfaces sharp insights about family, middle age, and the skins that people shed—and regrow—as they crash through the lake of life. If twenty years has ever felt like a blink, you will feel very seen by *The Missing*."
—**Chris L. Terry, author of *Black Card* and *Zero Fade*, co-editor of *Black Punk Now***

THE MISSING

by

Ben Tanzer

7.13 Books

ALSO BY BEN TANZER

After Hours: Auter (forthcoming)
Upstate (previously released as *The New York Stories*)
Be Cool
Sex and Death
Lost In Space
Orphans
My Father's House
You Can Make Him Like You
99 Problems
Most Likely You Go Your Way and I'll Go Mine
Lucky Man

Printed in the United States of America

First Edition
1 2 3 4 5 6 7 8 9

Selections of up to one page may be reproduced without permission. To reproduce more than one page of any one portion of this book, write to 7.13 Books at leland@713books.com.

Cover art by Alban Fischer
Edited by Leland Cheuk

Library of Congress Cataloging-in-Publication Data

ISBN (paperback): 979-8-9891214-2-7
ISBN (eBook): 979-8-9891214-3-4

HANNAH

If this was a movie or a television show, it would seem much too cliché to justify filming the scene as it's playing out. Gabriel and I are sitting on the couch, as is my father Ed, leaning forward, searching, hungry, waiting for something. Gabriel's parents, Bill, and Carolyn are at the kitchen table behind us, they're holding hands, grim-faced and stoic as ever. They look so old—reminiscent of Charlie Bucket's grandparents, except our parents can get out of bed, and we're not going to see any of them dancing in their nightclothes any time soon. Still, their skin is sallow, the bags under their eyes and their crow's feet take flight as we speak, the general fatigue of trying to stay strong during a trauma, breaking them down as much as it breaks us down.

I have no doubt this is horrific for them. As parents you don't want to outlive your children, much less your grandchildren. Which is not to say, we're about to get terrible news, or any news, but when the police ask you to gather, and your daughter's missing, while it might be good news, how good can it be?

There's a version of this scenario where while the police speak, they pause for some unknown reason, and your mind flashes to the things you'll never do with your child.

The birthdays you'll never celebrate.

The graduations and weddings that'll never happen.

The grandchildren you'll never meet.

And those are the big things—forget the lunches, phone calls, trips, and joyful tears.

Gone and never to be.

But whatever the reason for the pause, the need to gather one's words or clear one's throat, the police inform you they've found your daughter, unkempt, squinting and in shock, the real-world mashing into the surreal weirdness that's been her life on the lam.

But she's been found.

That's the point here.

They bring Christa home for a glorious, sad, amazing reunion.

There are so many questions to ask.

Just not now, not at this moment, not when the only important actions boil down to tears, hugs, making amends, and being home.

Home.

I look around our house for a moment. It's not shabby, it's homey, but Gabriel and I never did cross over into adulthood—did we? We never purchased nice furniture. The couch is the one I grew up with, and the rug is weathered, fraying at the sides, footprints worn into a path from the door to the kitchen. We planned on tearing it out and switching it to hardwood floors. What happened? I don't know. I do know the kitchen is more like those of college students, mismatched pots and pans, errant silverware.

Didn't I vow to do this differently than my parents?

Be better?

Gabriel touches my arm and I'm startled into remembering why we're here—we're supposed to talk to the police.

Officer John sits in front of us. He looks crisp in his uniform. His hat is neatly placed on the end table next to the chair. His shoes, gun, and belt are polished and shiny. His hair is beautifully slicked down, oiled, patches of salt and pepper peeking through.

Is it odd Officer John is someone we know from high school? That he was as notorious a drinker as anyone we knew growing up? How he was once someone who bragged at parties about driving drunk and who I now see from time to time working the holiday DUI checks? How about how he's a former star high school athlete now going slightly to pot, his paunch looming there in front of us, straining the otherwise wrinkle-free uniform? Or despite these things, he retains the confidence that former athletes, male athletes certainly, somehow hold onto for a lifetime regardless of what their life morphed into?

I'm the man, I own the room, and as needed, I own whoever is in it too.

He knows us—well, we know each other—but does he remember the one time we spoke?

Was it speaking?

There was a party near the end of junior year in high school. I drank way too much, and Gabriel was there, somewhere, and we weren't together yet. I was thinking about it—sort of—unsure and scared. Not wanting to ruin the one real friendship I had. Was I following Officer John around the house where this party was happening? A party I really didn't belong at. I was there because I'd gone with Alyssa, a girl I knew way back when, who was popular with her jet-black hair and olive skin. She had hooked up with Officer John, even though he was dating Maggie, a soccer goddess, which is why we were there in the first place.

So, yeah, okay, I was following Officer John—drunk and happy and feeling sexy and flirty. Why flirty? I don't recall. Were Gabriel and I fighting? I doubt it. We were all about a lack of confrontation then. We're barely good at it now. Preferring to let the bad energy, the cracks in our façade, drift away like puffs of smoke, floating there for a moment, and seeking attention, before ceasing to exist, unresolved and nowhere.

No, this approach hasn't served us well.

It has allowed us to keep the marriage going, stay together and get the small stuff accomplished—and we've done well enough with paying bills, parent-teacher conferences, tending to illness—but it couldn't, didn't help with Christa, how could it?

Jesus.

Gabriel was talking to Alyssa at some point, I remember now. It was too comfortable between them, and I didn't like it. It wasn't like Gabriel and I were together, we were friends. I hated it, even if there was no way something was going to happen between them. She wasn't ever going to hook up with Gabriel, never; she was too cool, and only trying to make Officer John jealous anyway. Not that Officer John noticed and not that Gabriel cared. Gabriel seemed like he would have made out with Alyssa on the spot if he could have. Check that, seemed, no, hard stop, he would have killed his mother to make-out with her right there on the couch even with the room packed with our classmates.

Okay, so fine, forget Gabriel, and if he was going to flirt and get it on with Alyssa, mostly wishful thinking—but still—I could too. Or at least pretend too, like he was. I wasn't going to make out with anyone anyway. Not with Gabriel there. This assuming I was even going to talk to Officer John, who was then shooting guard John and a senior. I didn't care about basketball, but we all watched John play. He was an artist out there. Jackson Pollack or Baryshnikov or someone like that. It was the way he moved without the ball. Or so my dad would say during games. Even adults loved watching shooting guard John back then. It couldn't be helped. There was a mythical beast in our presence, walking among the riffraff, and willing to share his powers for an allotted amount of time each week—and how couldn't we celebrate it?

What was the alternative, real life?

No, we weren't having that.

Had shooting guard John already drank himself off the team at the time of the party?

He had.

A god fallen to earth.

Did we feel for him?

We did.

So much.

Is that why I followed him around like a lost puppy that night? I don't think so. It wasn't empathy. It was his confidence and beauty, the cheekbones and swagger, a swagger he retained despite no longer being on the team.

He glowed and who didn't want to be around that?

Did shooting guard John and I find ourselves in the pantry?

We did.

I don't remember how, but we did, and I think I was willing to go in at first, but it was so cramped, and then shooting guard John was holding me really tight, and I wasn't sure I could breathe, not for long, and he was talking so much, pushing, asking for sex, saying he had heard in the locker room how I'd done stuff at parties before—that I was asking for it, seeking it, and now here he was cajoling me, pushing into me, his steamy breath slamming me in the face, the reek of Miller High Life suddenly everywhere, in every pore, and just as it felt like there was no room to move, shooting guard John looked at me and saw how freaked out I was. I could see him seeing me, and a sad, distorted look crossed his face. He pursed his lips, his eyes crinkling, he backed up, gave me a small wave, and left.

I stayed behind for a moment.

I took a deep breath.

I was appreciative he had walked away, and I hated having to feel like that.

I decided to never think about the whole thing again. When I left the pantry, there was Gabriel, smiling, looking for me—not making out with Alyssa—and wanting to ensure I got home safely.

Now, here we are, with Officer John, serious, and focused, the slightest smell of Miller High Life drifting across the room—I realize now we're never truly allowed to forget anything—and he's been talking for a while. The news isn't bad, such as they found

Christa dead somewhere, it's just nor can we expect the made for television tearful reunion and press conference where we thank everyone for their help, and man, we're so appreciative, and so happy to have her back safe and sound. Blessed really.

The thing is, we kind of expected this and we sort of believe Christa's okay anyway.

She's with Josh.

He works at her high school—maintenance.

He's nineteen and she's seventeen.

He has a stupid face and a bowl haircut.

Josh doesn't talk to his parents who live in some nearby town. I know this because Christa told me Josh stopped talking to them when they didn't approve of him dropping out of high school.

At the time I thought, what kind of parents do you have to be for your kid to willingly stop talking to you?

What do I know?

I know I didn't want her to see him. But I didn't expect them to last either.

We met him once.

He didn't make eye contact.

He stared at the ground.

His handshake was weak.

I didn't raise my daughter to be with someone like Josh.

But here we are.

Christa's note said, "don't worry, we'll be fine."

So yeah, Officer John's vibe is, there's no trace of her right now, and the police won't let the case go cold, but it's a small force, they don't know where to turn, Christa's at the age of consent, and when someone her age chooses not to be found, the police are kind of in a bind.

Officer John says, it's also important to acknowledge, that given Christa's note, and her age, this isn't a kidnapping, and not much of a missing person's case either.

But there can still be a happy ending.

It's only been three days.

We need to be positive, trust in the process, do our part, and the police will follow any tips that come in, keep talking to police across the country, and continue to check databases.

After his briefing, Officer John is gone, and we're right where we were before he arrived, nowhere really.

GABRIEL

Officer John is in our home, right here, in front of us. The home Hannah and I paid for ourselves, something I've always been proud of. It's also the home Hannah and I built together, and it's filled with personal touches that mean so much to us. The hand-carved bookshelf we bought on the cheap from an antique store just outside of town, the Lladró figurines and art deco lamps we found at estate sales, the colorful throw rugs with their array of geometric patterns we selected together with care and the couch we saved from Hannah's father's home and reupholstered. Some of the stuff is old, but it's ours, and it's a manifestation of how we want to present ourselves to the world.

But I'm getting distracted.

What's important is that Hannah and I have no idea what Officer John is going to say, and we're waiting with bated breath. Still, to act like it isn't weird to acknowledge that Officer John wasn't once superstar shooting guard John, and railroaded off the basketball team for drinking—are you serious?—drinking is a birthright around here, thus costing us the state title, and him the untold glories he deserved, doesn't make sense to me.

We'd kind of been friendly once.

Shooting guard John had been known for drinking, sleeping

with girls, and shooting the lights out on the basketball court. Most of us had never seen a player like him—not in person. He floated above the court. I don't know if he touched the ground then, on court or off.

The dude was golden.

Shooting guard John was also really into the X-Men, which seems dumb to focus on now, when he's come to talk about Christa, but this is how I knew him.

Officer John isn't talking yet. He's collecting his thoughts. You can see the words forming in his brain and moving to his lips, the jaw of his still handsome mug flexing and unflexing as he thinks about what to say.

It's stunning how some people retain their looks. Yes, there are spots of grey in his hair, some crow's feet jaggedly running amok around his eyes, and the slightest paunch creeping over his belt, pushing against his crisply ironed uniform.

It doesn't change the fact that his looks have largely held though, which is mesmerizing in its own messed-up way.

Again, my focus needs to be elsewhere, it's just hard not to think about high school and what it must have been like to be shooting guard John: idolized, girls dripping off him, giving it to him, and even with his awesome girlfriend Maggie around the whole time.

Maggie had these freckles, these crazy, dancing, verdant eyes, and this curly brown hair she would shake out as she walked around. She was a soccer player, and it was like someone had poured her into her jeans. Her calves were steel, but it was her laugh, you could hear it from down the hall, hearty, real; it stopped time.

Yet shooting guard John insisted he and Maggie never slept together—ever.

Shooting guard John always said he respected her too much, but it never quite seemed real. It also seemed to be a reasonable explanation for why he slept with everyone else.

Or tried to anyway.

I always assumed he and Maggie were sleeping together the whole time and his real goal was to make her not look easy—pure, above the passions that drove the rest of our behaviors. It didn't explain why she put up with his endless cheating, but people do all kinds of things until they can escape high school; and she had escaped. A soccer scholarship out west, gone, never to come home again.

Today there isn't any acknowledgment that any of us ever knew each other. Officer John is barely making eye contact with anyone in the room. He's mainly staring at his spiffy, spit-polished shoes. It must be tough to be here, knowing what he does, facing things no one wants to face.

Still, he could be a little more personal, couldn't he?

Officer John could show some emotion, caring, a recognition that we once knew each other and that in our shared past there's a connection—he feels it and feels for us.

That's not him though, is it?

Officer John opens his mouth and words soon spew forth.

Before the words reach me, enter my brain, begin to form clear sentences and ideas, and I translate what he needs us to know, a bitter, skunky waft of Miller High Life drifts across the room.

That smell is high school, another world, or parallel universe we once trod, and as I take it in, I drift into a memory I haven't recalled in many years.

There was a party, not one I was invited to. It was for older students, athletes, cooler ones, and shooting guard John was telling me about it in study hall at the end of my sophomore year, and way before he was kicked off the team. Shooting guard John was at this party. Maggie was off in some other part of the house, and Hannah's sort of friend Alyssa was drinking and dancing and fucking around. At some point Alyssa was stumbling about the house, and there was some athlete dude she was dating, and he got her to a room, and they'd had sex, or he had sex with her whether she'd wanted to or not. It's not clear what she remembered, or even registered, which was hilarious to this guy. He told shooting guard John about it and suggested that since Alyssa loved John—idolized him—and would be willing to have sex with him any time—not that she would tell John, or ever make a move, he was shooting guard John—if John wanted to take a go at her, this guy didn't care. But neither would Alyssa, which was the point. And so, John headed to the room, and there she was, naked and half conscious, and she seemed happy to see him, if not surprised. She didn't know him, not personally, and she couldn't really resist him, which John thought was hot. There was a moment when he was telling me this story where he seemed to think maybe it was wrong that he'd had sex with her. Alyssa didn't say yes, but she didn't say no, and she was drunk, and slept around so much anyway—had it really made a difference? Which might've been true—her sleeping around—though maybe that was just something people said back then. For a moment, even as I was thinking about how terrible the whole story sounded to me, I was jealous shooting guard John had the opportunity to sleep with her. Alyssa was someone I wanted to have sex with too. I almost never got invited to those parties and I was never in those situations regardless. Even as I had the thought, I fought to strike it from my brain. I knew how horrible it sounded and the embarrassment over my reaction lingered over the years.

It does right up until this moment.

I hate it, and I hate myself, and I'm reminded of this as I sit here and I realize this is the guy looking for my daughter, Alyssa was a girl Christa's age once and everyone is complicit in the sexualization of girls from childhood onward.

Hannah touches my arm.

I'm startled by a reality in which Officer John has been talking for a while, and now I'm talking, unprompted and unknowing, reacting to whatever I think has been transpiring while I was lost in my memories.

"How can we expect you to protect our daughter, much less women, anyone, when everyone and everything is conspiring against that, sexualizing them, ignoring their raised hands in class, telling girls they shouldn't care as much, grabbing pussies and supporting the patriarchy at any cost. Girls are objects, worthless, here for men to stalk and intimidate, bully. What girls would even want to be part of a world we've built at their expense? We raised Christa to be tough and sensitive, recognize that life isn't easy, to be her own person, follow her own path and tell her own story. Maybe raising her like that has something to do with why we're here now. Maybe we pushed her out the door, but Christa could be anywhere, doing anything, and how would we know? And how will you know? What are you going to do to make this better? How are you going to find her?"

Hannah touches my arm again and gives it a quick squeeze.

I catch my breath.

I must get control of myself.

We don't know anything, but we do know Christa is with Josh and while that's horrible, it also means she's safer than she would be if she was alone.

We met Josh once.

I wouldn't have talked to him in high school. That's embarrassing, but true.

He's a worm, slight, not cool.

I'm amazed we raised Christa to find someone like Josh appealing.

He must be easy to deal with though and maybe we're not?

Now we must find her.

Officer John looks queasy and confused. He adjusts himself and rubs an imaginary spot off his shoes.

There's no trace of Christa.

She seems to have gone by choice.

The police will stay engaged.

But we must stay positive.

We must do our part as well.

Cool?

Then he's gone and we're nowhere—nowhere good, nowhere bad, just nowhere.

Later that night after our parents are home and Hannah is asleep, I go on Facebook and search for Alyssa. It takes a moment, she's not really friends with anyone we grew up with. But there's some random chick from high school Alyssa's friends with—they're friends on Facebook anyway—and there she is. The same jet-black hair and olive skin. She's older, mostly around the eyes, and in the stray grey streaks which flow through her still amazing hair. It's not like I haven't seen her since high school, but it's been random, drunken. Still, I've found her. She's living the big city life. Drinking. Working. Yoga. Running around. No kids. Seems to be single. Oddly, she's been attending Burning Man for years and there are endless shots of her in leather outfits and covered in dust like an extra from *Mad Max*. She also actively attends protests and was especially active around the Women's March. She hates Trump and may be vegan. She goes to brunch a lot. She looks happy, or some approximation of that—who knows on Facebook? But maybe she is happy, and if one can get that, happiness, one should, and one should revel in it—even if it makes the rest of us a little jealous and sad.

And yes, hard stop   I'm sad.

My daughter is gone, and we don't know why, not really. We just know Josh is involved.

He seemed fine enough, decent, harmless, and even if I didn't get whatever Christa saw in Josh, I wasn't worried about him. I wanted to be cool about the relationship, and Hannah didn't. Sometimes you must support your children when you don't want to and let them see the error of their ways in their own time, which is what I chose to do. To push too hard or go on and on to Christa about how she was wasting her time with this loser or how he was too old for her, wouldn't have worked.

Do I regret that now?

Of course, I would do anything necessary to hold onto her now.

Still, we don't know how we pushed her away. What we know is we're somehow supposed to function in this new adjacent reality. Yes, it's only three days, but people really can disappear, go away, not be found, even in today's wired world—and we're supposed to accept that.

Like this is our new normal.

As I sit here and stare at Alyssa, I wonder how this works, the idea that people can just come and go from our lives as they see fit. Is this part of some larger narrative we participate in? That we're connected, and afloat as well? And whatever this life is, ultimately, we're supposed to recognize that we're small and doing our best to hold on?

I hope not, because that doesn't feel normal to me and never will.

HANNAH

Holding on is what I've always done, that's nothing to me, but the feeling of ongoing panic is new—if that's even the right word.

One time, Christa and I got caught in a freak snowstorm when we were driving to a party at some cousin's home somewhere off the beaten path and hours away. It was spring, or aspired to be, and we didn't check the weather. Not that we ever checked the weather, which seems like something real adults must do. They understand the importance of knowing what's to come, so they can plan accordingly. I never became that kind of adult. I wasn't raised in a home like that. Live and let live, push forward, keep moving, never sweat the small stuff, and figure things out along the way. That was my house growing up.

Did anyone ever teach me how to do the laundry?

Yeah, no.

It seems funny now, but everything does.

So, Christa and I packed our bags, got into the car, started driving, and within an hour, the snow started.

There were flurries at first—dusting the roads and our windshield—a layer of confection sugar whipping about. Cars would slow down at times, but it felt like little more than a belated belch of winter, smoke trailing a plane, a brief memory of something here and passed.

Soon it was coming down in waves, buckets of snow morphed and contorted into a sheet of white, dancing in front of the window and enveloping the car in a crunchy hug.

The car started to slide under my grasp and as I slowed, some cars joined me in a communal trudge through the elements. Others continued to treat the weather as if these were normal conditions, weaving between and around us, their red lights dotting the road, a telescopic sniper sight, scoping out its victims, here then gone.

I began to wonder if I could stay on the road at any speed. A car zipped past, jerked to the left, dissolved across the center line, corrected itself, jammed to the right before skidding off the road and liquefied as it merged with the towering snowdrifts now encroaching on the shoulder.

I felt this vise attach itself to the middle of my back, and like a rash, it started climbing up my spine, neck, shoulders, and head before it seeped into my brain.

My thoughts grew disjointed and trippy. I wondered if we were still on the same astral plane we'd been on when we left the house. We were engulfed in darkness, but for the inches of light in front of our car. I didn't trust myself to believe the other cars I saw were even there and I imagined the ways we might die that night—run off the road by an out-of-control semi, rolling into an unseeable pileup and crushed by the cars coming in behind us, White Walkers emerging from the shadows and gorging on us whole.

I couldn't let Christa know how I felt. This was my burden. I had to protect her, and I would see it through to its inevitable conclusion, fingers melded to the steering wheel as we pushed into oblivion.

"Mom."

For a moment the voice was disembodied, traveling from some parallel place.

"Mo-o-o-m!"

The voice was clear now—Christa, of course; who else?— firm, but shaky.

"I'm scared," Christa said. "Can we look for a hotel?"

A hotel, I hadn't thought about seeking refuge and safety. We pulled over at the next exit and found a place to stay. We awoke the next morning in our toasty room, buried under our enormous bedspread, legs and hair brilliantly intertwined, the sun piercing the space floating around us. The panic purged from my body and mind—dissipated across the universe.

I got out of bed, stretched my arms above my head, opened the curtain and looked out the window, the skies clear for miles.

Had the night before even happened?

Fundamentally I knew it had, but that I could have felt such terror and violation hours before and now this—nothing and calm.

How does that work?

It was panic, that's how it works. You're unmoored and out of control. No longer able to trust who you are and for that moment, what you've always been, confident and clear-eyed.

Do I feel panic now, with Christa missing, here but a moment ago, now gone?

No.

Christa's fine.

She wrote us a note and said we shouldn't worry.

I choose not to worry.

I must.

Caught in the storm I was aflame—my senses firing off in all directions seeking balance and answers—feral and focused on survival. I thought we might die, though I couldn't even trust that feeling. Every second of that drive is embedded into my memory and DNA, but it still feels like it was a dream. In comparison, this feels real, a constant source of anxiety, even if I awake each morning and expect to find Christa's legs intertwined in mine, both of us ready to tackle the day like we did on that trip, after the snow, and after the fall.

I decide I'll send Christa a text and write, "Hey."

That's it.

Christa never tells you what she wants in her first text—she writes "Hey," challenging you to write back.

Or not.

As if she doesn't care either way.

Christa not texting Gabriel or me now to tell us she's okay feels like a challenge as well. If the two of you want to know I'm okay, ask, go ahead, I'm here.

Could that be it?

We didn't see her when she was right in front of us, too caught up in being worried about everything to slow down and show actual concern?

I text Christa.

"Hey."

I'll keep doing so until she writes back, or we truly know she's fine.

GABRIEL

I WANT TO TEXT Christa and I'm trying to decide what I want to say.

I've called her dozens of times since she left, and she hasn't answered. Not that she answered her phone when she was still here.

I don't always leave a voicemail. I don't want the mailbox to fill up before we connect.

It's all silly, really.

There haven't been any pings on her phone and probably won't be.

Christa's too smart to use it. Or even turn it on.

That doesn't mean she isn't carrying it around with her or won't turn it back on at some point. And when she does, we need to be there. Hannah and I. Christa needs to know we care. Hannah and I haven't discussed this, but Hannah knows to text her as well. If Hannah doesn't know this, she'll be unhappy I assume she does and I didn't say something to her.

I don't have time for such a discussion.

I must act.

Fathers must act, and Hannah will appreciate that.

In the movies, a child goes missing and what transpires next is some kind of concerted effort to figure out where the child was last seen. Everyone involved in the search sweeps out across the area. People hold hands in fields, focused on finding the body or evidence—a scrap of clothes, identification, a phone. Others pray. There are press conferences fraught with the tension of wondering whether the child is nearby or worse, the abductor, as he or she trolls the safe space created to engage in the search—primal and full of flop sweat and stale coffee. The police work in concert with the state police and the FBI, private detectives, and volunteers. AMBER Alerts take flight to all known corners of the world. Somehow there's nothing, and then a grizzled veteran investigator arrives unannounced, maybe even unexpected. They're played by Morgan Freeman or Forrest Whitaker, Robert Duvall, Bill Camp or Elizabeth Marvel. Angela Bassett would be welcome. The investigator is made-up of sinew and cheekbones, motherly and fierce, and having survived Ike Turner, capable of anything. Yet somehow, and against all reasonable odds, reality is suspended, because when absolutely nothing makes sense, it's the father who saves the day through sheer will and exceptional attention to detail. Fathers find clues and track people down. While we're expected to ignore the racist or misogynistic undertones of this narrative, somewhere along the way it's the father who identifies the sign or call, the trace of life afloat on the winds of fate. The case is soon cracked. Hugs abound.

We find this to be an acceptable storyline, we even expect it, and so what does that say about me?

I drive around town, up and down the streets where we've always lived, worked, and breathed. The same dilapidated houses at the bottom of the hills near our home giving way to sprawling homes along the river that bisects the city. The barely energized local businesses struggling to survive downtown—their awnings and signs cracked and crumbling. The gray-streaked skies and dead gray lawns, the fall air a mix of leaves and flame. I go throughout the day, before and after work, during my lunch break, not bothering to eat or sleep, as the phone doesn't ring with information about where Christa has been spotted. She isn't anywhere and I can't make her appear despite my desire to do so, willing her presence from the nothing I see outside my window.

I also hang flyers around town.

On telephone poles and abandoned buildings.

It starts with, "Have you seen this girl?"

It includes a photo of Christa I love. She's sitting at a table in River Diner. It's one of our places. She's smiling. The sun is coming through the window. Her hair glows. She looks carefree and beautiful.

It also says, "She was last seen with this man," and includes a photo I took from Josh's Facebook page.

I wrote "man" so it would feel more urgent.

I encourage people to call the police with tips, but also include my cell number for those who prefer not to call the authorities.

No one has called yet.

I don't know how Hannah feels about the flyers.

I do know Hannah wants both of us to mostly accept that Christa is fine. Josh will make sure it's so. I also know Hannah needs to believe Christa is okay and I'm almost willing to accept this for Hannah and her well-being. But I just can't accept it. It would be irresponsible. I'm going to do what I can to find her.

None of which addresses the main thing I just don't know and can't understand—why Christa doesn't want to be found, seen, or heard?

We don't know what we did to cause this.

What clues we missed.

Or, what we failed to do.

Listen, be present, focus on her, her life, needs and choices, ask the right questions, and pay more attention, or less.

What was it?

We can fix anything we failed to do in the past—we will fix it going forward, no hesitation.

Which is something fathers do, they fix things, and if I haven't in fact been able to fix myself much of the time, well, that's beside the point right now.

After another fruitless stretch of driving around, I drive up to the front of Josh's building.

It's a three-story walkup on a sad little side street by the high school, and he lives on the second floor above a scuzzy pizzeria where students go to for lunch. This might have been a nice neighborhood once. Now it's like much of the town, run-down and holding on, but not sure why.

I roll by Josh's a couple of times a day, but I never see anyone walking in or out besides the couple who live on the third floor and run the pizzeria.

They always wave when they see me, but they know nothing. Nothing.

I ask.

I close my eyes.

I see Christa before me, but not the Christa I know today. This is a different, younger one from a trip we took to Amish country when she was a kid.

We stopped at a tiny storefront museum called Train City, USA that advertised itself as possessing the largest model train set in the world. There was a small gift shop in the front of the building where you could buy model trains, postcards, key chains, taffy, and T-shirts that read "My parents visited the largest model train set in the world and all I got was this lousy T-shirt" and "Rome. Tokyo. Mexico City. Train City, USA." The back room was sprawling and every square inch of it was covered with a model train set that seemingly went on for miles. There were jagged, snow packed mountains reaching far into the sky as the trains passed through, skiers and snowboarders whistling down them in an array of bright colors, hair long and flowing, and free BASE jumpers hurtling off the top of the peaks, unfettered and glorious. It also had sweeping forests filled with epic pine trees and towering redwoods and a golden gondola shuttling Jimi Hendrix, Elvis, and Marilyn Monroe from one small town to the next, each town filled with stores, streets, homes, people, cars, and pets, bubbling with life and hope. There were zoos and circuses, elephants trumpeting and lions basking in the sun, baseball stadiums where the games never ended and a not actual life size Cape Canaveral preparing for hourly shuttle takeoffs. And there were rivers and streams with real running water, splashing and kinetic and soaring bridges crossing great expanses of land, which included national memorials such as Mount Rushmore and the Gateway Arch, national monuments like Devils Tower, Chimney Rock, and Yellowstone, where Old Faithful sprayed the surroundings with watery wonder.

Christa was lost in its detail. It was amazing. The pine trees weren't just painted green and brown, they had real bark, the branches bristly to the touch and the Redwoods, cracked, thick, and asking for a deep hug. The clothes were hand sewn too. You could make out each individual stitch. And the animals had actual fur, soft to the touch and alive.

For me, or Hannah, it was just cool, but for Christa, it was transformative, a pilgrimage, akin to how people experience travelling to Lourdes or the Western Wall. The whole ride home she talked about how she now had a purpose, how she was going to build something just like it in our house, modeled on our neighborhood. She wanted to understand the details and minutiae of what makes things work. She talked about how she needed to touch things for them to be real and this she could touch with both her hands and her brain at once. She spent the rest of the trip sketching it and thinking through the materials she would need to bring it to life. Watching her work was mesmerizing, moving, and I promised her we could work on it when we got home. But we didn't. I got busy with work or life or whatever we get busy with, and the sketches were put away and ignored. She became a teenager, now she's missing, and here we are.

Is that why Christa left?

The profound disappointment of living in a world that failed to recognize her needs to the point it became too much to face each day. Especially when her own parents came to represent that disappointment. Maybe it was too much to have that staring her in the face, and invading her thoughts, and the only way for her to escape the constant reminder that life was destined to be a disappointment was to escape, leave it behind, and start anew with someone who was willing to look Christa in the eye and say I see you?

HANNAH

This is what happens now: you begin to focus on your shortcomings. They haunt your every breathing moment. You beat yourself up, and you can't stop hating yourself.

It's a penance. Punishment. Period.

So, let's do this, let's be honest, and let's hurt each other.

There didn't have to be a fight. Or maybe more accurately, it didn't have to go so far. I could've chosen to tune out Christa's nonsense. I could've chosen to ignore her eyeroll. And I could've chosen to talk less—much less, way less.

I could not have said anything about anything because it's ephemeral and stupid in the greater scheme of things. Why does Christa's bad mood—and her even worse attitude—mean anything to me? She's a teenager, and it was a meltdown, and regardless of what it was about, a demand of some kind from me about something she didn't want to do—clean her room, fold her clothes, put away her dishes—I'm sure I said please, and I'm sure I said it calmly. The first time and even the second time, then maybe I raised my voice the third time. But it was now the third time, so what the hell, at that point, seriously. That's the crux of it though, Christa doesn't want to do what she doesn't want to do, and what she doesn't want to do is anything I want her to do, regardless of how many times I ask her to do it.

Still, it could've been avoided. Do this please. No? Okay, then there could've been a consequence, and if she ignored the consequence, there would be more, rinse, repeat, endless and terrible. But that's it too, right? When Christa was little, I would throw one consequence at her after another as I wanted to make her stop no matter what and regardless of what she was doing. "You've lost television for tonight. Okay, tomorrow too. Keep going. Are you testing me? Okay, three days. Should we make it the entire week? Okay, all week." It was like being in a fugue state. I was enraged that this little kid should have the power. She'd taken control, and I couldn't take it back. It wasn't me alone back then either. It was Gabriel too. Gabriel hated to punish Christa, much less invoke consequences. He wanted to be cool. He was cool. And it was goddamn annoying how much he wanted to be cool and how hard he tried to achieve it. But at least he could try back then. Back before he couldn't. Before the night when things got out of control, and everything went to hell. After that Gabriel was neutered, screwed, incapable of punishment, rage, or anything that looked like it might be actual discipline.

So, it was on me and me alone.

I was alone.

Me who had no mother and no supervision, I'm supposed to deal with this sixteen-year-old girl who thinks she knows everything, while I know nothing. My mother wasn't there to fight with and even if I knew how to fight with Christa, I never believed for a moment that we wouldn't have the kind of relationship where things couldn't be addressed or fixed.

I was never going to let her get away.

We would sit down.

We would talk.

We would explain our feelings.

Work through things.

Wanting something doesn't make it so though.

Moving from a problem to sitting there, calmly, mind clear,

engaged in a dialogue, things making sense. It's what I aspired to, but I never got there.

Yet did there have to be another fight, and did it have to end like it did? No, how could anything have to end like this? There was eye-rolling, something disrespectful happened, words, stupid, certainly, asshole, maybe, aggressive body language. Ultimately, it wasn't any of those things which upset me so much. It was her unwarranted—as far as I was concerned—rage, which was so readily accessible I couldn't find a way to absorb it or react calmly to it.

Who is she to be so mad at me? I wanted to know, to understand it, and what I said was: "Who are you to be so mad at me? You have two parents who care about you, even if we care too much. We've never laid a hand on you. Not that not hitting your child should accord anyone any kind of nobility. But we're there for you in every way—especially these days. We sit together for dinner almost every night, and sometimes its late before we're able to do so, but we do it, and we check in with you to see how your day was even if you don't respond or you share these incredibly inane stories about who's fighting with whom in the bathroom, in the hall, on the bus, people we don't know and don't care about, fighting all the time. But we keep asking you open-ended questions and labeling our feelings. We use 'I' statements and we try to help you learn how to self-regulate. All the stuff I never had when I was your age. And that's what you hate?"

I wanted to add, "I don't fucking get it—or you—and I never fucking will."

I didn't do so, however.

But did there have to be a fight?

I must come back to that. Did I have to say what I said, and did it need to end like this?

No, enough, no.

"These are basic rules," I said, "easy to follow, simple, pick up after yourself, be respectful, and don't yell at me."

"But you yell at me," Christa replied. "All the time."

"Would you agree you yell first?" I asked.

I shouldn't have asked. It doesn't matter what I do. I'm the parent, it's a trap, and now I'd entered the rabbit hole.

"Who cares who yells first," she said rolling her eyes, "yelling is yelling. Plus, you're a fucking hypocrite, and you know you're a fucking hypocrite, and it makes me sick."

That should not have upset me.

What did I care if a seventeen-year-old girl thinks I'm a hypocrite? Seventeen-year-olds are supposed to feel like their parents are hypocrites. It's how they separate from us. And yes, even in the middle of this horribleness, I saw the irony. So, okay, I know it shouldn't have bothered me so much, except it bothered me so much. My mother was a hypocrite, and I didn't want to be her. Then there was Gabriel, and he was such a hypocrite, and Christa never said that to him. I haven't lived my life like him, and I resent him for that. Gabriel has allowed himself the option to take care of himself and follow his own needs. I haven't. Mothers never do. They can't.

How didn't she see that?

Why didn't Christa see the myriad ways that Gabriel did and did not do his best by us—while I was always there?

That she and I were a team, and together we'd been taking on a world only too happy to conspire against us?

How there was no one who loved her more fiercely than I did, and I would always have her back?

But also, how I've been decent, and I've been cool.

I've always told the truth, to Christa, to Gabriel, to my father, to myself, always, and knowing this about myself, and with such certainty, set me off, period. Did I hate myself for being set off, and for knowing it wasn't Christa's fault? How my behavior in the moment was a manifestation of my personal history and my own limitations, and she'd entered something she couldn't control?

Yes.

The thing is I couldn't control my response to that either. I sucked. I couldn't stop myself, exit the ridiculous place we'd found ourselves in, or refrain from saying things I didn't want to say. Nor could I not be the asshole I didn't want to be, in the moment. I couldn't or wouldn't. What kills me, is I thought I was going to be better at this than my mother. I was going to be more understanding, more present, more everything. I wasn't going to repeat her patterns.

I was better.

I was there every day and fighting the good fight.

My mother wasn't.

It's just, okay, I might have been fine enough, but I wanted to be better than that.

I chose not to be my best self.

And it was a choice.

"Look, honey," I said, and I was calmer, and yes, cooler, "maybe down the road, you'll have a roommate or a significant other, and they'll think your horrible attitude and your yelling is funny, or whatever, and then you can know in your heart of hearts that you were right all along, and that, yes, your mother is a hypocrite, and you can even come home and tell me about it. But until then, you live here, under our roof, as our guest, with our rules, and you're going to follow them, and be respectful while you do."

It could've then gone a lot of ways, and her storming off into her room and slamming the door would've sucked, but it would be better than what followed.

"I do have someone," Christa said. "Josh, and he loves me for who I am."

"Josh? Are you for real?"

I didn't call Josh a predator, which is what I thought and what I wanted to say. Gabriel had counseled me to stay cool and not push too hard or we would push her away.

"Then be with him," I added before she could respond.

"What, so you don't want me here?" she asked, one hand on

her hip. "That's what you're saying, you want me to be with Josh, because I want it to be really clear."

That would have been the perfect time to pause, I know that, but…but.

Did I not want her to be here?

The proper response if one is a parent, or any type of guardian, or human, would've been "of course I want you here, I love you. This is a temporary state of distress. It won't mean anything tomorrow."

That's the person and parent I wanted to be and mostly had tried to be.

But could I have said it and meant it?

Did I really want her here?

No, not always, I didn't, and no, I couldn't say otherwise.

Gabriel wanted to have a child, I didn't, and so I resented her—which I hated.

But love is love is love and I loved her and it's terrible and wonderful.

It's everything.

So, yes, it would've been a great time to pause before I proceeded, but I didn't.

"Do I not want you here? And do I want you with *Josh?* I didn't say that. I don't want those things. I also don't want you here screaming at me if you don't want to be here."

Christa then calmly walked into her room, made a phone call I couldn't hear, packed her backpack, and walked out the front door. She did this when she was a little kid too. She would grab her bag and cram a pillow and stuffed animal inside it, maybe a book, and walk out. At first, I followed her in a panic, my heart pounding, wondering where she was going and what was going to happen to her if I just let her go. I would ultimately insist that she turn around and march back into the house. Why was I so weak? I didn't know what would happen to her, and I didn't want to find out. But also, my mom walked out just like that. Not in a rage, but she walked, she never came back, and I couldn't allow that nonsense to repeat itself. No, no way, forget that. Later I stopped chasing Christa, and I started calling her bluff, not giving into her emotional blackmail. Instead, I would sit on the couch, freaking out about what it meant not to chase her, to have faith she wouldn't go anywhere. Nothing was so bad here at home she wouldn't return. Nowhere else was better. I would force myself to believe she would walk back into the house.

And she always came back.

"What the fuck," she said the first time. "Are you seriously not coming after me?"

I didn't respond. Lines had to be drawn, fewer words needed to be spoken. Fears had to be managed. Plus, an eight-year-old saying, "what the fuck," was surprisingly cute.

It got less cute, way less cute, but not in the beginning. It was the only thing that saved me back then.

So, the night when she walked out and got into Josh's car, I held my breath, and when I saw the note she left, "Don't worry, we'll be fine," matter of fact, just as I would be, I grimaced, smiled, tightly, I put it in my pocket, got a beer, put on the RAMONES, sat on the couch, closed my eyes, rubbed my temples, and waited. The minutes passed, then hours. It got dark. She didn't call, or text, anything. No "what the fucks," and no "I hate yous." Just nothing. I texted her—of course. Not immediately. But after two hours passed, yes, and thirty minutes after that, then fifteen minutes, then every few minutes—my intensity and panic growing with each message. I demanded she answer me, the three dots present at first, then not. I called her friends as well, what few there were to call, but no one had seen or heard from her. Or Josh. Or so they said.

What I didn't do was call Gabriel. Not at first. He didn't come home until late that night, and there was a moment when I wondered if he was at a bar or in someone's bed, but he said he was done with that. He was always at work, and I know he'd been at work—that's who he's been for years. He would work until at least dinner and later when he could—anything to stay focused and occupied—and if I didn't hate him, I would admire it. Anyway, I couldn't call him. I couldn't bear it. What would I have told him? I've lost our daughter because I couldn't ignore her eyerolls. I kept talking and talking. I didn't like being called a hypocrite. I pushed her away in the very way you asked me not to, and maybe, just maybe, for a little while I enjoyed the intense silence and calm that followed, and I didn't want to relinquish it?

I couldn't tell him any of that, I didn't—not for hours—which is how Christa being missing started in the first place.

GABRIEL

WHAT MIGHT I SAY here? How it feels like Hannah drove our daughter away and how she's too absorbed in Christa's every feeling and emotion. Or that Hannah is too sensitive to each tic and disrespect. I wish she was more chill. Except it isn't about chill, which is too simple and reductive. Not when it's about anger and feelings triggered by Christa who Hannah doesn't want to turn out like her, or worse, reminds Hannah of her own mother. How it can feel like a pattern that continues from generation to generation—a pattern Hannah isn't able to break free from. Not when frustration and resentment build, then harden, her ability to think straight is skewed, and the desire to be the person she wants to be is compromised.

Might I say something about that?

I could, but what'll that accomplish? Will it bring Christa back? Will anyone feel better, or become more laser-focused on wherever the hell Christa went when she left? Will it allow me to suspend time and space long enough to move in reverse?

If so, that means I could've figured out a way, or a reason, for me to have left work early, come home, walked into their fight, broke the tension somehow, and redirected the craziness. Maybe I could've distracted them like when Christa was a child, "Hey look, is that a purple bird?" That kind of thing was amazingly effective back then, and maybe it could've been that night as well. Say it did work though, or something just like it, and they both walked away to their respective haunts, Christa pissed at the world, Hannah and me, but home and safe, and Hannah mad at me for intervening in such a way I looked like the hero and she looked like the asshole—but it also meant she didn't need to tell me that Christa was lost.

I don't do that by the way, make Hannah look bad in front of Christa, even if, let's be honest, it might be better at times such as this. Hannah doesn't do that to me either. We're a team and we're imperfect. Not always on the same page, but united, for Christa. We can do that. We agreed to it early on. We're a unified front, and we work out the details and disagreements in private, and away from the maelstrom that is home.

It's about love and how one lives it in a world quick to embrace rage, disrespect, and falsities. It's also about choices, and we always try to stay on the right side of that.

Much, or all of this, excludes the greatest imperfection in the story, however, me, my behavior, and history. If we're going to talk about rage, disrespect, and falsities, the story isn't Hannah's alone, it's also mine.

To begin, I'm not a decent person.

Full stop.

I'm a good father—better than mine was certainly. I converse and listen. More than that, I'm loving, caring, mostly available, and for much of the time Christa has been in the world, I've been a calming presence. Able to bandage knees, fix bad haircuts, read children's books long into the night, and past any acceptable bedtime. I can have sex talks and manage parent-teacher conferences. I can be present, absorbed in every word of every story, whether it's who's fighting with whom in the bathroom, in the hall, on the bus, and despite Hannah and I not knowing the people Christa's talking about—and not caring either—just they are people she knows who for some reason must fight a lot. I'm right there. I know someone named Carrie banged Joseph while he was dating

Kim—whose mother doesn't like her dating Asian dudes, though even she would admit that Joseph is kind and hot—and they'd just sort of broken up, on the bus, or in the hall or whatever. It was the same when Christa was little, and she watched those terrible television shows, *Caillou* and *Wizards of Waverly Place,* and she shared her wacked theories on what the story lines meant. How Caillou had cancer and his bald head wasn't supposed to be funny. Instead, it was the story of his parents imagining what it would've been like if he had lived. And the world-building that happened to and around the Wizard family was a commentary on homosexuality and the other in the not quite modern world we exist in now, living a public life, yet not, still needing to be careful, and always at risk of being ostracized. I loved it then and I love it now. Christa's awesome, beautiful, weird, and yes, angry at us. But she's going to be a great grown-up, fun to hang out with and full of fascinating theories about the world.

I can't wait to have the opportunity to not be like I am with my parents—my mother anyway—to build something with Christa, which is other than cordial. Existing with her as adults in the world together. Talking about life, love, and the wonderful things that sometimes feel like they're just beyond our grasp. Christa will be the better version of Hannah and myself, and when I slow down, move away from the present, and see the possible futures that abound, I know I can't wait for that either.

Hannah has been unable to see it. She's been too caught up in the worry and the day-to-day reverberations of adolescence, the outbursts and drama, the inability to manage any of it, to see where and who Christa might be—full of energy and humor, able to care for others and remain steady—the very things Hannah is and has been with me and my utter bullshit behavior.

She also hasn't wanted to contain her rage about Josh being in Christa's life and resents me for wanting it to be okay and not treating it as potentially more problematic than it is.

But she resents me anyway. And should.

I haven't been a good husband, and I haven't been present for her in the same way I've tried to be for Christa.

Am I proud of this behavior—because a willingness to brazenly talk about one's flaws and look like an asshole can also sound like bragging.

I'm not proud of it.

But I don't think there's any other way to do it. One must be honest, look in the mirror, and at those you love, and say, I'm damaged, and my errant behavior has been as unacceptable as my drinking, and I want to conquer it, or control it. Or at least not have it be me, own me and shade my every decision, looming like a bogeyman.

I've been unable to say that, however, to Hannah certainly, even if I can say it to myself.

I drank through much of Christa's very early life. I could be present, and I could be there for her, but I couldn't face the rawness of being a parent with any kind of sober honesty. The exposed nerves involved in doing it right. My parents made it look easy. They weren't loving towards me, not like they were towards each other, but I wasn't missing anything, nor did I rebel, or even see any reason to. I was good, alone, a lot, with my thoughts, and books, but I was good. Later though, with Christa, no one told me if you're going to be all-in all the time, it's impossible not to be worried most of the time too. Always wondering if your child is going to stop breathing or get hit by a car. End up with leukemia. Or get kidnapped like the girl in my neighborhood when we were kids. One day that girl, Lori, was going door to door selling candy bars to raise money for color guard, and when she knocked on this one door, the dude dragged her inside. They found her later that night. It wasn't hard. The guy looked like a predator with his buggy eyes, thick glasses, ill-cut hair, and dirty, mustard-stained T-shirts. We avoided his house as children. It was an unwritten rule. But Lori didn't. Not that night. Why, I don't know. They found her half-dressed in the basement, dead. He'd barely covered her up and hadn't even tried to really hide her. He cried when they found her. He couldn't explain his behavior. He said it was impulsive and he'd never done anything like that before. He also said he was alone, people didn't talk to him, he craved contact with someone, anyone, and there she was. He wanted her but couldn't have her. She said, "No, please, no," he explained when questioned and her rejection had set him off. Lori didn't want him, it made him angry, and he took her. She was there and then she wasn't. That was it. Later, you'd see her parents around town, shuffling, wide-eyed, and staring at the ground, always on the verge of tears, shells of their former selves, haunted by her memory. They were lost without her, and without any kind of reasonable explanation for any of it.

How do you not worry about that kind of thing?

You can't not do so. What you do, is you set those feelings and fears aside, you bury them in the backyard, channel them elsewhere: work, sports, food, politics. You compartmentalize. The key thing is you place those feelings and fear in a box you lock up in the outer recesses of your brain. Then after doing so, you take a moment and acknowledge you are powerless in your ability to protect your child.

You have no control over anything, but yourself and your choices. You teach your children how to be safe and smart, and then you let go.

First, you make them sleep in their own room, and you will yourself to sit there through their crying, and then when they stop, you must believe they didn't cry themselves to death, and they're truly asleep—red-faced and salty, but alive. Later, you let them leave home without you, walk to school, go out with friends, go to the mall, get a job, climb into cars you don't recognize and with people you don't know. The whole time you also keep asking them how they're doing? Who their friends are? Where are they hanging out? Are they drinking, taking drugs, having sex? Are they happy? It's a lot, even when you care, especially when you care, and I didn't understand this going into it. I should have. I wasn't cavalier, I just didn't know and could never quite get the letting-go part. Nor could I get past my anger at not being able to let go of these things. I couldn't believe I wasn't above it. How I wasn't too cool for that, or calmer, way calmer. Internally. Hadn't I always been good at cool and calm? I had been and I wasn't any more. I tried to channel my anxiety elsewhere, work mainly, and when needed, sleeping with other women, and sometimes, men.

The cheating only happened when I drank, and back then, there was nothing like drinking. The first moment the drink would hit my tongue was electric, and then I'd be numb, and there was nothing better.

Drinking isn't going to work now though. There can be no drinks. None. It's been too long, and I can't go backwards. I need to look forward and I need to channel my crazy, spiky, sad anxiety into being present, perfected, and finding Christa.

HANNAH

Super Gabriel, no, he would never make me look bad, and of course, he's going to channel his not drinking manic, spiky energy into finding Christa, and saving her.

It's what he does.

One moment he's nowhere and the next he takes over, makes it about him, his goodness, and the desire to fix everything.

Well, forget that and forget him.

Of course, I was too attuned to Christa's moods. Someone had to be the realist, the bad guy, the mother of dragons, and Gabriel was always the good guy—when he's home, but more scared too, always, and I never understood why.

I also never understood why he couldn't understand how marriage works.

How it's about balance, someone makes money or spends it, and the other person balances the checkbook.

Someone wanders and the other person stays home, and when things are working, one or the other pushes their partner to join them on paths previously unexplored.

One partner is light, the other dark.

Sun and moon.

If one is the extrovert, talking smack, sucking up the air space, the other must pull back, be cool.

There must be stability and equilibrium—or it implodes.

And as parents, we must remind our partners that we have no control over bogeymen. What we can control is what's in front of us and sometimes not even that.

It comes with the territory, and it's not that complicated.

"Hey, you were around Christa's age when I first met you," Tracey says punching me in the shoulder, bringing me back to reality.

We're outside of Neary's Bar & Grill and Tracey's standing there in a low-cut T-Shirt smoking a cigarette, looking as earthy and sexy as ever. Tracey's only five years older than me. She just seems so much older. Almost weathered, but not quite, and as beautiful as the first time I met her, really, with her crazy blonde curls, and this amazing body the laws of gravity have decided not to mess with.

My feelings about Tracey are not sexual—not that they couldn't be. Check that. I could maybe have feelings for women in general. I think. I don't know. I've barely explored my sexuality. I've been focused on Gabriel for as long as I've been focused on anything. I felt something for him, it was good, we were connected, he felt safe, and that was that. Regardless, Tracey has been a sister, mother, and rock for me, and I'd never allow myself to mess with that.

"That was a long time ago, right?" she says when I don't respond. "How are you doing?"

Tracey wants to talk about Christa.

I don't want to focus on Christa.

Does this make me a bad person, or worse, a bad mother? It's easy to feel like a bad mother.

Trust me.

Also, do I care?

I want to breathe, and I want to lose myself in something else, disassociate, which I know I'm capable of, because I've always been a pro at it. You must be when your mom runs away, and everyone looks at you with pity. Or your husband has sex with people who are not you, and you run into them in stores, restaurants, and parent-teacher conferences. I'm not always self-aware enough to know when I disassociate, but tons of childhood therapy ensured I can trigger it on my own most any time I want.

It's my defense mechanism and my escape.

Gabriel can drink and sleep around. This is my thing. I own it and there's never been anything negative about it to me. It is what it is, and it's a necessity, because sometimes it's easier to smile, ignore people and think about other stuff.

"Hey babe," Tracey says, "are you tuning me out?"

She knows I am. She's been around long enough to know my game.

"Hannah, come on...."

I'm already lost in memory.

I was fifteen, and yes, nearly Christa's age when I walked into Neary's Bar & Grill with my father the day I first really met Tracey. My father had recently acquired a double chin. It was as if someone had taken an extra layer of skin from somewhere else on his body and slapped it onto his neck. It wasn't pretty, though I was hopeful the gray hair that now peppered his sideburns would at least lend itself to some respectability down the road. His chin though, there was nothing distinguished about it, and there was never going to be. My dad wasn't old exactly, or terrible to look at, but he wasn't Robert Wagner either. At thirty-three, he was already far from the dashing figure he once was. That said, he was a single father, which must have aged him horribly. Also, what did it matter if I found him attractive, the question was whether anyone his age did? My mother Lucy must have, at least once, but she'd been gone a long time at that point. She'd taken off with the neighbor stoner dude and if the rumors were true, they'd joined a commune built on free love. I could say I resented it, but she was pregnant at eighteen, married at nineteen, and alone at home as my father went to work and stayed there. I knew he'd thought it was the right thing to do. It was the family business, and it was his duty. His family had their little store and that was it. Maybe there was even part of him that wanted to stay away from his young wife and kid. I got that too, but I couldn't imagine how hard it must have been on my mom.

I could imagine what it might have been like to have received a postcard from my mother occasionally. How hard would that have been? She could've just said, hello, I'm checking in, how are you doing? But that hadn't happened. We hadn't heard from her. We were not going to hear from her. We would never know what happened to her. And it was fine with me.

I looked at my father again and wondered how this could happen. One day you're young and full of hope, and the next your wife is long gone and you're a single dad with a double chin and an angry fifteen-year-old daughter.

It didn't seem right.

My father poked his tongue out and ran his fingers across it, before parting his hair to the side with his hand. He rubbed his face, adding a little color to his cheeks. He straightened his back and squared his shoulders. He did something subtle with his face to minimize the extra chin I was obsessing over.

Interesting, why did he suddenly seem to care about his appearance?

The dude never cared about what anyone thought about him.

I looked up and saw Tracey, one of the waitresses my dad was friendly with, walking towards the table. Tracey was like nineteen or twenty. She was thin and had incredible breasts, which threatened to explode out of her required one-size too small wife beater T-shirt like the fireworks display held downtown every Fourth of July.

She was also nice to me.

Always.

"Hey beautiful," Tracey said.

"Hey to you," my dad said, beaming.

"I was talking to that daughter of yours, Ed," Tracey responded. Looking at me, she added, "You're more striking every time I see you, young lady. Thank God you look like your mom."

"Thanks," I said, "now if I could just grow a chest like you, I'd be set."

"No rush, honey," Tracey said. "Once you have them, the boys will follow you around like a pack of dogs."

"That sounds pretty cool."

"Due time," Tracey looked at my dad. "Do you want the usual, handsome?"

He nodded, and as she walked away, he tried to inconspicuously stare at her butt, which like her breasts was fantastic, but still.

"Ewwwwh, you're so snagged," I said.

"Please don't," he replied.

"Lighten up Francis. It's not like you're going to get any play anyway."

"Of course not, honey. All I care about is your happiness and whether I can age with some grace. That's plenty for me. The rest of it, who cares, right?" my dad said, with the slightest smile.

In that moment, something clicked.

My father had slept with Tracey, maybe he even had sex with her on the regular. It was a thing. He was a man who had sex, which was great for him, and horrific and weird otherwise.

"Oh my God! You boffed Tracey. How crazy is that?"

"Shhhhh!" my dad said, raising his index finger to his lips like he did when I was five years old. "We're in public."

"Fine, "but is it true, have you slept with her? Because as gross as it is to contemplate, inquiring minds want to know."

"Yeah, well, enquiring minds are probably going to be disappointed then," he said, as he made some adjustment to his posture and shifted from Sex Guy into Dad Mode, which is what dads do. "Sadly though, I now have to ask, do we need to have the talk?"

It was at that moment, history would reflect, that time briefly stopped, worlds collided, the sun lost its ability to heat the planet and dogs and cats started to live together.

"Do you mean the sex talk because you're out of your ridiculous, possibly sex-addled mind, motherfucker, if you think I'm having that talk with you. No, seriously, please."

"First off, language. C'mon, you're a young lady. Second, my mother is your grandmother. Third, and most important, your mother isn't around. If I don't ask, who's going to?"

He seemed sad as he said this last part, and while I could have tossed him a bone and let him play dad there, it just wasn't happening.

"How about, no, and if it helps, I don't ever plan to have sex, much less end up like you and Mom, okay?"

"Works for me."

At that point, Tracey arrived with a pitcher of beer, and he chose to drink over talking, which is much better than the alternative. "Hannah! Jesus, come back to earth already," Tracey says back in the here and now.

"What?" I say, snapping to attention.

"Are we not going to talk about Christa?" Tracey punches me in the shoulder for a second time.

"She's coming back."

"I know she is, she's a smart kid—like her mother."

"Plus, Josh will come to his senses soon enough, right? Who could possibly want to run off with her?"

"No one, but also, you need to talk about this with someone. It's not healthy."

"My dad did a pretty good job with me when I was kid, right?"

"Yeah. He would benefit from a little more talking as well though, especially with you, but he loves you, and if he wasn't, you know, perfect, he was right there."

"Gabriel and I should have done a better job," I say, looking away. "I thought we were right there too, but you know, look how trash everything is."

Tracey turns my face back towards hers, gives me her best sympathetic mom look, a tear rolls down her flawless skin, and pulls me close. For a moment, I think I'm going to cry, but I don't—my mom would have hated that. No weakness, no getting bogged down, keep pushing, keep looking forward.

I steady myself and here, now, again, I must acknowledge as good a job as my father or Tracey did with me, my mother's opinion is the only one I care about. She may be a ghost, but she's always right there.

GABRIEL

"Look, speaking of ghosts being right there, or not, I should be clear. I don't have Hannah's baggage. No lost moms, I didn't have to take care of my parents, or myself as a kid. I didn't spend my child-hood hanging out in bars. I had a stable home. Two parents. Not that two are required, but I had it, plus love and support. Things were taken care of. It was safe and Hannah doesn't know safe."

I say this to Officer John after I pop into the police station to see him and ask what's happening with the search for Christa.

It's now a week and we still don't know anything about anything.

Christa doesn't return my texts.

I haven't seen her at Josh's.

I reached out to Josh's parents before I came to the police station. They seem unmoved. Josh is nineteen, and they don't care what happens to him.

Which is to say I went to their house, I introduced myself, told them why I was there, and asked them if they had heard from Josh or had any idea where he might've gone off to with my daughter. They had not heard from Josh, they had no suggestions about where he might go off to, and they didn't care. They were normal looking. Regular haircuts. The dad, Bill, had on a flannel shirt, green and blue, the mom, Mary, was wearing a sweater with a French Poodle on it. They both wore glasses—his Buddy Holly style frames, hers, round and oversized. They didn't seem alarmed to have a stranger at their door. They just didn't care about their son and wherever he might be.

They're exact words were, "It'll work itself out."

What did they think would work itself out?

Josh would create a life with Christa and all would be fine.

Josh and Christa would come home?

What?

I don't know and I didn't ask. I had no idea how to talk to these people who didn't feel remotely like I did.

Still, there was a moment, as I was standing there, looking at these flannel-wearing, normal-looking, coffee cup-holding adult humans when I wanted to scream, "What kind of people raised a man who runs off with a seventeen-year-old girl?"

Then I thought, these kinds of people—people who don't seem to care about anything.

I also thought, what kind of father doesn't punch that kind of man in the face when that father finds out his daughter is involved with that kind of man?

I didn't know the answer to that, I just knew I didn't want to be that guy when I first met Josh or when I met his parents.

I didn't scream at Josh's parents either, instead I lingered for a moment, and I wondered if something miraculous was going to happen—Josh and Christa would suddenly appear, or Josh's parents would realize they knew where Josh and Christa were—but nothing happened, and I walked away.

As I sit here looking at Officer John, and I think about Josh's parents' complete lack of concern about his disappearance versus my feelings about Christa, I ask myself, why I'm so worried about finding her?

Christa's with Josh and that's cool, right?

No, it's not, Christa is seventeen. She's not a child, but she's too young for whatever this is.

Also, is my reaction due to not picturing her life play out like this. This being Christa falling in love and leaving in a huff?

That would be correct. I didn't picture it happening like this and this isn't right.

There's a proper way and proper time to do these things and when that time comes, I'll be cool.

This isn't that time.

I'll add that I've never been to a police station before this either. It's what you would expect if you ever watched even one cop show: crusty desks, wanted signs on ancient corkboards, a coffee machine, stale donuts, and tweaky fluorescent lights. The biggest surprise might be how unlike television things are. There are so few people here. No hustle or bustle. No one is handcuffed to a chair. There are no errant screams pinging off the walls. It's Officer John, me, another officer reading the newspaper and a receptionist playing Candy Crush. I don't know if this is because there's so much going on, or so little, but if it's because it's so little, why can't everyone be looking for Christa? I want to ask Officer John this question, but it feels too forward and aggressive. Also, even as I want to focus on the search itself, I'm happy to have the opportunity to just talk to someone. To free the endless thoughts and fears roaming the recesses of my brain. This is a place where you can feel safe, if not actually hopeful, it's refreshing, and when Officer John nods my way with the slightest acknowledgment he's listening, I continue.

"There's so much I'm not good at, or at least exceptional at. I wasn't a good husband—I own it. Look, if I'm going to be transparent, not being an asshole most the time is who I prefer to be. I'm good at recognizing how flawed I am. I'm not a success by any stretch of the imagination, which I understand is a construct that society has foisted up on us, men especially. What we're supposed to do or be in the world, how we interact with the economy, what kind of consumers we are, and what we produce. Do we have any kind of impact on anything? By any, or most, standards, I don't bring much to the table.

"I wasn't a high school athlete which seems to be important to some people. I never had many friends. I didn't finish college. There was Christa, alcohol, numerous women, men, and look, how often one hooks up can be a sort of metric for success, right? But if you're married, or unless your wife is cool with your behavior, doing so makes you the worst, and yes, that's me.

"I never cared much about being anyone at work, but I always worked, and I always provided. I go to the office, and if a truck or shipment is supposed to be somewhere at some time. I'm the guy, I make things happen, and if it isn't happening, I fix it. I get things where they're supposed to be. People have always appreciated it, and I've always appreciated being appreciated, validated. It's good, which is also a kind of success, being happy, people telling you you've done well, taking care of stuff.

"Which I guess also brings me back to the now, reality, why I'm here—not wanting to dodge my responsibilities by justifying my worth or trying to feel better about what I've done or not done over time. The only thing I need to be successful at now is finding Christa, and I know I can be of help, because the search for her and what needs to be done is a confluence of the things I'm best at.

"I'm relentlessly optimistic and obsessive and is anything more important than those traits when searching for someone who's missing?

"This optimism is not such that I believe we live in a world that's fair. It's not. It's much better if you're a white male as I am, or if you're lucky enough to be born in this country, which is not intended as jingoism—just reality. But life is not fair to most of us. I remember complaining to my mom about something not being fair when I was kid. It wasn't anything important and wasn't to her certainly, and she looked at me and said, 'Who told you 'Life is fair?' She didn't wait for a response, nor did she add, 'what do you have to complain about? You live in a stable home. Everything is taken care of. The world is at your feet. Don't be a jerk, and it'll all be yours.'

"What I took from that is the world isn't fair to many, but that doesn't mean I can't thrive, or at least find my place, fix things, be loved, happy. It's not cool, but it is what it is.

"The obsessiveness, that's something else, and something I always was. It wasn't enough to read comic books or watch professional wrestling if I couldn't know the details of every character's backstory, their origins, families, strengths, weaknesses, hopes, fears. Can we talk about laundry? My parents didn't care much about laundry. They sent our clothes out and forgot about them. So, I asked them to buy a washer and dryer. I had to. Laundry had to be done, and folded, and piled neatly, and it still must be that way, which Hannah and Christa find hilarious, purposely nudging the clothes out of order when they're neatly lined up across the living room floor, driving me crazy. No one complains though about having neatly folded clothes or being around someone who can fix things that aren't working. At work, I'm a hero. People love it when stuff is done after I stay late so everything is in place for the next day. I'm a throwback. All these young guys talking about apps for this and that, automation, AI, scheduling appointments on Outlook. But someone must care about flow, harmony, detail, and I do, and I will, always.

"All of which perfectly suits me for helping you find Christa. I know we'll find her, she and Josh will slip, there'll be a phone call, receipt, or text. There'll be a clue, and it'll be sitting there in plain sight, and I'll catch it. Someone else might miss it, but I won't. And if Hannah can't get as wrapped up the search as I am, that's fine. Hannah will find her way, and she, Christa, and I, will be together again.

"And no, I don't think I'm saying this to distract me from the fact that I can't believe we haven't heard from Christa yet, and I'd rather not think about how crazy making this is. I just believe we can find her, and I think you believe it too."

"Uh, yeah, okay, thanks," Officer John says, lowering himself to wipe a speck of invisible dust off his shoes, which have been propped up on his desk as I was speaking, and are now on the ground. After he's done, he looks up, and as he leans forward, he places his elbows on his desk to face me. His handsome mug looms there, a moon, celestial, beautiful and taking up the whole room.

"I know this is hard," he says, "trust me. I also know we're doing everything we're capable of to find your daughter…"

"You're looking for Christa and Josh, right?" I say interrupting him. "I only care about Christa, but it seems to me if you're looking for two missing people, it's more efficient, you'll get more leads, and you can cover more ground or something?"

"Yes and no."

"Yes, and no?"

"He's not technically missing."

"How so?"

"I spoke to his parents, and they don't care about this like you do. He's nineteen, he's a man, and they don't talk to him. They have no intention of reporting him missing. He's moved on and they seem fine with that."

"Yeah, I had the same experience when I spoke to them. I don't understand that attitude, but I also don't understand why it matters in terms of your approach to finding Christa and Josh."

"As far as the parents go, what can I say. From their perspective Josh and Christa left by choice. You care about your daughter, which I appreciate, and Josh's parents don't care about him. If they don't care we're not going to expend our limited resources focusing on him."

I want to say how illogical this sounds, but I don't, my head is spinning.

"Okay, fine. What are you doing then to find Christa? No offense. It's just so quiet here. Isn't there something someone can be doing?"

"No offense taken I know this is terrible for you. I'm following up on every tip we get, I'm making calls to other police stations around the country, and tracking arrests or traffic stops that involve suspects that look like them. I'm doing everything I can and there's nothing yet. I'm sorry about that."

I believe him, and yet there's no urgency in his voice or demeanor.

"Do I need to talk to your boss?"

"Why?"

"So, I know everything that can be done is truly being done?"

Officer John leans forward and a waft of Miller Lite passes between us.

"Everything is being done, but if you want to do more, why don't you create a Facebook page or something like that?"

I ought to say more, but now, I just feel lost and unmoored.

I'll create a Facebook page, though I don't trust he's doing everything he can. I know what doing everything you can looks like, and it doesn't look like this. I'm going to let it go for now, I must, I can only control what I can control. Still, why doesn't Officer John refer to Christa by her name? She has a name and when you forget the name, you forget the person, and I can't allow that, it's not fair to Christa or us.

HANNAH

FAIRNESS IS A BIG thing to Gabriel even though he acts like it isn't. What Gabriel fails to understand, however, is that people will disappear from your life—gone, end of story. I understand it though. I expect it. It's hard to live this way, but at least I'm prepared for things to go south. And they will go south. Trust. Gabriel will tell you that his mother long ago told him that life isn't fair, that he heard her say it, that he gets it, and because he hangs on to her every word—my words not his—he knows it to be true. But does he live it? Or breathe it? He does not. I do. Expect the worst, it'll usually happen, and then move on. Find small moments of joy, grab them, hold them, cherish them, and always keep it real. I enjoy miracles in the abstract. Small, everyday things, that shouldn't work, that feel almost senseless, but make sense, and work. Not really miracles at all. Finding Christa or her walking back through the front door won't be a miracle—but her first steps were. How her pudgy legs righted themselves, the wobble and shakiness becoming something else, upright motion and propulsion? That was magic. "No fear," I yelled at little Christa as she took one step, then another, weaving like a drunk across the room, hands in front of her, finding balance, and promise. Life itself, making, creating, finding a path. These things are small miracles, and I celebrate them. How or when Christa will make it back to us is something else. Someone will make a choice, maybe her, maybe Josh, and she'll be home, and it'll have nothing to do with the universe intervening. Am I sad about this? I'm wrecked by it and wonder now why we ever encouraged her to walk in the first place. Once she could walk, she could leave and since I know people leave, all we did was set the inevitable in motion. It's sad but letting go always is. This doesn't mean that Christa and I couldn't have had the kind of relationship my mother and I didn't. An adult relationship. Phone calls. Beers at Neary's. Manicures, maybe. Whatever Christa wanted. And now, I don't know if it'll ever happen, and I feel sick. I want her to go when it's time. This isn't time. But I can't get lost in that. And I can't get lost in sadness. That sadness is in a box, the box is wrapped up, and double-sealed, and set off to the side somewhere where I don't have to look at it—or think about it, all the time. Does that mean I don't care as much about Christa as Gabriel does? No, I refuse to accept that. But I also accept what life is and isn't, and Gabriel doesn't do real life very well.

Regardless, I can be there for Gabriel, and fake my belief in him, or my belief in his belief that there's a puzzle to be solved. That Christa's absence can be erased. I've been faking so much for so long. All women do, and all partners must—it's how relationships sustain themselves over time. You can't believe in everything the people you love care about. Early on, you fake an interest in the wide range of things that are important to them, some of which you also kind of care about, and much of which you don't. Do I care about *Close Encounters of the Third Kind*? I don't. It's not real and can't be real. Aliens in general, as some ephemeral possibility, and the idea that we aren't alone, I wholly embrace that. But some ridiculous movie about abductions, mashed potatoes, and Devil's Tower? No, I'm not having it. Don't give me science fiction, give me science. Gabriel needs the story though, the belief in things that just won't, and can't, happen. He also needs those around him to believe, and he needed me to believe that *Close Encounters* had something profound to say. Done, I believe it, just don't forget that left to my own devices, I choose to believe in what's real. The launch of the Challenger Space Shuttle when Gabriel and I were in high school was real. Maybe it went bad fast, but the takeoff was life and science and facts combined to create something great and worthy of awe. That it went so awry is tragic and has haunted my days ever since. But that's life too.

Which is to say, marriage is endless compromise, comprised of small lies, small glances, and hope, and when there's nothing else to give, unadulterated support not forthcoming from anywhere else.

Which is also to say that when Gabriel says we need to dig further into Christa's life, look through her diary, search for secret email accounts and retrieve her old text messages and images— invasions of privacy that would otherwise be anathema to me, I say yes, whatever you think is best, let's do that together.

When we learn what we sort of already knew—Christa was a mostly normal teenaged kid, some friends, but not as many as we'd wished for her. People knew her, but while she always had stories about being around drama, she didn't fight with that many kids or have much drama herself. What we also knew, is that she didn't leave much of an impression in school. She was there, she had a nice smile, and she was kind to her fellow students, but she didn't participate in anything, she was somewhat spectral, floating through the halls, a teenage contrail, here, then gone, an image evaporated as if never there in the first place. She was angry at us, but in the way, teens are, we were boring, liars, fucking hypo- crites—that word, again—and we just didn't understand her; no one really did. Except maybe Josh. At first there were stolen looks between them at school. He walked her home occasionally. They started to hold hands. Things accelerated at some point. The way he looked at her made her happy. She wrote that, even if she also wrote, she wasn't entirely capable of feeling happy, not when she was also sad as only teenagers can be. The world was dark. The people running the country were insane. Children were in cages because their parents wanted them to live in a country where there's supposed peace and prosperity and that country didn't want to share it with them. There's so much violence and posturing. Women were hated in every way and everywhere and vilified for speaking truth to power. The oceans were rising, and crops were dying, and it had started to blur together into a kind of rot, and maybe none of it mattered anyway, because the planet was overheating and becoming a place where soon enough no one would be able to live, not her children, or their children. Not that Christa was ever going to bring children into such a world, or ever become a parent anyway. Screw it—my words, not hers. She was also never going to become the kind of liars Gabriel and I are. Can you even be a parent and not lie she wanted to know? Small lies, big lies, secrets, what's the point of even being a parent if you needed to lie to your children much of the time? Why bother? Why indeed? Mostly, Christa seemed to have lacked hope.

This is as painful for Gabriel as anything else. He can't understand how he didn't impart that to her. I get it though. Life can, does, really suck, but it also makes me sad that I somehow failed to show her that there are still little miracles to be found every day. I was unable to provide her with a richer, fuller embrace of the world. Show her how you must believe in science and babies taking their first steps and if you do then there is hope. There are small rays of light everywhere, and you can discover these miracles when you recognize they really are right there, waiting for you if you just look for them.

When Christa comes back, I'll tell her these things, and I'll keep telling her them, even if she acts like she doesn't care about any of it.

It's my job.

GABRIEL

Hannah wants to talk suck and how life isn't fair? Okay. There's much I don't know right now, starting with where Christa is. We have no clue or clues. But that doesn't mean I can't be hopeful or that Christa can't be found and will be fine. And to do that, I need to get this Facebook page right. If people see this, they'll be moved to action. They'll keep an eye out for her. Which photo of her is best though? What captures Christa's essence, and that which makes her unique? Because it's not just what she looks like, long brown hair, thin lips that sometimes, somehow curl into a question mark and the small tidal wave of freckles that flood her cheeks during the summer—an ant colony burst out into the world. It's about who she is, and what she exudes, and it's being able to truly see her. Maybe it's the eyes that are most important. When Elizabeth Smart was kidnapped, her abductor marched her through town, and no one noticed it was her. Elizabeth Smart was covered in a makeshift burqa, and someone would've had to see something in her eyes to see her at all. Is there a good photo of Christa's eyes? The photo on the flyer I made doesn't speak to her eyes. Not that Christa is a kidnapping victim or necessarily near town. She's not Elizabeth Smart, who was stolen from her home by handyman she didn't really know. So why am I obsessing over Elizabeth Smart? We know Christa is with someone she knows, and she chose to be with. We also know the police have talked to everyone—friends, Josh's parents—and it was pointless. No one had anything to share. They didn't know anything. No one really knew Christa though. She was a mystery to them, and us as well apparently, and so why Elizabeth Smart, why not? I'll take any insights I can glean from anywhere.

And yet, I need to keep reminding myself how Christa left on her own.

We know this to be true.

What we don't know is if she really left in a fit, called Josh, ran out, and kept going. Or if there was already a plan? There's no proof of a plan, but we don't know what's been going on in her head. Maybe Christa and Josh knew they were going to leave at some point, they mapped it out, waiting for the right moment and the fight with Hannah was the final push.

Regardless, there's no abduction, no religious nuts, no handyman. Christa isn't being marched through town. She left because she doesn't want to be around us or any of this anymore. That's what it is, right? It is, of course it is. This is about us and how we raised her, and compared to an abduction, it's too confusing and too abstract for me to make sense of. It means we couldn't talk or figure things out. That Christa didn't feel she could communicate with us then, can't now, and maybe never will.

It also means we might not have the adult relationship I envisioned for us—sharing stories, meals, trips, grandchildren, and I'll learn to live with this state of things, even if I can never accept it. I can mold myself to embrace this new normal if I must—the normal where Christa says she must live apart from us, my beliefs about the state of our relationship aren't right, that's that, and she's fine. But if this is the way it's going to be, Christa can at least let us know she's okay, and she's not coming back. Not for now anyway. She must find herself away from us, and that's that as well.

It would help.

A lot.

It would just never make sense why Christa feels to be the person she needs to be involves cutting us out of her life.

When Chris McCandless disappeared, his family had no idea why either. Is that fair? There's that word again, fair. It means nothing to anyone, and maybe it didn't to Chris McCandless either. He seemed to be done with the material world and was possibly angry at his parents—his father in particular, and the hypocrisy of his father's behavior.

But when is our behavior not the root of our children's struggles?

Never, I guess. The small reverberations flowing over time, the lies, anger, and recriminations chipping away at their belief in us, the way we choose to live, or raise them. The healthy definition of this is individuation. There must be a break from the parent, a fissure, but it can be done in a more transparent manner—college or boarding school, a job away from home.

It doesn't have to be like this, disappeared and final.

I don't accept it, nor will I, especially when there's been no communication. Christa is missing, and she can be found, and if I can get this Facebook page right, and if I can find the correct photo, the one that says, this is me, see me, I'm Christa, and I'm right here in front of you, which you will not realize until you look at me, really look, and really see me—and when I can accomplish this, she'll be home, where she belongs, with us, safe and loved.

Also, I know now that I should have pushed a little harder, taken a chance, and told Christa I didn't approve of her relationship. Maybe even punched Josh. I didn't. I wanted to be cool, and I regret it.

HANNAH

Safe and loved. That sounds nice. It's something Gabriel doesn't believe I had growing up. How could I he thinks when I grew up with the chaos I did? Maybe I didn't feel safe. I don't know. I don't spend any time on such nonsense. Nor do I spend much time thinking about the past. It's done. But I know I felt loved by my father, and how much love does one need to receive to feel loved?

Should I ask my father what he thinks?

No way.

He's right here though, so close, I can touch him if I want to.

I'm sitting with my father behind his house. It's our house, I guess. I don't know. I haven't lived here in so long. There's a deck out back he built with his bare hands. The nails are askew or missing, the wooden slats, long warped twisted into gnarled sine waves, repeating again and again until they suddenly drop off into the perpetually muddy grass otherwise known as the backyard. There are also some rusty chairs my father never puts in the garage, instead condemning them to battle the elements year-round as they slowly became one with nature and the deck. The remains of a blackboard he added to the side of the garage for basketball games we never played and were never going to play. A grill covered in sap and pine needles, the top melded into the base, fused forever together by time and neglect.

The grill is a bit like Gabriel and me.

Too on the nose?

Too bad

I went from this house to my house with Gabriel, a straight line and a life fused together, which once seemed fine enough and now seems ridiculous.

Also, how does this happen?

Is grabbing hold of someone then desperately clinging to them better than what I grew up with? I said I'd do better than my parents did. But is this better? A sad, tenuous marriage and a missing daughter who'd rather be with a nineteen-year-old janitor with a bowl cut than us?

How have I fallen so short with this adult thing?

Meanwhile, where was I? Right, the grill. Did we ever grill anything?

"Did we ever grill a fucking thing back here?" I ask my dad, immediately regressing into the role of angry daughter, something I've worked so hard to outgrow, but can still fall into so easily around him.

"Language, baby," he says, like I'm still thirteen years old. "And no, grilling was your mother's thing, and after she was gone, I didn't see any point in it."

"We couldn't grill because you couldn't stop her from leaving," I say, as I adjust my chair and catch my sandal on one of the twisted nails.

"I wouldn't say quite like that," he replies. "I never wanted to grill, but I did for her. When it wasn't for her, I didn't see the point."

"What about me? Did you ever ask what I wanted?"

"No, I didn't. Did you want me to grill?"

"I definitely did not care about grilling."

"Well, fuck you then, sweetie," he says, with a sad smile, his lips curling up and down in one motion.

He then touches my leg, and I do my best not to cringe. It's almost more intimacy than I can bear in a moment where everything feels so lost and unfixable.

To ameliorate things, I try to ruin everything. Or at least deflect the energy elsewhere.

"Okay," I say, "what about that stupid backboard? Why did you put it up?"

"Your mother was worried you didn't have any friends and thought someone might come over to play basketball."

"For real? Did you make any decisions on your own, old man?"

I may want to ruin the moment, but that's supposed to be funny. He gets that, right?

"Well, I know I made all the goddamn decisions after she left," he says, rubbing his eyes, and looking away from me and off into the backyard.

I guess he missed the humor thing.

"Lighten up, Francis."

He must appreciate a *Stripes* reference, right? We saw it together. We had dinner and went to the movies every Friday night from the moment my mom left until I married Gabriel. I never let anything get in the way of that.

No response.

Nothing, which is not nothing—he's disappointed in me.

He thinks I'm not upset enough about Christa. He thinks he raised me wrong—I'm dead inside, or a robot. But he's wrong. I'm like him, and like my mom, I suppose. Head down, plow forward, things will work out, forget everything else.

My father knows how he raised me, doesn't he? If he's disappointed with the results, isn't he somewhat to blame?

But maybe that's it too?

He feels responsible for this.

Me.

Christa.

He and Christa were never close and even though he helped

us with her at times when she was little, there was a distance. I always felt he held something back, scared that if he got too close, it could blow up and that would be unbearable for him.

He became weird around her, and it was uncomfortable to watch.

I could have pushed him to be less like he was, and I could have pushed Christa to see his goodness, but it always felt like too much work.

Now she's missing, and I know he thinks he could have prevented it if he'd only tried harder along the way.

It's who he is.

Still, even being who he is, he looks especially tired today.

It's not just the bags under his eyes, or the sagging jaw, or even the color of his skin, which is so gray as to be one with the sky, because it's always gray here, the horizon, stretching on forever, infinite, without end, and muted as hell. It's not any of that, though. It's more a world weariness, and the sense that when one lives long enough, sadness and loss stretches on without end too. Life is punctuated by amazing things, but they're merely blips on the connective tissue. One long gray sky where all relationships are at some point destined to become something awful, or worse, nothing meaningful whatsoever and so everything sucks.

Yet we're sitting here together, which proves this point of view is at least somewhat incorrect.

Still, there's Christa, she's missing, something has been destroyed, and we somehow must talk about her.

Or not.

I don't really know what he wants to talk about, and I really don't want to ask.

"My father was shell-shocked from the Korean War," he says, something I well know, and something he knows I know, but there's no way I'm going to stop him from telling me again. "No one knew what that meant back then, or what PTSD was. We didn't know trauma. We just knew that people were damaged and scared, that it was hard for them to leave their rooms, face things without drinking or rage. You just accepted it. I accepted it. My mom was nowhere too, you know that. She left me during the war with my grandparents and didn't come back. They were tough, and I promised never to be like them. It was Depression-era stuff. No risk, no joy, get the work done, and be thankful. I worked for them in their candy store, and when my dad came home, they gave it to him, but he couldn't leave the couch, and I started to run it. I went to school when I could. I took care of my father—made sure he got his meds, didn't choke on his vomit when he passed out, and got the bills paid. When my dad blew his brains out, I got as far from there as I could. It's just I only made it as far as Neary's down the street and met your mom. She was so young, and on the run, and beautiful with her red hair, just like yours and Christa's, and she took me home and said she'd take care of me, and the day you were born, it was like Jesus in the manger—a miracle. The three of us were something too. What a team. And when it came to you, I was happy to have someone like your mom to make the decisions for us. I knew how to take care of adults, not children. Not that it mattered. Even after she left, you were easy, and you knew how to take care of yourself. Still do. I just hope Christa learned how to take care of herself as well…"

He starts to cry.

"God, this is awful…," he adds.

The tears soon become rivers, then puddles, and tidal waves. It's the worst thing I've ever seen, and I would do anything to be anywhere else right now. But I start to worry our warped deck is going to float away, and I take him in my arms—just as I did the day my mom left—and I hold him until the deck comes loose, and we drift into the neighbor's yard.

GABRIEL

Did we raise Christa to take care of herself? That's the question right now, right? I hope so. Not that we can know until we see her again. For now, it's just speculation, fear, and memories. I had no idea there were so many memories, or that they're everywhere, every turn and corner, every block. She's in the ether. It's how love works. It imbues everything it touches, and it never fades away. And so yes, there are the obvious things. Maybe it's a song we once sang in the car that comes on the radio, pick anything by Demi Lovato, Ke$ha, or Taylor Swift, though I hope I'm not the only middle-aged man to burst into tears listening to the song "TiK ToK" at the mall. Or it could be a movie, *The Hunger Games*, or *The Hangover* (not that I ever told Hannah that Christa and I watched the latter). It's seeing a book she loves, such as any or all of the *Harry Potter* series, which instantly transports me to a night where I'm in a bookstore at midnight, maroon and gold scarf and wand in hand, picking-up a copy of whatever is coming out, and ordered months in advance—me pretending to enjoy the fake Butterbeer and Jelly Belly BeanBoozled Jelly Beans, while knowing I'll never quite get the flavor of spoiled cheese out of my brain or teeth. Even seeing a jar of peanut butter reminds me she's not here to make her a sandwich for lunch.

It's an extended narrative, a life, stretched from birth onward, and the detritus, good, bad, and indifferent, that gathers along the way, sticks to your DNA, molds itself to the objects that surround you, and never, ever let you forget that there is someone you love who you can't see.

Maybe I encounter someone Christa goes to school with on the street, someone I met picking her up somewhere, I make some uncomfortable joke in front of them, and they don't know what to say, and I don't know what to say, and it's terribly awkward, and they look sad, and I want to say, "hey, it's okay," except I don't—I only say it in my head, and then I want to hug them, except I can't do that kind of thing anymore. Impulsively hugging a teenage girl, can you imagine? Even if you care about them, and even if it's not remotely sexual, everything is sexual now, and I get it. It's not a personal affront to me. Things change, times change, and we must be hip to that, something Christa would be more than happy to point out if she were here. To her, everything I do or say, or think is homophobic, racist, or misogynistic. I can't reference a black friend or refer to someone as a girl. And nothing can ever be gay. No way, which is fine.

Do I want to live in a world where people don't care about those things?

No, I only want to live in a world where I don't have to think about her absence so much.

But I don't live in that world. The memories also wash over me when Hannah does something as simple as tilts her head—slightly askew and away from me when she's embarrassed. Christa does this well, and yes, she got it from Hannah in the first place, but who cares, it's her. Or the crooked smile they both have. It's devastating to see Hannah smile. Then there's the hair, always on fire, a blazing inferno. Impossible to escape. Every room is saturated by it and sometimes the whole sky, which may be otherwise filled with darkness, but is explosive and aglow, as far as the eye and heart can see, when either of them enter the picture.

Christa Hannah Christa Hannah Christa Hannah Christa

Hannah Christa Hannah Christa.

It's all night, all day, every day. Christa's right there, a continuous jolt of sense memories on repeat, which serve to remind me what is and is not. Any of which might make someone, me, want to have a drink, which might in turn bring someone, me, to Neary's staring into the window, swallowing hard, and sweaty—not moving, not allowing myself to, and then not thinking about drinking, but thinking about Christa, again, always, and the last time we'd been here together.

I couldn't believe I was going to have the conversation without a drink. That's what I was thinking, but I didn't drink anymore, and the plan was to sit Christa down and do the conversation properly. It was Hannah's idea—father-daughter time. I know it was a test. Hannah wanted to see if I could show responsibility. I got it. It wasn't so long before then I had been a sloppy mess. Hannah wanted me to be more like her father Ed, the saint who raised her as single dad and did his best to take care of things. He didn't always do it well, but he got things taken care of, nonetheless.

Not like me.

Not that Hannah would ever say that.

Not that she even totally believed it.

It was just the way she asked me to do things, or looked at me, judging me, for those times I wasn't where I was supposed to be, or home, drinking too much, too often. I'd always been able to rally, but I wasn't her father. Compared to him, I sucked, and God forbid I ever said something negative about Ed. There was no room for that. To Ed's credit, it hadn't been easy to say anything negative about him. He'd always been pretty good to me, even when I wasn't good to his precious daughter.

But holding the sex talk with Christa, how could that possibly be my job?

I didn't know how anything worked and no one ever had a talk with me. Most everything I learned, I learned from Hannah. But maybe that was part of her point. Hannah had always taught me and Christa and whoever needed it about how things work, and she was always taking care of everything, for everyone, and now it was my turn.

Ughhhhh.

Still, I loved Christa, I loved Hannah, and I knew I could step up.

Should I have taken Christa to Neary's for that talk? No, it was a bar, and somewhat inappropriate for both of us, but I hadn't been drinking for some time and Hannah wasn't the only person testing me. I was testing me too. I wanted to remind myself I could handle the stress, that bars had once been my downfall, but no longer were, and I was doing what I needed to do despite being in one.

The plan was to be mechanical. Christa was still kind of young for this to me—just nine years old, but from Hannah's perspective Christa couldn't be too young to learn about sex, not when Hannah was the product of a teen mother. What if that skips a generation? Maybe that was part of it too? Maybe Hanna wanted to believe Christa wouldn't want to disappoint me and wouldn't take Hannah seriously because she was the mom, and Christa's a girl, and on and on and on.

So, there we were, me knowing that Neary's wasn't exactly the proper choice, and Christa looking at me with her huge, saucer eyes, full of anticipation and a small grin, because she knew what we were about to discuss.

"What's going on?" she asked as she tilted her head away from me and gave me the side eye.

"Th-i-i-s is the talk," I said.

"Fuck, really?" she deadpanned.

"Mouth," I said, before adding, "please don't make this any harder than it has to be."

"Fine, go." She placed her skinny little-kid arms on the table and cupped the side of her face with her hands. "Hit me."

"You know how…it works, yes?"

"Yeah, sperm, egg, fertilization, baby, right?"

"Yes, okay, but do you know how the sperm gets to the egg?" I sought to both assert myself and drill down to the must-knows.

"Uhhhh, yeah," she said, with a tinge of false bravado before sweeping her hair out of her face and setting the room on fire.

"A boy has to put his penis in a vagina," I responded. "That's clear to you, right?"

There was no response from the other side of the table, just horror, and Christa looking away, down, anywhere, but at me.

"Yeah, I guess, but does that mean…?" she finally said.

I let her statement linger for a moment.

She might've been thinking about herself in that position someday, or me and Hannah, or penises and vaginas across the millennia—I didn't know, it didn't matter, it seemed profound to her, and I went with it.

"It does," I replied.

"Oh, yuck," she said, as her mouth scrunched up.

"Oh, yeah, super yucky—beautiful too—though nothing you want to rush into."

"Rush, how about never?"

"Yeah, well…it's not like that isn't music to my ears, but no, sex can be great. Let me tell you about the rest of it."

And I did, which was the last time we ever spoke about it. I tried to check in occasionally after that, but Hannah eventually took over.

I think.

I'm not sure what I know as I remain in front of the window. Well, I know one thing, wherever Christa and Josh are, I hope they're practicing safe sex. I also know this seems like a nutso thing to worry about in the context of her being missing, but it still matters. Christa needs to take care of herself, and she can't count on Josh to make good decisions. He's a teenage boy, and he won't be thoughtful enough, often enough. That's how it is and has been for time immemorial.

I know as well that I want a drink, and it's not just grief, or memory driving this desire, though it's that too. It's mostly the desire to be numb and not face the realities before me.

I put up the Facebook page and titled it "Have you seen Christa?"

I got the picture right.

I shared my phone number.

I encouraged people to contact me with tips.

I checked it obsessively and I waited for something, anything.

At first, people mostly shot me text messages. "Good luck" or "sorry," "Jesus loves you." There were some jerks, "she's hot, man, I hope I see her," and some psychics, "can you send me an article of clothing?"

I even spoke to some people who were kind and sad.

"I've been there with my daughter, I've been lost, and I feel your pain."

They mostly wanted to talk, and I talked to them, but they had nothing to share, but pain.

There were the occasional leads, a 7-Eleven in Erie,

Pennsylvania, a soup kitchen in Columbus, Ohio, squatting in a deserted building in Denver, Colorado. All of which I passed along to Officer John.

But then nothing.

No calls, no messages, no tips, no leads, no jerks, no psychics.

One week became two, then three, now it's a month since Christa went missing and there are no signs, no leads, and no follow-up from Officer John, because he doesn't care enough; and because he has nothing to say.

It seems impossible, but it's not, Hannah always said people can just leave, disappear from your life, and I didn't appreciate just how easy that is.

It's not that I didn't believe her, but the possibility of it didn't mean anything to me. And I never thought it would apply to Christa anyway—Hannah maybe, but Christa, impossible, how?

Isn't our connection so strong?

Father and daughter?

Jesus, look at Ed and Hannah.

Doesn't it mean something to Christa?

Here we are though, and if there's nothing, isn't it better to feel nothing too?

No, it isn't, ultimately.

I'm not going to drink, not now, not one minute from now, not tomorrow.

I'm also not going to focus on what a failure I've been as a father or my inability to fix this. I can't obsess over that, because once that starts, it's over.

I turn away from Neary's, I close my eyes, take a deep breath, and I repeat the mantra I've adopted for times of stress, *"I am not empty, I am open."*

It's a line by the Swedish poet Tomas Tranströmer I once read in a horoscope. It works, and when needed I repeat it until I'm centered.

"I am not empty, I am open."

"I am not empty, I am open."
"I am not empty, I am open."
I'm good.
I also need to get more help if I'm going to find Christa.

HANNAH

Am I in the kitchen?

No, I'm not, no I am, but this isn't where I want to go. Where do I want to go? I want to go to the bathroom, no, the basement. I want to get the laundry. I walk down the stairs to the basement. This was once the scariest thing to me, the creaky stairs, the cobwebs, the oozy, rich darkness. It's all a fear pudding, thick with a slight layer of crud on top. The feeling of being alone, lost, and naked. Unmoored. The surety that someone, or something, must be waiting for me at the bottom of the stairs, full of glee and looking to kill me, or worse, defile me in some way, the damage and taint crossing eons.

With each step I realize that I'll never quite lose the fear of what may await me. Adulthood teaches one this shit isn't real. Pragmatically, if not statistically, speaking, this isn't what I need to fear. What I need to fear is losing my way, work falling apart, finances disintegrating—the realization that what I dream of and want for myself isn't going to be.

Gabriel and I will not take great vacations to exotic places.

We won't take surfing lessons.

Or join a country club.

We won't be able to pay for Christa's college, which will leave her with debt, and unable to spread her wings, worry-free.

We won't retire at some reasonable age.

We won't be the kind of adults who at some point go on cruises or drive around the country in an RV, lazing around in the afternoon, smoking a joint as the sun drops and day blurs into night, taking naps, entwined with one another, our creaky bodies briefly transported too somewhere better and more peaceful.

We'll scrape and scrimp, and we'll be fine, but we won't be better off than our parents.

That's not happening.

Then there's Christa.

She's not here.

She's not coming back.

And we're supposed to accept that, somehow.

This is my fear and the reality.

Did I see Officer John?

I know I saw him when Christa was first missing.

Is that it?

No, wait.

I was with Tracey.

Was it at the police station?

No, Neary's, when was that?

It doesn't matter.

We left. We stood there. Outside on the sidewalk.

No, we're inside. We're having drinks.

That's right.

Tracey steers me away from him.

He's drinking at the bar, talking to someone young. Blonde. He's stroking her arm. He's still in uniform, smiling, full of swagger, ever the big fish in the small pond, and I grab an empty bottle of beer and start to approach him from behind. I'm so close I can see the oil in his hair, the jet-black interspersed with gray and much more obvious up close and personal. My throat tightens. I can't breathe. A phantom hand has me in its grip. I find myself in a space too small for me, and as I grapple to climb out, Tracey takes the bottle out of my hand and steers me away.

This happens, right?

There are moments these days when things fly around in my head, take shape, settle there, and feel so real—conversations, confrontations, but it might be the idea of these things that have a hold on me, not something happening, merely the wish that it had.

It's not Officer John's fault that Christa doesn't want to be found. How could it be?

But he's the perfect receptacle to channel my sad, angry energy into. He represents something—lost hope, the male gaze, sexuality, fear. Yet he's not quite real either, more object than human, which means he can take it, absorb it—and he doesn't even have to know.

Wait, what, why am I here, standing in the dark, in the basement?

I want to be in the bathroom. No, I want to be in the kitchen? I'm at Neary's. Where is Tracey? No, I'm not in Neary's and Tracey is not here. I'm in the basement. I'm where I belong, but why did I come down here? The circuit breaker? No, not that. I came down for more toilet paper. No, not that either. The laundry, yes, right.

I walk over to the dryer, I open the door, I reach in, but there's no laundry.

What?

Did Gabriel already get it?

I pause.

Why am I here?

My throat tightens.

I try to swallow.

I try to make it go away.

I'm so cold.

I wrap my arms around myself in an embrace.

Why am I suddenly so scared?

I walk up the stairs. I trip. I bang my shin. I fall forward.

Catch myself. I leap back up and keep moving. I get to the top of the stairs, breathless, my hair matted down to my forehead, sweat trickling down my back.

I stop.

When did I get here? Why does my shin hurt so much? I look down. There is a spot of blood spreading across my khakis. I watch it grow, at first just a drop, soon a pond or small lake, now a vast unknowable sea, crimson and dark, spreading across the floor, and then everywhere across the universe.

I'm mesmerized.

I wonder what it would be like to lay back and go out with the tide. Where might I go: out the door, down the driveway, across town? Might I land in the river and where would that take me—to the ocean, space?

Now I'm floating above myself. I look at the small creature that is me. This speck. I'm standing at the top of the stairs. I have no idea why and no access to the great universe that exists past the planets, the stars, and the galaxy as we know it.

It's so vast, and I'm so free.

No.

I'm back and one with myself again, panicked, gripping my head in both hands.

Focus Hannah, you got this.

Everything goes black for a moment. Little lights ping about like the stars which now inhabit my fragile brain.

I rush to the bathroom to clean up the blood.

Why am I here? My shin hurts. I look down. There's blood as wide as the ocean. Right, my shin's bleeding. Why is it bleeding? Did I get the laundry? Why was I scared? The basement, yes, no, does the basement still scare me? Wait, not the basement. It was the dark—the unknown.

It's not that. It's a different kind of fear.

It's isolation. Loss. A grief I can't quite articulate even as it crawls up my neck and envelopes me.

Oh fuck, fuck, fuck.
My shin hurts.
Why am I here?

GABRIEL

WHY ARE ANY OF us here? Is it to love, and be loved, or make the world a slightly better place, for a little while?

Is it to make sure those we care for are taken care of and happy, or at least content?

I hope it isn't that, because if it is, I'm a huge failure.

And not just with Christa.

Not at this moment.

When I wake, Hannah isn't by my side, and I experience a moment of profound panic.

It's still dark, a slight chill in the air, and as I lie there, staring at the ceiling I feel the slightest additional fluctuation in the uncomfortable flutter I awake to in my chest most mornings regardless of how much sleep I get or how calm I feel at bedtime. I rub my chest in a circular motion—feeling the pinch and contraction, the slight ripple and vibration that is my anxiety expressing itself in this most banal of ways.

Why I feel this way is not a mystery.

I know well enough what's going on.

There's no need to pretend otherwise.

While I'm not consciously thinking of Christa at this moment, she is my every thought when I'm otherwise supposed to be in a deepened state of relaxation. The thoughts we bury and run away from during the day will find a home in our dreams. In my case these thoughts are manifesting themselves in this somewhat awakened state due to the mere recognition Hannah isn't where I believe she should be.

I go to bed worrying about Hannah as well.

She's off.

We're off.

Of course, we're off, but Hannah's keeping something from me. Whatever's going on in her head. I can see it, but I don't know what it is, and I haven't asked.

Do I want to go to bed worrying about her too?

No, not really.

I want her to feel better, and I want us to be with Christa again or at least achieve some kind of peace with whatever will be, but do I want to take care of Hannah? I thought so. Once. It's just that wanting to fix things and make them go away isn't the same as caring for someone. Or being there for them and being present.

You learn these things with age.

Why you do what you do, what drives your decisions, what you really care about.

I do anything for Hannah I can. Same with Christa. I recognize her need to have parents who are supportive of her, each other, and in general, modeling it, living it. It's good parenting. But Christa isn't here, and she may not be back, and if that's the case, is there a point to any of this? This meaning, being here, and why? It's an old feeling, and it's creeping back into my brain. A desire to escape the tough stuff—run from expectations, responsibility, reality—some of which is related to the panic that has become omnipresent, and I can't manage or control it.

This panic I speak of is the panic of being alone and lying in an empty bed I'm too scared to leave. The irony of this situation isn't lost on me. That I can wake up anxious and confused by the lack of Hannah's presence next to me is as obscene as it is sad. How many nights has she awoken to the indentation on my side of the bed, empty, a vast chasm between us, our marriage some kind of arrangement or partnership, living like siblings, or friends. Hannah being forced to wonder where I am—in someone else's bed, asleep in my car, or dead on the side of the road? How often do I ease into our bed in these darkened hours, freshly bathed, clothes stripped of bars, smoke, cigarettes, sex, foreign scents, other beds—Hannah forced to pretend otherwise? And not out of misguided loyalty, but because she merely wants to make it to the next morning with a semblance of her sanity.

Well, for her sanity, and for Christa's.

This is unspoken, but Hannah isn't ever going to repeat her mother's actions, there can be no leaving, and if I take advantage of it, which I do, shame on me.

My truth telling doesn't change our current reality, however. Christa's gone, missing, one moment here, the next not, and if it can feel real to me that her absence might invoke questions about my relationship with Hannah, then it can do so for Hannah too.

What loyalty does she have to me?

When did I engender such a thing?

Why does she have to stay?

Hannah is here for Christa, not me, or us. For Christa, and if there's no Christa, there's no us anymore, right? I should check that. I don't know if this is the truth. I don't ask. I don't drink. I don't sleep with other people. I don't stay away from home. It is work, home, Christa, meals, mantras, sleep, and on and on.

What does this mean to Hannah now though?

I don't know. I could ask that too, but she's not here, and now we've gone full circle—my chest pounding, and soon to burst.

"Christa?"

I hear this drifting through the halls, dreamy, gossamer, and silken.

"Christa?"

Could it be a ghost or memories assuming some kind of astral form?

"Christa?"

I might be losing my mind, yes, easily—I follow the voice anyway. I leave our room and walk down the hall towards the den.

"Christa," Hannah is saying this over and over, an echo of herself, her voice reverberating across the ages.

Should I have known it was Hannah's voice? Yes, but when everything is confused, everything is confused.

Hannah is sitting by the back window and staring into the dark sky as morning washes across the room. The sun is creeping, melty and orange, hints of purple threaded through the clouds, appearing as veins, or maybe conduits, lazily forming and unforming before us.

"Christa, Christa, Christa," Hannah says, a tear trickling down her cheek as she places her hand on the window.

"Hey," I say softly, careful not to startle her, "what are you doing?"

"Christa," she says smiling, something dancing behind her eyes, something making her happy, though I'm not sure yet what it is. The only surety is she doesn't recognize I'm even in the room.

I think about when I hurt her, how different her eyes look—filled with rage and sadness. The betrayal clear and sharp, cutting, even if her words are not. Even when she nods in agreement with my lies and acts like she accepts them as truth, or at least the only means available for quantifying the terribly weak man before her.

If I accomplish nothing else in this life, I can only hope she won't ever have that look again. That I won't hurt her in that way. There has been enough of it for a lifetime and exponentially so in this primal search for Christa. The hurt is now everywhere, and Christa's name now taken flight across the room.

"Hey," I finally say, "Christa's not here."

Hannah notices for the first time someone else is in the room.

"I know," she says. "How could she be?"

"She could be," I reply confused, "but she's not, not at the moment, not yet?"

"Christa," Hannah says again, before turning to the window and pointing outside.

What?

Oh.

Outside.

Morning.

The slight chill in the air.

Hannah is not thinking about our Christa.

She is looking, waiting for a launch which isn't going to be, and an astronaut who isn't going to triumphantly appear at the door to give her a hug.

Here, now, I should probably ask myself if this is a concern—if she needs help—but I don't. Instead, I stare at her, hesitant and unsure of myself, and at some point, Hannah stands up, runs her fingers through her hair, smooths her shirt, and says she's sorry she freaked me out. She was having a moment. She needed some alone time. Things are not okay, and she can't imagine when they will be, but she's cool.

She then kisses me on the cheek and goes to get ready for work.

HANNAH

I'VE ALWAYS THOUGHT ABOUT my mother, and flight, and I wasn't surprised when I found myself watching her fly away from me. I willed her to soar and keep soaring, and it's not like I wanted her to—I didn't—but I'm a mother too, and I knew how it felt to feel trapped, and to wish you could fly and so I respected her wishes and desires.

I didn't trust her flight would go well, however, which isn't to say I was convinced any of this was the truth. I knew I might be spinning a narrative about our mutual desires, which allowed me to forgive her for leaving and myself for questioning whether I ever wanted to be a mother myself.

Then, suddenly, my mother was no longer flying.

Instead, she was hurtling through the sky, falling, plummeting towards the earth, the river waiting below to eat her whole. She had been wearing wings. The wings were made from feathers and wax. They'd been working beautifully, as she'd been climbing towards the sun and away from that which imprisoned her.

But that was no longer the case.

Things had gone awry.

The wax had melted.

The wings faltered.

It might've been the sun and the heat having its way. Or maybe it was hubris, the idea of a woman wanting to be free of her marriage and her child, liberated to explore the universe and the secrets it held. It wasn't going to happen though. There would be no freedom and no more flight. She achieved all she would be allowed to achieve. It was done, and there was nowhere left to go, but down.

I thought I might still be able to catch her though. I was also flying far into the sky, and I sought freedom too. I understood how universal this feeling was and I wanted to be a person who so understood someone else's need to be free—in this case their own mother's—they'd be willing to rise above any emotions that might otherwise tell them to feel anger, confusion, or loss.

I wanted to be that person.

But was I, or was it more accurate to say I hoped my mother's flight didn't go well? Maybe I felt so betrayed by her that I never wanted her to feel free?

This felt like a philosophical argument for another time though and for people who had time to ruminate on such arguments, whereas right then, that was real and there was no time. My mother was in free fall, spinning, contorting, battered by the wind, and I was reaching, diving, hoping, thinking that maybe I'd be able to catch her if I could get a little closer.

But no, it wasn't happening and wouldn't happen. She was almost gone. The calm surface of the water was waiting to suck her into the roiling grasp that lied below. Waiting there hungry to consume her and quash the dreams of a woman who dared to want more. I might have been able to shoot a web at my mother and grab her before she reached the surface. This presupposed I could make a web—something I somehow inherently knew to be true. The question was whether I could fire one web off above me somewhere, anywhere, nearby to stop our respective falls, while still firing another one at her, and swinging us both to safety— triumphant and beautiful.

Which led me to ponder another question: how could I ensure my mother wouldn't end up like Gwen Stacey, plummet averted, necked snapped in the process? None of which speaks to the reality of the water getting so close or how I might not have the ability to shoot webs regardless. It doesn't matter. I wouldn't reach her in time despite how hard I was trying to do so. With that, I took one more look, but she was no longer even my mother, she was Christa, and she was reaching for me, pleading with me, her hair a firestorm engulfing everything I could see or know. But it was too late, and I turned away, not wanting to see what came next.

Splaaaaaaaaaaaaaaaaaaaaaaaaaaaaaaaaaaaaaaaaaaaaaaaaaaaaaaaaaaash.

Christa was gone.

I was lying in bed covered in a layer of cold sweat, shivering, and even with Gabriel curled up next to me, the shape of his body as familiar to me as my own, I felt so alone. There's an obligation to learn how to be alone. Embracing love may be the window to making connections to a life outside ourselves, but ultimately, even if we embrace love, we're alone in the world, and we'll go to the next one by ourselves as lost as when we came into this one. As a child, I came to understand loneliness like anything was a state of mind. We were only as lonely as we allowed ourselves to be. We could control the feeling and replace it with something else—work, activity, engagement with the natural world, something more spiritual. Not that I've ever been religious. Still, I knew we were one with the universe and with each other. I didn't know if science supported this, and I may have had to contradict myself to believe it, but I did. I knew it was truth, and it was in accepting the belief we're never truly alone, I was able to believe it.

While this belief sustained me, it was the awesome possibilities of the universe, and by extension, space that especially transfixed me when my thoughts drifted to what the state of being alone even meant. I would consider the narcissism involved in believing humans alone exist in this vast universe. It was an offense to the very nature of nature.

I'd always believed we could contact creatures not us, but not unlike us either.

We were already connected.

I also believed it was space travel, which offered the greatest potential to unlock these connections and expose what we already knew; and that it was the space shuttle program which offered the greatest hope to make this so. It also held that no single American figure had spoken to me as much as Christa McAuliffe did. She was the perfect embodiment of life's great potential and the ongoing tragedy that life isn't fair.

That life couldn't be fair.

That life wouldn't be fair.

It's true I once fantasized how Christa McAuliffe might come into my life. She would recognize I was motherless and in need of a stabilizing feminine force, and guidance, and that my potential was unlimited and awaited the opportunity to be released out into the universe she was destined to know so well. It's, of course, not true, that not reaching whatever potential was intended to be mine was the fault of Christa McAuliffe and the tragic twists of history. But it's also true, when I left Gabriel's prone body, his earthly shell, and I wandered down to the living room, it was in search of our big windows and their access to the vast galaxies lying just beyond our reach. It may be that when dreaming of my mother, recalling Christa McAuliffe, and continuing to place my own Christa in a little box, here, but not here, nearly in reach, but not quite; in believing that's the only way I know to manage the horror of her missing—six weeks and counting—a reality so unfair and scary it had been slowly ripping me in two, I became overwhelmed as I stared out of the window and into the unceasing darkness that is the world. One moment I was sitting there, attuned to what had been going on both inside and outside my psyche, in control, and connected, and the next I was sitting there, and Gabriel stood before me, freaked out, and confused at my confusion, as I didn't know how much time had transpired since I sat down, much less remembered anything after coming to the couch.

I could've said something to him about how scared I was, how alone I felt, and how unaccustomed I was to be sharing these things. How life suddenly felt so impossible, my memory felt shaky and unreliable, and I needed help. I could've said these things, or just that I needed him. But I didn't. I didn't know how. Instead, I acknowledged his presence, his fears, and apologized for alarming him before heading into work and another day of managing the loss, pain, fear, and confusion by myself.

It has always been this way, and it always will be.

GABRIEL

With Hannah, there may be no mother, but the endless reverberations of loss, pain, fear, and confusion wash over years and generations, taking root first in her DNA, then Christa's, and just might in her children as well if such a thing is to be. There may also be a need for Hannah to control her emotions, pack them away, and keep them at arm's length. But there's also one constant: Ed the saint, always and forever, and when my cell rings and I see it's him, my first thought is how much I want to avoid his sad, judge-y eyes, and how I'll not be able to do so. Which isn't to say I can see Ed's eyes—Ed does not FaceTime, but they're there. They're always there.

"Gabriel, it's Ed, Hannah's dad," he says, as if I don't know who it is thirty years into our relationship. He always introduces himself to me by name when he calls, as if I might forget his voice, or he believes he's somehow too inconsequential for me to remember.

"Hey Ed, you know I know it's you, right? You're saved in my contact list. Also, I know your voice by now. Anyway, I appreciate your calling, I do, but I'm kind of busy…," I start to say. I'm not busy. It doesn't matter. He cuts me off.

"I'm going to come by in thirty minutes so we can go for a run," he says. "Start hydrating."

Ed is worried about me, not sorry, or empathic, or even angry, though he might be feeling those things too. It's just if he wants to run—he's worried.

The first time I stopped drinking, cold, hard stop, no rehab, no meetings, no nothing, merely the fear of repeating behaviors I couldn't bear to face again, Ed played a big role in helping me channel my crippling manic need to drink by dragging me out to run. It was an odd juxtaposition for me. He hated me for being weak, and in his estimation, not doing right by his daughter and granddaughter. Still, while he didn't forgive me, he didn't drop me either. He knew something about drinking to forget. He also felt regardless of how well he'd done on his own with Hannah, two parents are better than one, and if not always better—it's not always better—that having one parent disappear for any reason didn't serve anyone. At first, as I sweated through work, and sleep, and re-built what it meant to function as a sober person, feeling emotions I wasn't accustomed to as they exploded in directions I couldn't understand, and had no way to manage regardless, he would come by every night and make me run with him. We almost never talked, and he was slow as hell, which was excruciating in its own way, but it was rhythmic, and consistent—every night, one step, then another, arms and endorphins pumping, the stress and obsessions melting away with every drop of sweat flying off my back. He knew he could help me get through it, and even if he barely cared about me as a human being, he most definitely cared about Hannah and Christa, and everybody benefited.

We haven't run together in years. We didn't need to. Those concerns had long faded away. I was good, Hannah and I were good enough, and things were stable. I might ask if being good is good enough, or even enough, and whether that's part of aging? How with age, we allow a kind of stasis to set in, accepting how much easier it is to embrace it than fight the inertia slowly engulfing our brains, motivation, and hope.

It's a good question for another time, but not now, not with

Christa being wherever she and Josh may be, and Ed wanting to go for a run. To Ed's credit, whether I want to acknowledge it or not, things are not stable anymore, and even if the temptation to drink and destroy things feels minimal to me, Ed doesn't know this, or care about it—he's concerned, and we're on.

Watching Ed stretch is almost as painful as what it was once like to run with him. He's like a dry sponge that someone believes they can wring water from if they just keep twisting and mashing it. He's not limber. His paunch is now a ring of old man fat that slaps his thighs as he bends over. Perspiration dots his forehead, then pools on his neck and clavicles after mere moments of effort. It's almost unbearable to be around him. Ed doesn't care though. He doesn't worry about being cool, looking good or how people perceive him. He's certain about who he is—solid, dependable, a mamma's boy—and attractive enough to suit himself. That certainty has allowed him to move from stage to stage with only a modicum of doubt.

He knew he wasn't enough for Hannah's mom Lucy, and how caring for house and home, providing, wouldn't suit her for long. But he believed he could prove to her she was wrong, and she wanted to believe him. He also knew he was punching above his weight class even falling in love with her and her fiery, magical hair that lit up the night sky like a lightning bolt or fireworks. In the few photos I've seen, Lucy was near feral, a magnificent beast unleashed from some parallel world to grace this universe with her presence for but the briefest of moments. I know it was his certainty, however, that made Ed attractive to her. He wasn't concerned with whether she was untouchable—the concept didn't mean anything to him— and Lucy had never met someone like him. Plus, they had their messed-up fathers in common. Both men were nearly incapable of leaving their homes, shattered by the violence they'd encountered: Ed's father in the war and Lucy's in his own home at the hands of his own father. Lucy wanted the stability Ed offered until she didn't. Ultimately, she wasn't going to be caged by any person, and she never understood that Ed didn't care either way. He never wanted to cage anyone. He just wanted a cage to call his own.

Which is why we're heading out into the streets, muscles long unused, lungs burning from the start, as we wind down the hill away from home and into the night. Ed's going to be sure I maintain, even if I feel like I'm going to die along the way. This is not an exaggeration, or paranoia either. My chest is a pounding jackhammer and there's nothing to distract me from how scary it is.

I'm reminded of when Hannah was close to giving birth. She couldn't stand to be anywhere for long, if it didn't provide a distraction, and we started going to any movie we could. When we went to see *Moulin Rouge* one night, Christa reacted to the blasting music and started kicking and punching to such an extent that we could see her little feet and fists protruding from Hannah's taut, near translucent belly.

I'm certain if I lifted my shirt, I would see my heart doing the same thing.

One sign of knowing you're running at the right pace is you can speak, and though Ed and I don't speak when we run, it's impossible to do so tonight. To talk would require summoning oxygen no longer available to me on this planet and may never be again. My goal is to not die on the side of the street, which no doubt is Ed's goal as well: make me focus on not dying, so drinking won't feel like a reasonable alternative.

As we roll down the streets and away from the house, we pass the decaying low-slung apartment buildings that serve as housing for local college students, affordable refuge for single parents, and last gasp housing for so many others. We hit the cluster of businesses that anchor the neighborhood—the 7-Eleven and its wealth of frozen burritos, the garage, its overpriced repair work and the guarantee they'll break something else even as they repair the latest problem, ensuring you're never quite allowed to escape their oily clutches, and Gino's, the greasy, and perpetual fire hazard of a pizza place, with its spongy, slime-encrusted walls and booths. Soon Ed and I move onto the off-ramp that takes us towards the *closed* bridge.

No one can agree on how long the closed bridge has been closed to cars, but they can agree it doesn't seem to be held together by much more than hope or prayer at this point, and it seems especially wise not to cross it with too many people at any one time. The bridge sways and creaks with every step, and there's a moment where I want to ask Ed if he feels safe crossing it after all these years. He's lost though to thoughts I have no ability to disrupt as stays focused on placing one foot in front of the other, step after step, rhythmic, and stolid.

On the far side of the bridge is the Korean War memorial statue. The statue depicts a soldier in full sprint, rifle in one hand, helmet in the other, backpack swinging behind him and as we get closer to the statue Ed blessedly starts to slow down before coming to a full stop at the statue's base. I come to a stop as well, and immediately double-over, hands on my knees, the sweat stinging my eyes, my thighs raw and lightly chafed.

It dawns on me how Ed might view my flaws as an explanation for why Christa's missing, and he's been awaiting the right chance to punish me. It doesn't seem like his style, but grief screws with people in unpredictable ways.

"My father always insisted that the statue portrays a proud, American soldier running into battle, headstrong and fearless," Ed says, never turning away from the statue itself, which makes me question whether he's talking to me or to himself. "But I wonder if that's true. The statue is perceived, and even accepted, to be in forward motion, but what if that's wrong? What if he's static, and running as hard as he can, but unmoving, stuck in place—wanting to be anywhere but here, yet going nowhere just as quickly?"

Personally, I'm not prepared to tackle this conversation, then again, I'm still not sold Ed is talking to me.

"What if the soldier is more like Sisyphus," Ed continues, now rubbing his eyes, "and what if he'd do anything to get off the hill, he's stuck on, but since he can't, the action and adventure, even the hope he has, is happening in head? Sisyphus may always be moving, but he gets nowhere. He has no choice and how's the soldier any different than Sisyphus?"

At this point, Ed looks at me, and with an intensity that leads me to believe I better have an answer to these questions. I assume the soldier is Ed's dad in this story, but I don't want to guess wrong about that. People describe Ed's father as a hero. He saved his battalion by killing a whole unit of enemy soldiers by himself in some depraved hand-to-hand combat situation. Ed never talked about it, but people did—they admired his father in the way people love heroes, as the other, somehow supernatural. They also pitied him. Ed's father was a shell of a person, and terrifying to children. A wacked-out combination of Captain America and the Hunchback of Notre Dame. By the end, people avoided him, and they felt terrible about doing so.

"Ed, I want to provide you with a meaningful answer," I say, "but I'm not sure I know what's going on here. Plus, I'm trying not to barf on either one of us, a battle I might lose as we speak."

"That's the problem with you, Gabriel," Ed says, slowly, each word spit out as small daggers which embed themselves in my chest. "Everything is a joke to you. You're never present."

"You know Ed, and I say this respectfully, I'm sure you're feeling this loss of Christa just as I am, and we may have different ways of processing it. I also know you're worried I'm going to end up drinking instead of dealing with it responsibly. And I appreciate it. I do. But I'm grieving in the ways I know how, and humor helps. What surprises me is I've never thought of you as kicking a man while he's down. I think we have that in common. Regardless, I'm not going to kick back. What I'm also not going to do is kick your ass, because maybe this is how you grieve."

I'm calm when I say this last part, but I speak low as I say it, so it will sound more menacing.

Ed looks at me one more time. He's quiet. He wants to take a swing at me, but he doesn't. Instead, he turns around and runs back across the bridge, which sways with every step he takes.

As I watch Ed fade into the night and prepare to somehow run again myself, I pause and wonder if Ed knows me better than I know me. He might be right to be concerned. He's aware I feel like a failure because he knows exactly what that feels like. He's also aware how this undeniable sense of failure means I can't breathe—and this has nothing to do with running.

I choose to let these musings pass without further thought, and instead, begin to put one foot in front of the other. The long slog home begins.

HANNAH

I NEED TO OWN something: ever since Officer John came to the house, I find it hard to breathe, to stay focused, and to not feel all my fears at once as they run around my brain—the lost mothers, daughters, and lives wasted. I can manage it. One can manage anything for a while. I'm not sure, however, I can maintain it. It would make sense to ask Gabriel or my father for help, talk to Tracey, or even reach out to Gabriel's mother Carolyn, who's been more decent and caring towards me since Christa's gone missing than I care to admit. Checking in. Finding ways to touch my hand or make eye contact when we're together. Letting me know she cares, and she's present, but doesn't want to push.

Maybe I want to be pushed—or need to be?—maybe, but I'm not going to ask for help.

I'll take it, if it's thrust upon me, but I can't ask for it. I'll push through before I do so. It's how I do things, and it works, mostly, usually. It might be I'm testing the people around me to ascertain if they care enough, if they see me, can read my thoughts, and understand what I'm going through without me having to say a thing. But this is also about knowing that to ask for help is to receive help and I've avoided asking for help for a long time now. Help means something therapeutic, something probing, and I don't want to be probed when I can't breathe.

To get help is also to talk about my mother, and I've done that already, when I was a kid. It was fine. But to work through my feelings about her again, now that I'm a mother myself, and what it means, the cycles and repetitions, the damage, and reverberations across generations and the patterns we repeat and cannot escape—love, loss, withdrawal, and nourishment, always pushing and pulling one another until everything in its wake is destroyed. I don't want that.

A therapist will say, "tell me about your mother" and what will I say?

She left, she didn't come back, and I must be right with it.

It's not that I never saw my mother again either, that's not true, not exactly. It's just seeing someone is not always seeing them, and I've decided not to assign any value to it. It's not as if I didn't think about her over the years. Even if I preferred not to, I couldn't help it. I long ago inured myself to believing I would ever spend time with her again. I also stopped allowing myself to care about the possibility of doing so. Which is why I was surprised how hard it hit me the one time I saw her after so many years of not seeing her—so sure I didn't care, and it wouldn't mean anything if I somehow did. I felt stupid and babyish, when I even reacted, but it was such a gut punch, low, hard, and fast, snapped wrist and well-placed, my ability to breathe stolen from me, my only option to lean forward and grip my shaky knees.

I had dropped Christa off at childcare one morning. We could only afford to do that twice a week because I hadn't yet gone back to work. But those hours were such a gift that at times I would merely sit on a bench in the park or stand on the closed bridge and take in the air and silence that exists only when someone doesn't need you so completely your brain can only function if attending to their needs and wants, and struggles to understand how it ever had the ability to block out anything before that person existed. What I didn't do during those brief interludes of freedom was think about what might be or have been, if there wasn't a Christa, or if I had a mother to help guide me through the bullshit, fear, pain, and confusion.

It would have been unacceptable to me, and while I never, ever remember wanting to go down the path of parenthood before Gabriel and I decided to do so, I was never opposed to it. Not exactly. I just didn't think about it. I also knew if some child unearthed itself, picked us and not someone else, I was never going to disappear from that child once it came into the world. I would never even allow myself to entertain the thought of it. Not even during my weakest moments when I wanted it more than anything. And so, when Christa was here, born to us, in this world, our world, those thoughts were placed in a box. The box was closed, and it was stored somewhere far away—and unreachable. Like the box, I chose to be locked in for as long as it took to get Christa to adulthood and out of the house, a semblance of balance and stability a necessity.

Which speaks to the importance of those mornings away from her, and the chance to breathe and guard against my brain exploding across the sidewalk—no undo stimulation or surprises, no emotions, no nothing. But it wasn't to be, not that day. Because that day I was walking to the closed bridge and, as I passed Neary's, I looked in the window to see if Tracey might be there. Instead, I saw my father sitting with my mother, her red hair streaked with grey, crow's feet splaying out below her temples, her skin otherwise flawless and glowing, as her smile still lit up her eyes. They were signing papers, speaking, at times laughing, as if this was normal, everyday life. Like someone disappears, reappears, and one makes small talk with them. Like nothing happened. Unless of course, this was something normal for them. She wasn't truly gone or wiped off the map my father and I had to navigate. She wasn't some weird fantasy for him, because for him, she was a reality. It was only for me she was something else, something spectral, a vapor, not real. I stared at them for an unnatural and ungainly length of time, willing one of them to look out the window and catch me staring. I pictured time stopping when they did, everything at first in slow motion, then grinding to a halt. The universe capable of recognizing how insane the moment truly was. How in some way, some force, some greater power would halt everything, everywhere, and leave this moment to exist as the most meaningful thing happening in the world.

It didn't happen.

I also pictured rushing in for some kind of dramatic display—the wronged child, having her moment, grabbing a twisted, unfair world by the neck, and not letting go until all the air has been squeezed out of it.

I didn't do that either.

Instead, I stared and stared and waited for something, anything to happen, but nothing did, because this wasn't a monumental moment for anyone but me. On the other hand, my head hadn't exploded, nor had I been moved to violence. It was more of an ache, or an emptiness, which took hold in the bottom of my stomach, and refused to go away.

I took one more look at them and questioned for a moment whether I even truly saw what I saw. How do we ever know if we can trust ourselves about anything we think we know?

Maybe I was crazy?

My brain willing something to be I wanted so badly, but fought against, and now, suddenly, inexplicably, had caused this impossible thing to bloom, grabbing a moment it had created, shaped, giving it form and life, because I wouldn't allow it to happen otherwise.

I pressed my hand against the window in some sad romcom gesture that would even embarrass Meg Ryan, and I walked away. I pictured heading to the closed bridge, standing there, eyes and hair ablaze, arms raised to the gray skies, and as the bridge swayed and creaked below me, channeling my rage and hurt like Dark Phoenix before incinerating the town and world around me, nothing left behind, but the hope for a grander, kinder future.

There was also the fleeting thought that much of my anger,

while buried, was saved, and directed at my mother and my mother alone, but was that fair to her? Did my father deserve some of the blame as well?

I couldn't process that.

I didn't have any more space for any more pain, and I couldn't burn anything down, despite my great desire to do so.

Instead, I walked back to childcare, and when I got there, I swept Christa up in my arms and I squeezed her until she was soaked in tears and the staff had to look away.

I also vowed to never allow myself to feel that way again, vulnerable, and unhinged, something I wasn't always able to do, and something I hated about myself.

And here it is now, days, or weeks, since Officer John left our home, and that ache is back again. The emptiness. It lingers and squeezes me—fear and anger suffocate my thoughts and actions.

I think back to how valuable those mornings were. The utter freedom I felt. The ability to breathe.

The idea that I might be able to escape how I feel suddenly seems more important to me than anything in the world. I want to breathe again, I must—and while I was prepared to let Christa go and form whatever life was to follow, if I knew where she was at this moment, I would hug her so hard and so long, time would cease to exist.

GABRIEL

Hannah is in the hospital.

She had been home, we were home, and we were lost. We searched for words, connection, something bigger than either of us to help make sense of what felt senseless and seemingly unfixable. There was a loss, and a lingering ache, no resolution or closure. Not that either of us had ever believed anything ever gets fixed. At best, you patch things up and afterward you hope doing so helped. Still, we were together and then we weren't. Hannah was gone. Not in the back room looking out the window, but somewhere else, somewhere lost. I knew it. She was slipping between worlds. I ignored the signs, and it might've been self-preservation on my part. I didn't want to slip into whatever rabbit hole Hannah was drifting into. I didn't want to become merged with her in a unified anguish. I wanted to be strong even at her expense. But whatever was driving me I was selfish, and it was a lack of commitment to the commitment I made to her. Which is also what it must come back to: have I been in this, and I have I been present? It's what we agreed to.

I haven't always been present, and I hate myself for that.

Who we become when we don't police ourselves.

Slipping away.

Losing self.

Becoming the worst version of what we might be.

That's the thing.

It's seven weeks since Christa went missing.

I'm trying to be present for her.

I can barely check the Facebook page, but I do.

Nothing.

I text Christa once per day, first thing—when the day is still fresh.

"Hey, we love you, we're thinking about you, and we hope you're being safe."

I can't tell Christa to contact us or tell her what we need—I can't push.

I contact Officer John and I did so today.

He has nothing to share.

He said I might try the local media again—they might think this is a story now.

I call the newspaper after I speak to Officer John, and someone calls me back.

"Do you feel she's at risk?"

"No, not necessarily."

"Remind me, is she with a coach or teacher?"

"No, it's her boyfriend, but there's been no word or sign of them."

"Yeah, that's tough. This feels like a personal matter, and I'm sorry, but there's not much of a story here."

So that's not happening.

I reach out to one more person.

Bob Morton.

I Google local private investigators. There aren't many. There's Bob Morton.

"Yeah, this is Bob Morton, P.I.," he says when I call.

"I'm looking for someone to help me find my daughter Christa," I say. "I'm desperate."

"How old?"

"Seventeen."

"Okay, runaway?"

"Yes, she left with her boyfriend. Josh. He's nineteen."

"By choice?"

"Yes."

Bob Morton pauses for a moment.

"Okay," he says, "I need you to email me everything you have. Police reports. Phone records. Key witnesses."

"I can do that. How much does this cost?"

"For the basics—calls, internet research, reviewing tape if its available, some travel— $25,000."

I pause for a moment. $25,000 is a lot. It's money we don't have, and I don't want to talk to Hannah about it regardless. It's Christa, but I never like to talk about money with Hannah. There are always too many questions and too much anxiety. She'll ask whether I did my homework and know what I'm getting us into. This conversation will be a headache. Plus, Hannah is in the hospital. Maybe I can spend less and not have to tell her.

"What can you do for $10,000?"

$10,000 I can keep from Hannah if needed.

There's another pause.

"I can talk to some people, make some calls, take one local trip."

"Okay."

"Okay, send me what you have, everything, a certified check for $10,000, and I'll see what I can find out. I'm sorry about this. It's way more common than you know. I'll be in touch."

That's done.

I prove to myself I'm not giving up. Still, I'm also reminded I must stay focused and keep it together. Which means going to work, not drinking, being present.

I'm also reminded how I can't lose anyone else.

Which means I must find a way to put more energy into Hannah.

Maybe I can't fix what's happened with Christa, but that doesn't mean I can ignore Hannah either.

Hannah was confused when I found her.

She was at her father's house, looking for him, not remembering he would be at the store. She was knocking on the door, gently, a low thud with each contact, her knuckles raw, and starting to bruise. She was missing a shoe, a splotch of blood by her toes flooding across her sock. She didn't recognize me at first. There was a look of familiarity. Fleeting. More like she was thinking maybe we had met once at a party. That I represented some slice of history, here and gone. I wondered then if it was all gone, first Christa, now Hannah, and this fear caused my knees to buckle. It was a selfish reaction, and one born of self-preservation, a focus on my needs, unconscionable.

I tried to focus on her.

"Do you know my father?" she asked.

"I do," I said. "He's a good man and a great father. It's an honor to know him."

"Do you know where he is?"

"I do, and if you get in my car, I'll take you to him right now. I know he'd like to see you." I reached for her. Slowly. No sudden movements. Nothing abrupt. Avoiding any triggers and with no intention of taking her anywhere besides a hospital.

This was not exactly a terrible kind of untruth, but I was lying to her. I told her what she needed to hear and what I wanted her to hear, because I wanted to help her. Still, I lied, and I paused to consider the implications of that. I lied to her for many years and made her feel crazy. It was wrong, and I knew it even as I was doing it. I've tried to make up for it ever since, being kind, not demanding, taking care of things and her. But I couldn't help but wonder over the years what kind of damage I caused and what it might have to do with what she's been going through since Christa left. This had been primarily about Christa, her absence, and loss, and how bewildered we were about it. Even knowing that, however, I can't accept it as the whole truth. We would've been bewildered by Christa's absence whatever the circumstances, but I'd also been stuck on whether Hannah wouldn't have been better prepared to deal with it if not for my terrible behavior?

I could measure how the repercussions of my behavior accumulated over time and how it altered the people most touched by it. Good behavior and kindness would've ensured some kind of joy and an absence of decay. My bad behavior, though, was insidious, a river of toxicity that crept and warped everything it encountered, and what's to say Hannah hadn't been transformed, even in small ways, by my choices? No one could say she hasn't been. I can't. That moment at her father's door was different—I hoped—a moment intended to offer comfort and respite. I might've once argued my earlier lies were to protect her from knowledge, she didn't want and not merely an effort to protect myself from myself and my boorishness. But those too were lies. Lies built one on top of the other as they compounded and molded themselves into a thick band of deception—a web which wrapped itself around my brain and altered my ability to ever be truly honorable.

I hadn't been a good person, and I've poisoned Hannah and by extension, our life together. This I'd come to accept. I could also accept how once were in the hospital, lying to Hannah about taking her to see Ed was different. It served a purpose. At some point I thought I would tell Hannah about the conversation and when I did, I would do so patiently, and truthfully. I would explain how her behavior was temporary. How stress caused by trauma such as we had been experiencing can lead to memory loss. How really, it was unavoidable and not a sign of weakness. She wouldn't want it to sound or feel like weakness. As I took her to the hospital though, I also realized that she must start talking about what she hasn't been. How she needed to talk to someone professional and maybe I don't need to discuss any of this with her.

That I understood was for the future, however.

Hannah needed to rest.

I needed to take the time to ruminate on my many failings, my great desire to help her feel better, and the importance of my finding a way to be present for her as well.

HANNAH

I'm in the hospital.

I'm suffering from memory loss and confusion. I'm aware of it and believed I could deal with it on my own.

Christa leaving has triggered memories about my mother, Christa McAuliffe, and terrible thoughts about how alone and abandoned I feel. I spend most days able to keep it together and I mostly shake off the long-time negative energy I carry with me. I can't do it anymore. I'm not able to shake anything, and it's unbelievable to me, to be so weak. I know Gabriel hates for me to talk about myself this way, but he doesn't know my mother.

I don't really know her either, but I know how she thinks.

More unbelievable to me, however, is that as I awake the only person in my room is Gabriel's mother Carolyn. She's always been distant, but not lately, not since Christa left. Before this, Carolyn was cold—no life, no energy, no love for me.

I don't reject the suggestion that the tenuous nature of our relationship is my fault. Why not, everything is, right? If someone is to be blamed for something, it'll be the mother and in this case I'm the mother in question. It's the reason we're here. Men need someone to blame. Women need someone to blame. Society needs someone to blame. Mothers are perfect in this capacity.

This is my first time in the hospital since Christa's birth and being here makes me think of Carolyn, even as I try not to think about Christa, my mother, or why I'm here in the first place.

Seventeen years.

Has it been that long since Christa was born?

It's tough to look back on that day.

It's said, if you count the duration of time that passes between each contraction you know when it's time to go to the hospital. But what if you can't figure out when one contraction starts or finishes, and what if the time between the contractions seems murky, lost in the haze of fear—the pain associated with the tightening and constriction of my uterine muscles serving to only further cloud my ability to make sound decisions?

Further, let's say on that day I had to count on my generally capable single father and mostly capable husband, to have the answers, cut through the murk, and maintain a sense of calm? Let's also say neither of them had the capacity to be the person I needed them to be at that moment. It might've been one of those times having a mother around could have been useful. It might've even been useful to have the mother of my mostly capable husband around, but it's possible this person, Carolyn, may have decided not to be of assistance.

Was this because she thought we fell in love too young, which could've only been my fault? Or that despite her somewhat indifferent attitude to Gabriel when he was growing up, she still felt he was hers, and hers alone, and I had somehow stolen him? That I entrapped her precious son and in doing so exacerbated his drinking and general poor behavior, which from her perspective had nothing to do with his upbringing, genetics, or the twisty winds of fate? Or might it be she saw me as a lonely, feral motherless girl, who was looking to fill the empty space in my life by whatever means were afforded to me at the time?

But maybe that's how I saw myself then, and then I never quite let go of those feelings, despite years of being a dedicated wife and mother and somewhat decent daughter-in-law.

Has Carolyn believed Gabriel would've called her if not for me?

Still, the primary difference between Gabriel and me in this narrative has always been that I'm the woman, and one thing most people agree on is they resent powerful women.

Most women.

It's true Gabriel wanted to do this parenting thing way more than I did from the start, and I acquiesced to his desires. I wanted him to be happy. I was also tired of feeling like a freak, and it seemed like such a normal choice to make.

But did he listen when I first told him I wasn't sure I ever wanted kids?

How my sense of mothering was warped and damaged and for the most part, I was okay with who I was—someone who didn't need a child—until he started to push?

Did Gabriel or anyone else care that being a mother isn't a requirement?

How about the very real reality that I didn't find pregnancy to be easy or euphoric the way people like to describe it? How my morning sickness was intense, cliché, but intense, crippling. My breasts hurt throughout. People always wanted to touch my stomach. Some didn't even ask before they did so. I didn't like people touching me. Period. I needed them to respect my space. Apparently when pregnant, however, there's no space that's just your own. Suddenly, you're everybody's property. Then near the end when things couldn't possibly be more unbearable, I couldn't find a comfortable position to sleep, and I had to pee all the time.

So, there were those things, plus the exhaustion, doctor appointments, eating right, dealing with Gabriel's hovering, my dad's sheer bafflement about how any of it was going to work, and me worried about who was going to care for him, paying for every-thing, not thinking about my mother, wondering how I would ever be able to breastfeed, the slight uptick in Gabriel's drinking, the medical bills I couldn't comprehend, the need to build a crib, trying to be happy, potty training, getting a break, getting a rest, foreseeing and creating a future for us, teething, starting school, dating, breaking up, the sex talk, learning to drive, having sex, getting married, making sure the outlets were covered, obsessing over whether we used the right cleaner on Christa's mattress, and those people touching my stomach unasked—Jesus, I hated it.

It's also possible at a moment of profound stress, Carolyn, the mother of my mostly capable husband, wanted to be helpful about something—truly, I believed that—but I couldn't hear it, or handle it. With all due respect to my father, I wasn't accustomed to having an adult who wanted to be helpful, or act like a parent in such situations. So, okay, I was unprepared, if not unqualified to deal with it, and there might—okay there was definitely a moment when Carolyn offered some helpful, albeit unsolicited, advice about how best to care for myself while pregnant, and it was probably as simple as, "do you really think you should eat that," and it might have triggered some long lasting, never quite closed, much less healed, lost mom wound, and I might've replied, "you're not my mother," and maybe it was enough for her to forsake me.

Okay, it's not a maybe scenario—it happened, Carolyn stepped back, stopped trying to be helpful, and I was never able to fix it.

Which is why there was no mother available as I tried to figure out how far apart the contractions were, just my befuddled father, and my mostly capable husband, and that's how it was going to be and how it remained for years.

Except as I awake—and on the day, I'm going to meet with a therapist—Carolyn sits there, calmly, maternally, staring at me, half smiling, half grimacing, and as I start to wake up to the world, she grasps my shaky hands in her surprisingly warm ones.

GABRIEL

The idea is I'll accompany Hannah to her first therapy session. It'll be a show of support and a reflection of our united front in the face of our "profound state of loss and grief." Those are the therapist's words, not mine. Therapy has never been my bag. There's nothing wrong with it for others, nothing wrong with anything as far as I'm concerned if your decisions and behaviors don't affect me or anyone else negatively. Talking I get—mothers, spouses, friends if you have them—talk as much as you need to. But therapy, no, you can't fix me. People can't be fixed. We are who we are. We're on a path, and we must make the path work, ourselves, even, when, if, it involves diverting the path elsewhere.

I can support Hannah though. I can do anything for her. That's easy. I love her, and I owe her, and so I'm sitting here, next to her, holding her hand, ignoring her stringy, greasy hair, and oddly beige skin, which is off-putting, and which I know has everything to do with being in the hospital, but somehow bothers me more than it should.

I don't even think of myself as a guy generally caught up in the vicissitudes of beauty, but here I am, as much a male as I ever was.

The therapist meanwhile is cute, young, and the young are so fresh. Her skin is dewy, and I'm not sure I ever saw a use for the word dewy before now, but there it is, the proper word. Her skin glows. Her hair is long and brown, and there's this bounce to it. It's engrossing. She's also wearing a crisp blue blouse with one button too many undone, a tan houndstooth skirt that stops abruptly before her knees, and brown leather boots which rise just above the top of her calves.

I mean, is there a hotter look than that?

There isn't.

When the therapist smiles at me, I need to remind myself why I'm here, and how not every smile has implications or reflects interest beyond being polite. Really almost no smiles mean anything more than that. I know this. The therapist is being appropriate, friendly, and I'm being a man. It's how we think, even apparently when we're in a therapy session with our wife, our daughter is missing, and nothing could be less cool or pertinent.

Hannah isn't speaking. She's present, but not giving anything. Which I believe is what's truly behind the therapist's smile. Her desire for someone to say something.

I'm surprised therapy works this way—the support person jumping in, but I also don't think much about therapy or how it works.

"When I was a kid," I say, "we would ice-skate at the park by school where the tennis courts froze every winter. They would use the locker rooms attached to the public pool next to the courts as the place we could change in and out of our skates. The boys and girls always drifted towards different sides of the room. This one day, I found myself alone and surrounded by the neighborhood girls, who were dressed in pink and lime-green CB ski jackets and Levi's, and I heard, 'Did you guys know that Gabriel read, *Are You There God? It's Me, Margaret.*?' It was Alyssa, the ringleader. It was true I'd read it, but I read anything I could get my hands on then.

"'I saw him reading it in the lunchroom,' Alyssa told everyone.

"The other girls were nodding in unison. I'd grown up with most of them and I'd never been so close to them before this.

"'So...,' Alyssa said.

"'So…what?' I replied, but I knew. Margaret gets her period, which is exactly what Alyssa said next.

"'Uh, Margaret gets her period,' Alyssa said. She walked away then, her point made, and everyone followed her. Everyone but one girl, who I hadn't seen in the back of the room, and I knew I'd never seen before. She had red hair, like fire, and she had a kind smile, and she was smiling at me. She must've been. There was no one else left, but why she was smiling didn't matter, she was, which made me smile, and it had to mean something. Why else would she smile at a stranger?

"'Hey, it's fine you read *Are You There God? It's Me, Margaret.* No secrets, right?' the girl said, nodding at me as she walked by.

"I decided I had to get to know her, somehow, no matter what.

"So, I did.

"The girl with the hair on fire had been going to the Catholic school on the other side of town, and now she wasn't. She was now going to our school. She lived with her father. There was no mother. She didn't have any friends yet. This was an opportunity for me. She didn't need to know I didn't really have any friends, how I spent most of my time reading, or after that first chance meeting how I started thinking about her all the time, and when I didn't see her my stomach hurt.

"I carefully studied the route she walked to get home and when she left school, I'd find ways to conveniently intersect with her, running along parallel streets and making the turns that would inexplicably leave me turning onto the same street she was on as if by magic and the miracle of timing.

"She didn't know what I was up to or how I prepared what I was going to say in advance, even scripting her likely responses, so I would know what to say and how it could play out.

"*So, did you see* Close Encounters?

"*If she says no, I say cool, what have you seen recently?*

"*If she says, yes, I say cool, what was your favorite scene, the mashed potato scene, that was cool, wasn't it?*

"*And so on.*

"Anyway, I knew we were meant to be, and I guess that's what I wanted to share. I was certain about us and here we are."

I stop speaking at this point, and I'm not sure if I went on too long, but I'm really pleased with myself for stepping up and giving the therapist some material to work with.

"Hey, wow, thank you," the therapist says, smiling again, but with a different vibe, quizzical, carefully picking her words and trying to form her next sentence. "I appreciate your participation—it was interesting, helpful. I know you're both going through something. It's tragic, and scary, and I want you to get the help you need as well, but this time with me, is more about what Hannah needs. Also, I know how hard it can be for people who may have never attended therapy themselves to hear this, but silence is okay. Respecting it and giving it space. Letting it breathe. The words will come, and we don't have to push it. Does that make sense?"

Yeah, no, I guess it didn't make sense before I pushed it.

I do know my opinion doesn't carry any weight.

That I have no authority or any idea what my wife needs.

That the therapist doesn't want or need to me be here.

Not that I say so.

This is about Hannah.

I get it and I don't need help.

I was trying too hard to fix something which didn't need fixing.

I can stop.

I will stop.

"Of course," I say. "This is about Hannah and what she needs, and if I ever need something, I can find a way to get it."

The therapist smiles again, and it's less weird, and more like when I first walked in.

Then things get silent.

HANNAH

"WHAT WOULD YOU LIKE to talk about today?" the therapist asks.

Super Gabriel is not at my therapy session today, which means I must talk. I know Gabriel's not much for silence, not when he's not drinking anyway, and that he likes to save me, but I've never thought of myself as someone who needs saving.

God, I hate him.

But I hate me too.

Sigh.

"Let's not talk about Gabriel and how he has to talk when he doesn't know what to do," I say.

"Okay," the therapist says.

She's young, but maternal, kind-looking, focused, ready to absorb whatever I share with her.

"But I do sort of want to talk about Gabriel," I say.

"Great, go ahead," the therapist says.

"When I was in high school, senior year, my dad didn't know I was dealing weed. We never had a lot of money to throw around, it was low key, and my dad wasn't going to try and figure it out anyway. Gabriel didn't approve and the two of us had a quiet understanding about it at that point. I was doing what I needed to do, and Gabriel was staying out of it. We were more than friends by then, but what that meant wasn't clear to us. I just knew he was more important to me than anyone else. Gabriel and I met every day after school to check-in. It was intentional as opposed to the old days when he would *accidentally* run into me as I walked home then make some ridiculous excuse about why and how he just happened to be where I was—followed by those inane conversations about things like *Close Encounters of the Third Kind*. Which for the record, I found annoying, but never told him. I knew enough even then how it would break him in some way. Anyway, the point is, by then, we walked home together nearly every day.

"'How was your day?' he asked one afternoon.

"'Pretty quiet, except for this thing with Mr. Sibby,' I replied.

"Mr. Sibby was the music teacher. He was also known as Mr. Grabby, and everyone, the girls—even the boys—tried to avoid him.

"He was youngish and wore these handmade hippy clothes his wife had made him. He also had this long, flowing hair parted in the middle, and he oozed moistness—always saturated in these odd mixes of flop sweat, organic hair products, hemp lotions, and healing oils.

"'Yeah, it's best to stay away from that dude when you can. What did he do?' Gabriel asked, trying to come off casually, but tensing up regardless, the small muscles around his jaw grinding and belying his efforts.

"'Well, he didn't grab me, or anything, if you're worried about that,' I replied, 'which is not to say you are, worried about that, or me, but he didn't. He did come up behind me and start rubbing my shoulders like he does with everyone, but he didn't rub up on my ass, which is a blessing I suppose, or accidentally brush my breasts, not that there's much to brush there anyway, right?'

"That was an intentional stab at humor," I say, looking at the therapist.

"Understood. But was it for me or Gabriel?" she says.

"Oh, for him. Things between us were weird and awkward and vaguely sexual then. I never knew what to say," I reply.

"Okay," she says.

Okay, whatever okay means.

I continue.

"'So, uh, no comment,' Gabriel said, trying not to stare. 'Hey, do you think he's really married to one of his former students, or is that like a rumor?'

"'Definitely not a rumor. It's a former student teacher who found her husband in bed with another man and then fell into Grabby's arms. Whatever, I'm just trying to avoid him.'

"'Of course,' Gabriel said. 'So, what did he want?'

"'He wants to buy weed. He knows, somehow, and he said he'd never report it or anything, but he wants me to hook him up.'

"'And?'

"'And what—no grab, no dope, no anything.'

"'Good, though can you please stop dealing? I'm happy to give you money,' he said, knowing I would ignore him.

"Gabriel then moved on to something like a detailed explanation of the movie *Dune*, and the ongoing failure of book-to-movie adaptations.

"Not that I truly minded hearing about *Dune*, again, because what I didn't want to think about was Mr. Grabby, which I didn't until the next day. But then there's music class, which is my last class, and he's lurking there when the bell rang, cornering me outside the door.

"'Hannah, are you going to hook me up or what?' Mr. Grabby said, placing his palms on the wall over my shoulders and leaning in so close I'm engulfed in his usual nauseating mix of sweat and ooze, mixed with something new, and different, some toxic mélange of male desperation, desire, intimidation, and knowing impropriety.

"'Yeah, about the weed. I'm not into dealing weed to teachers—you know? It seems like a bad business practice,' I said, looking to squirm away from Mr. Grabby's hovering mouth while briefly catching a glimpse of the raging erection poking through his sad, flowy, drawstring pants.

"There's also a string of spittle caught between Mr. Grabby's lips, the lower lip fat and bulbous, the upper one not fully formed, more like a hyphen splayed across his stubbly face.

"'I'll be honest, Hannah,' Mr. Grabby said, dropping his left hand and stroking my shoulder. 'If you don't want to hook me up, it's fine, but I don't want to be the guy who's forced to tell anyone about this little side business of yours, you know? I'm cooler than that. I'm down. Really. It's just…I have responsibilities to the students at this school and their safety. Well, I'm sure you get it. Now if you want to make some other kind of arrangement—we could discuss that?'

"As I stared into Mr. Grabby's suddenly crazy eyes I realized something I should've already known and promised myself I would never forget—men are no different than dogs when they lock into the scent of sex and it's combined with a sense of vulnerability or fear, or whatever it is, wafting from you. They go on the attack. They think they can't help themselves. It's fucking repulsive.

"'Aren't you married?' I said, forcing a smile, and stalling him, hoping I'd figure out a way out of this.

"Mr. Grabby leaned back for a moment, and I could see him sizing me up, looking me over, my still-slight, bendy hips, flat stomach, and small breasts. All of which turned him on to no end—he even licked his lips—and somehow made him even more repulsive than he'd already been mere moments before. Mr. Grabby then shifted his attention back to my face, studying me and reveling in his hard on. I could literally see his brain churning in front of me. How much could he push me? What form should it take? Should he go for the hard sell and strong-arm me, or should he attempt something nicer, softer, less threat and more flattery? He knew he could've backed off. As messed up as things at home must have been for me—and he, of course, knew how to sniff that out—there were so many vulnerable kids from messed up situations in school. The possibilities were endless.

"But I was a challenge, and he liked that. He was a sick, predatory scumbag.

"'It's great you have a moral compass. I admire it. It makes me feel like we're doing our job here…but my wife—the marriage—there's an agreement,' Mr. Grabby said, straightening his back, squaring his shoulders, and dropping his hands to his hips. 'So, like it's cool, promise.'

"It suddenly became a showdown between the two of us. I had no more answers, dodges, or feints. It had also gotten dark and quiet. How exactly did schools become this quiet I thought? Seriously, where was everybody?

"'*Unnnnnnnnnnnffffffffffffffff.*'

"Mr. Grabby suddenly let out this small shout, his face briefly frozen in shock, as his meaty chest flew forward, his knees buckled, and he fell towards me. I barely sidestepped away from him before he lightly bounced off the salmon-tiled wall and tumbled to the ground in a heap. The fuck? Had he suffered a heart attack?

"No, it was just Super Gabriel to the rescue.

"'Oh man, are you okay, Mr. Sibby? You know what it's like when you're running down the hall and you're looking for someone who's supposed to have already met you outside and then you don't even recognize there's someone else standing right there in front of you. Like you're so happy to find the person you're looking for and you can't focus on anything else,' Gabriel said, as he winked at me and reached over to help Mr. Grabby off the ground.

"'It's fine, Gabriel, thanks. But let's be more careful in the future, okay?' Mr. Sibby said, brushing himself off.

"Gabriel stood there, not talking, just being.

"Who was this?

"Mr. Sibby stood there for a moment as well. He looked so small. It was comical. He then walked away with a sniff. He didn't say another word.

"'Did you just shove him?' I said, hugging Gabriel with my still-shaking arms, holding on for an extra moment and almost kissing him. 'He's a teacher. That's crazy.'

"'What's he going to do? He was trying to feel you up. Forget him,' Gabriel said, smiling at me.

"'Yeah, fuck him, though, that may just portend the end of my weed dealing. I don't need that drama, right?' I said, even as I found myself smiling back at Gabriel and grabbing his hand, but just for a moment before we started walking home together."

I'm done and there's silence. I've been talking and talking and I'm not going to fill the newfound space. It's uncomfortable. God.

"I don't think of myself as someone who needs saving," I say. "But is it possible I haven't been averse to it either? That some part of me wants someone to at least want to save me when I might need saving?"

"Is there anything wrong with that?" the therapist asks, turning my nonsense back on me.

"I always thought so, but maybe I'm wrong?"

"Do you think you're wrong?"

I know what I'm supposed to say, and I can't just give her the answer she wants—can I?

"I want to know what you think," I finally say.

"I think you want to believe you don't need anyone, but everyone does, and there's nothing wrong with it if people help us when we want to be helped, and we ask for it. Versus when it's thrust upon us by people who might be well-meaning but fail to acknowledge what we may be feeling."

"Like this?"

"Like therapy?" the therapist asks, smiling.

"Yeah," I say. "No one has asked me if I want to be here."

"True," she says, "but we feel you're in trouble and need to take better care of yourself. Sometimes people also need intervention. Do you think Gabriel needed to intervene with this teacher when he did?"

"Yes, no, I don't know, Mr. Grabby was a pig, but he was manageable."

"Do you think Gabriel needed to intervene when he brought you to the hospital?"

"I guess, I don't know. I believed I had things under control, but I know I didn't."

"Okay, do you think there's some way he might have intervened with Christa, but didn't?"

"Yes, no, I don't know." I'm flustered, repeating a phrase I'm not sure I've ever said before today.

More silence, sitting in it, stewing, Jesus.

"Yes," I say. "Gabriel always wants to be cool. He's cool, he knows it, and I know it, whatever, but with this Josh thing, I don't know. What he needed to do is shove Josh a little—like he shoved Mr. Sibby. Josh is only nineteen-years old, but he could've been a little more scared of Gabriel. He should've felt Gabriel's presence. But that's the thing, Gabriel's actions, or non-actions regarding Josh, are only a symptom of what he needed to be. He needed to be more present. Gabriel wasn't present enough for Christa and he should've been."

"And you?" she asks.

"Me?"

"Yes, could he have been there more for you?"

"I don't know, I guess. We don't operate that way. I don't think about it. We became something more, we worked, and we stuck. It's what it is."

"Okay," she says not so convincingly. "Could you have done more for Christa?"

"So much," I say almost too quickly. "I was there, but yes—so much."

"Let's talk about how that makes you feel," she says.

And so, we begin.

GABRIEL

Do I want to talk about how things make me feel?

Can I talk about work?

The thing with work is it's been predictable. The parameters and expectations are clearly defined: make sure things flow, don't mess up, maintain relationships and be responsible for products moving from where they are to where they should be. It's straightforward, and I get it, how it works, what's needed, how to protect my superiors from having to think about things they don't want to deal with or even know about—and this has always been nice, fine, but is especially so now. I want to go to the office, take care of business, manage the paperwork, glitches, the flow thing, stay focused throughout the day; leave work, visit Hannah, be present, get her home; and not think about Christa too much, beyond actually thinking about her every day and endlessly—wondering where she's been sleeping for two months, what she's doing for money, if she's happy, safe, scared, lost, alone, confused, hungry, dirty, angry, missing us, hating us, resenting us, safe, all the while sending her positive vibes, praying that Josh is being decent, willing her to come home and allow us to reset our relationship, no questions asked, no admonitions, no anger, no blame, don't drink, do pass go, do collect $200, and then sleep, start again tomorrow, and the next day, the day after that, and on and on, no further disruptions, no chaos, nor confusion, rinse, repeat, onward and upward; embracing the clichés contained therein.

Is that enough for me?

Taking care of business.

Keeping my head down.

Staying straight.

I would say yes, it's fine, I'm fine, and if this is life now, it'll work for me until Christa is home, and then even after that.

What else do I need?

Nothing.

Truly.

Except, there's no heir apparent at work. The founder's son has a son who wants nothing to do with the business his father and his father's father built, the world is changing, going global, and we've remained small, local, no rules or formality—and how's this supposed to be okay if we intend to survive?

Not the way it's been working apparently. Nor, it's been decided, can anyone on the inside be trusted with running the place. The ideas the current team has aren't big enough. Everyone is too provincial and we're too stuck in old ways of thinking. Which is how we find ourselves in the presence of Stan Stuffy, high school and college football star, hometown hero, drinking buddy of the founder's son's son and all-around dick—now returned from whatever company he was running from wherever he was running it, to take the reins, and lead us into an even brighter and more profitable future.

We're ushered into a conference room for the announcement and a group introduction, and there's a moment as Stan Stuffy starts blathering about synergies and low-hanging fruit, how he's going to hit the ground running as he did during his years of football, that he's a change agent—and yes, change can be hard, but it's necessary if we're going to take the company to the next level, and everything he says becomes this mass of spectacularly empty nonsense that threatens to envelope the entire building in a cloud of stink, when I see Stan Stuffy scan the room, and give me the side-eye, shake his head, and dismiss me, and I know I'm done. I'm surely emanating a bad attitude based on his presence alone, but even if I can adjust it, I'm screwed, and I know it. I represent old ways that don't fly anymore, and there'll be no goodwill for years served, nor any assessment of my value. I won't be able to work with this guy because Stan Stuffy will never let me do so. I'm the founder's son's guy and I'm a dinosaur, detritus, and we can talk, or not talk, but the exit is on—and no history of hard work, loyalty, or diligence, much less my desperate need to work so I don't have to think about my missing daughter every moment of every day will prevent that.

I also recognize at this moment—more than ever—I've become my father's son. Stan Stuffy's beautifully coiffed and layered haircut and pinstriped suit alone ensure I want to reject him as the fake he is. He can't answer any questions about his ideas for the future of the company, much less wholly define what we do, which further engenders an endless need to overcompensate and focus on his football exploits, hometown bona fides, and his great success selling software in far-flung places around the world. Which solidifies the strong likelihood I won't be able to stomach working with him even if he doesn't want to get rid of me. Which is to say I'm my father: reject the fake, don't play along, never manage up, and be who you are regardless of the costs—even if being who you are means you don't get to be anyone. I've fought to become my father my entire life—his endless shadow enveloping me from the very shadows he himself lurks in, choosing not to engage with me, while still impacting everything I am. I've also fought engaging with the Stan Stuffys of the world. Both of which are reasons I'm who I am and Stan Stuffy is who is. Everything is now going to be impossible and even recognizing everything is about to go terribly wrong, it doesn't mean I know what to do next.

Said differently, I'm watching my own destruction play out in slow motion right in front of me, but I'm powerless, or at least unwilling, to do anything to prevent it. Something bad is looming, but whether it's my own resistance to embrace this reality, or my stubborn disbelief of what's surely to come, or both, I can't think of any good way for things to go well for me. In fact, the only question remaining is whether I'm going to figure out how to take some kind of control of my life or react to the changes as they come at me, fending for myself as best as I can.

HANNAH

"Last time I was here, we talked about being present, Gabriel, me, and maybe this time I should talk about my dad." I say to the therapist, who I'm ready to do the hard work with. Who has a name, Kelly, and who seems Irish. She has nice brown hair, though it's unkempt. She's tall and gangly, like a colt, or an athlete and always folded awkwardly into her chair, knees, and elbows askew, with Kelly not clear where to put them—as if she and the chair are having sex for the first time and she's still learning her partner's dimensions. And so, she's Kelly, but she's also still *the therapist*, period, and while I'm sure I'm supposed to be thinking about my missing daughter, I'm going to talk about my dad.

"I mean, my dad was present, just not exactly. So, for example, sometimes I fell asleep on the couch at night, and sometimes I chose to sleep there. Either way my father didn't wake me for school. My mother had been the one to wake me up in the morning and then she was gone, and my dad just never did after she left. I don't recall ever thinking about this as a big deal, I just didn't know what to do about getting to school before the bell rang. It's not like I could tell time either. I began willing myself to wake up early. I'd sleep in my clothes and take change from my father's pocket for lunch, eat cereal on the couch in front of the window and look for other kids to leave for school so I could leave when they left. I could do that, and I did, never following them too closely, or drawing too much attention to myself, and it mostly worked. Except for the morning I followed one of the older neighbor kids to school and it was dark and, about halfway down the hill, he turned around and screamed, 'It's not time for you to go to school yet. My class is going on a field trip and we're leaving early today. Jesus you're fucking weird." Then he turned around and walked away. I went back home, sat on the couch, and waited until someone else left for school—"

"Can I interrupt you for just a moment?" the therapist asks.

"Yeah!"

The therapist recoils. Was my response too strong or rude? She's in charge and it's cool with me. It's not my place of employment, and I'm not the professional in this scenario. I work in an office, I know what flies there and what doesn't—and sure, I've been in therapy before, but I was a kid, and I don't know how she wants this to go.

I could ask, but I won't. I can't give her that much power.

"We're in charge," she says. "I may ask questions, but this is a safe place where we can work together and discover things—as a team."

"That's cool," I say. "What are you thinking?"

"I'm wondering if any part of this memory seems odd to you, or what you might have done differently?"

I know she wants me to say something about my father specifically. How he was neglectful somehow, and I could've told him he was, but I'm going to make her earn that.

"Like what?"

"Like your father…"

"Like what…"

"He…"

"He could've done things differently," I say. "Okay, but we didn't operate like that."

"But you were a child."

"Look, I know what you want me to say. You want me to say he was neglectful. It's just, it was a different time, things were looser, and my mom wasn't there…he and I were a team too, you know, and I needed to do my part."

"I think we might take another beat on this."

"Okay, sure but let me finish first. After the neighbor kid yelled at me—shamed me—I realized I needed a better plan. I also realized you can't necessarily count on people, even well-meaning people like your father, to do the right things. Why should you? Anyway, one morning I was up early on a Saturday, eating cereal and reading *Family Circus* and Billy is talking about how he may not be able to tell time, but it doesn't matter if he has a digital clock. This light bulb went off in my head. I mean my brain literally explodes upon reading this comic. I think, digital clocks, of course, and I ask my father if he'll get me a digital alarm clock, which he's only too happy to do."

"Did he ask you why you needed one?"

"I don't remember. He might've. Is that important? What's important, to me, is after that, I could get myself up for school and I was way less anxious about it. I would, of course, check my new clock half a dozen times every night before I went to sleep so I could be sure it was truly set…turning it on and off so many times I got a callous on my finger, and I had to be certain it was on AM and not PM too, checking again and again, and that the volume was at the appropriate level. But it's also true I was able to get up for school on time after he got me the digital alarm clock, and I didn't have to sleep in my clothes or sit on the couch and wait for neighbors to leave for school. I still had to take money from my father's pocket for lunch, but that was kind of awesome. It was always the best part about getting up for school on my own anyway."

"What does this recollection mean to you?" the therapist asks.

"To me it means that I was forced to be independent from an early age and it has served me really well as an adult."

"But does it also mean you're more reticent to trust people to make the right decisions? And you try to control how they make decisions since from your perspective they can't possibly know how to make them as well as you?"

"Yeah, of course, why?"

"How does it sound to you when you say it loud?"

How does it sound? Not great, how could it be, but I'm not sure there's any other way.

"Not great, I guess," I say, "but this is about survival. You get that, right?"

"I don't believe survival has to be as hard as you describe. You can share more of that work with others. Gabriel, for example. You can expect more from him, trust him, drop your guard. You're going home soon and there's no time like the present."

Maybe, I think, I don't know, we'll see.

I also want to make a mental note: I don't want to talk about Christa, and the therapist doesn't mention her either. Christa's old news, a relic, somebody from the past we don't quite acknowledge. The therapist, Kelly, might say this is merely an oversight or how we're building towards something, but she and I both know better than that. Girls get lost, swallowed up, forgotten, and we don't care, not enough—not me, not Kelly, not society. It's baked in.

GABRIEL

"Hey," I say to Hannah, with a slight wave as I arrive at her room to take her home, "how are you doing?

I ask her this like I haven't been here every day for the last two weeks. As if I'm just another acquaintance. She looks fragile, not that she'd ever admit it or could possibly ever perceive herself in such a way, and I don't know what to say or do or what's best for her. I'm not going to ask her about therapy, for example, and though I want to tell her about Stan Stuffy, which she'd find funny—the name and his beautiful haircut anyway—I'm too scared to do so. What am I going to say? Work is not going to work much longer, and then what—what'll happen to me, how will I keep it together, stay distracted and not drink? Hannah will tell me to be more proactive, to start looking for work, call friends, and get an actual resume together. She'll want to take over and I'll want to let her, but it doesn't seem fair to burden her with this. It seems easier to say as little as possible.

Which is also why I won't tell her about my follow-up call with Bob Morton.

"Hey, it's Bob."

"Hello, do you have anything for me?"

"It's not great, not bad, but not great. That cop, Officer John whatever, he's worthless, and his boss, yeah, he's no help."

"I know."

"Josh's parents' also kind of suck."

"I know that too."

"I did learn they received a message from Josh's bank that he withdrew $5000 in cash from his savings account just before he and Christa left, which helps explain why there's been no activity on either of their credit cards."

"Yeah."

"I also learned after some calls that they found Josh's car in Youngstown, Ohio."

"Really, is that promising?"

"Eh, I drove out there—it's like five hours from here—I connected with a cop friend who let me look at the car. It was stripped bare and wiped down, except for a note that read 'Drive me,' along with the keys. That and some empty boxes of hair dye. Black and red…"

"And?"

"I'm sorry, that's it. No real trail after that. No video. I can keep looking…"

"But?"

"It's another $10,000 and I can't promise anything."

"Yeah."

"Should I continue?"

"No need, I guess. Thanks."

"Right. Sorry I couldn't be of more help."

Which is what I have as I pick up Hannah. Nothing. I got nothing.

"What are you thinking?" Hannah says.

"I don't know," I say. I want to change the course of the dialogue in my head to something more positive. "I'm thinking about taking you home today, and I'm flashing back to the first time you invited me into your house when we were in high school. I don't know, I'm free-associating I guess."

I'd walked Hannah home a million times and I didn't know what was different about the night she first invited me to come in.

We held hands on the way home. But even that wasn't unusual back then. It was a beautiful night though. It was also the day I leveled Mr. Sibby at school and maybe that was enough to score an invitation.

"Look, perfect, we're at my house," she had said. "Do you want to come in or something?"

I didn't answer, I just followed her in. I'd never been inside her home, and I didn't know what to expect. The house wasn't neat, not like my house, but there wasn't anyone like my mother living there either. There wasn't any mother, though there was one photo of her mom Lucy. Lucy was with little Hannah, and they were dancing on a lawn somewhere. Their hair was on fire, electrifying the sky. Hannah already looked so much like her mom back then. The same weird, ethereal beauty. It was eerie. Amazing. Hannah was already refined in comparison though. She carried herself with some class, while her mom seemed feral, a freakish burst of animal energy thrust straight from the earth.

At one point, Hannah started to cry, which I assumed had something to do with Mr. Sibby. A delayed reaction or whatever. I didn't know what to do, but I knew I wanted to be helpful.

"Do you want to talk about it?" I asked.

Hannah looked like she was going to scream.

"What?" Hannah snapped.

I didn't respond.

"What do you think is going on here?" Hannah continued.

I didn't know what I thought had been going on, but I knew it had to be about Mr. Sibby. I was sure of it. I also knew I had no idea what to say next—so I didn't say anything. Not that Hannah waited for me to say anything.

"Fuck you," she said, holding back the tears and grinding her knuckles into her eyes.

"Fuck me," I said, though I was at a loss for what to say next, "fuck you, a-a-a-and the horse you rode in on."

Neither of us said anything and it seemed like forever as

Hannah stood there stunned at the inanity of having someone like me standing before her.

"Sorry," she said, as she wrapped her arms around my neck, something she'd never done before, "but fuck you and the horse you rode in on, that's what you got?"

"It just slipped out," I said as I realized how hard I was. "I was in a panic, but look, I'm sorry. None of this is my business."

"Except that it is. You care about me, right?" she said, staring at me with a look almost as feral as her mother's.

That's when I became truly hard, and I started to freak out.

There was a pause, and we both knew it was the moment when we were supposed to kiss. It would be impossible to have ever watched a single teen movie and not known that. I also knew I was the dude, and while it would've been awesome if she just grabbed me hard by the back of the head, pulled me towards her, and mashed her lips against mine, she wasn't going to, which means either I had to step up—or there would be no kiss. I didn't step up. It wasn't a movie, and it wasn't going to happen after I dropped the ball. Not without a script, or a rehearsal, and not when neither of us could've imagined making a move towards one another, much less how to even do so.

"So, was that like our first fight?" I said instead. I stepped back and tried to create some space between us, between her and my erection anyway, the moment ignored, broken, and lost to the ages.

"I guess so," Hannah said. "It went pretty well, right?"

"Not bad, we might've overused the fuck-yous a little though? You know I don't really like to swear…"

"I do. Your mom thinks it makes you sound less educated—"

"Yes, and she also says, when you overuse any word, much less, fuck, it blunts the impact."

"I think my mom would have punched your mom if she heard her say shit like that."

I smiled.

"That works."

In truth, I had half-smiled, half-grimaced as I said it. I was kicking myself for not kissing Hannah when her arms were around my neck. I knew I had screwed something up, and my great fear was I might never get the same chance again.

I also knew I needed to get it right the next time, assuming there was one.

What I didn't expect was the next time was right then.

"You say that a lot," Hannah said as she stepped forward again.

"What?"

"That works," she said, as stepped forward even more and leaned in towards me.

It felt like an eternity by the time our lips finally came together, so much so, we both reached for the back of the other's head at the same time as we tried to pull the other one closer, faster, resulting in our teeth bumping, and both of us recoiling, laughing, and then diving back in and consuming one another. One moment we were standing there, the next we were on the couch, at first side by side, our lips smashed together, wet, and hungry, and then Hannah was on top of me, kissing my neck, my nose, ears, anywhere she could reach. I had no idea what I was doing, or what she was doing, but soon we were moving together, and I couldn't breathe, and I opened my eyes, and Hannah's were closed—she looked lost in something, and she was going really fast and hard, and then suddenly she rolled off me, and I didn't want it to stop, but she was done, with something, and I didn't know if she'd had an orgasm, or what one even looked like, but whatever it was, it was over. For the moment anyway.

"What, were we going too fast?" I asked. "I'm really sorry."

"No, it just—it stopped feeling good. Sorry, that wasn't cool," she replied.

I didn't know what to say, so I just stared at her, her hair afire, and the sweat on her nose and her freckles blurring together. She was beautiful and I knew I loved her and there and then I committed to never letting her go or hurting her again or anything like that.

"What?" she finally said.

"I don't know, you're so beautiful," I said, "and there's no rush to do anything. It's cool. I'm just happy to be here."

And I meant it—I really did.

I snap back to the present, I look at her, and I half-smile, half-grimace.

"I'm glad you're doing better," I say, "I'm glad I'm here, and I'm glad I can be the one to take you home again."

I mean that too.

HANNAH

I KNOW GABRIEL IS happy to be here and happy he's the one to take me home. He wants to be present. He wants to be here for me. He loves me and I know this.

Still, I kind of hate him and I've hated him for so long now.

I hate him for managing Christa leaving better than I am. I'm the tough one. Yet I'm the one in the hospital, and I'm the one who can't handle our missing daughter, as he plugs along—obsessive, as always, and fine.

I hate him for not being present in the way he should've been. He was a decent, loving father in the ways society values fatherhood over motherhood—expecting so little of men and then celebrating them every time they do what's expected well. But he was absent, and he wasn't a good husband, not like he could've been, and I can say that now, something I may owe to Kelly, but I prefer to claim for myself.

I also hate him for never quite going away in a world where people tend to leave and not look back. He wandered, but he didn't leave, he wouldn't. Not that my father has either. I know this. But my father doesn't count…he's, my father. Gabriel has distorted my worldview and I hate that too.

I hate him for being male, even if his maleness has nothing to do with Christa missing, though a lot to do with who he is and has been.

I also hate him for his version of the first time he came over to my house, which while right in some ways, is so wrong in so many others.

Yes, I invited him in, but when I did so, Mr. Sibby was the farthest thing from my mind. It happened and it was gone, done, one of the endless aggressions I—and women everywhere, encounter, every day. But as Gabriel and I walked into my house, I saw for the first time what my home must look like through his eyes, and in doing so, I wished I hadn't invited him in at all.

It was neat enough. I did my best, but it still looked like a bachelor pad. There was laundry, folded and not, and piled up in the dining room. There weren't any photos anywhere, except for a an old one of me and my mother dancing on a lawn, her hair, long and electric and splayed out across the sky. There were no little touches—not a woman's touch, or a mom's touch, anyway, which isn't to say that dads can't buy vases or placemats, little drawings of clowns, or who knows what. It's just my dad never did.

I started to cry, which I hated doing.

I had this feeling that while I wanted him to hold me until I fell asleep, all I could think about is how I never wanted anyone to look at me with the mixture of sadness and pity he was looking at me with ever again. I needed to be more self-conscious about my home life. I hadn't needed to before this, but if I was going to start stepping outside the bubble I'd been living in, I was going to need to better protect myself.

Even around Gabriel.

"Maybe you shouldn't be here," I said, stepping away from him.

"Do you want to talk about it?" he said, ignoring me.

He was trying to be helpful, caring, but I didn't care. Looking weak was not my thing and being angry was so much easier than being vulnerable.

"What do you think is going on here?" I said, clapping back.

"I-I-I-It just seems you've had to deal with a lot of crazy stuff, and maybe you've had to deal with this stuff for a while, but why should you have to deal with it by yourself?"

His eyes were burning, and he looked like he wanted to cry, or yell at me, or both. He was holding back, and I should've held back too, but I couldn't. Even being friends with him, or more, I had erected a wall, it had worked well enough, and now I felt humiliated.

"Fuck you," I said, "what do you know about anything?"

"I know what you look like when you're sad, the way your face starts to melt, and I care about you, so fuck you, a-a-a-and the horse you rode in on."

Neither of us said anything, and I started to giggle—then laugh. Gabriel almost never swore. But then I was crying, dropping my head onto his shoulder, wrapping my arms around his neck.

"Sorry," I said, "but fuck you and the horse you rode in on, that's what you got?"

"It just slipped out. I was in a panic, but look, sorry, none of this is my business."

"Except it is, because you care about me, right," I said, looking at him.

There was a pause, and we both knew it was this moment when we were supposed to kiss. It would've been impossible to watch even a single teen movie and not know that. In those movies there are tears, an argument, passion, a dark house, and no parents anywhere to be seen. That's how it happens and when it happens. And what I was supposed to do next was close my eyes and step up on my tippy toes, and Gabriel was supposed to lean in and lightly brush my lips with his, and then as he started to pull away, I needed to lean in, grab the back of his head, ready to consume him in one gulp, and as I did, maybe we would bump teeth, which would be terribly awkward and funny, but then we'd settle in, smashed lips and tangled tongues.

It would be electric and as scripted.

Well, if we'd been in a movie, but we weren't, and those things couldn't happen, not without a script, or a rehearsal, and not when neither of us could truly imagine making a move towards one another, much less how to even do so.

"So, was that like our first fight?" I said, stepping back and trying to create some space between us, the moment ignored, broken, and lost to the ages.

"Guess so," Gabriel said. "It went pretty well—right?"

"Not bad, we might've overused the fuck-yous a little though? It loses some of the impact when you curse too much. It's like showing too much blood in a movie. You must dial it back, or it blunts the overall impact of the scene."

"That works," Gabriel said.

He was half-smiling, half-grimacing, when he said that, and it was clear, he was kicking himself for not kissing me when my arms were around his neck. He felt he'd messed something up, and his fear was he might never get the same chance again. I knew that didn't have to be true, but he didn't. I wanted to believe he was also thinking he needed to get it right next time. What he didn't know was the next time was then.

"You say that a lot," I said, stepping forward again.

"What?" Gabriel said.

"That works," I said, stepping forward even more and leaning in towards him.

It felt like an eternity before our lips finally came together, so much so, that we both reached for the back of the other's head as we tried to pull the other one closer, faster, resulting in our teeth bumping. Both of us recoiled, laughed, and then dove back in, and consumed one another. One moment we were standing there, the next we were on the couch, at first side by side, our lips mashed together, wet, and hungry, and then I was on top of Gabriel, kissing his neck, his nose, and ears, anywhere I could reach. He wasn't the first boy I hooked up with, but it was different—personal, intimate, meaningful—I found myself moving with him, and when I did, I felt warm, and it was something I tried to focus on, that feeling, keeping it, but there was something so weird about it, and how couldn't there be: it was Gabriel. I loved him, but it was too real. I got distracted and my mind started to race. I flashed back to my childhood and how I had liked to lie on the floor in the living room, my hand between my legs, slowly moving up and down. How good it had felt, and how after being caught by my mom, and being told what I was doing was okay, normal, healthy, but I had to do it in the privacy of my own room, I'd stopped doing it, the excitement lost to the idea that maybe I was supposed to be ashamed regardless of what my mother told me. Suddenly and on top of Gabriel I started thinking too much—and I couldn't stop it. I lost my momentum and started to feel uncomfortable and not warm, my jeans rubbing me in all the wrong spots, the excitement and friction gone. I rolled off Gabriel who looked like his face was about to implode, his eyes pleading with me not to stop, not yet please, but I was done. It was over. The moment passed.

"What," Gabriel said, trying to collect himself, and then shifting, self-conscious about the erection pressing against his jeans.

"Nothing, sorry," I said.

"Were we going too fast?" he replied.

"No, it just, it stopped feeling good. Sorry, that wasn't cool."

Gabriel stared at me, and I became self-conscious that the moonlight was crashing in through the window and illuminating my face. All I could think was my hair must be matted against my sweaty forehead. The freckles on my nose, which I hated so much, must be merging, and blurring into one—my already pale skin red and flushed. I didn't want to look him in the eyes, except he was smiling, oddly, excitedly, and I became more embarrassed about the way he was looking at me than I was about the way I looked. Other people had stared at me like that, well Mr. Grabby anyway, but it didn't feel the same, and it certainly didn't feel so welcome.

"What?" I finally said, sheepishly, angrily, elbows up, ready to fight.

"I don't know, you're beautiful," Gabriel said, "and there's no rush to do anything, really, it's cool, I'm just happy to be here."

I knew he meant it, and it confirmed what I already felt.

Gabriel was special. I was too though and maybe we finally needed to see where this thing between us might end up.

I snap back to the present, and I realize I hate him for that night as well. For being there when I needed someone to be there. For being cool, even if he was so uncool later. For me never quite being able to shake that initial good feeling about him.

Gabriel takes me home again, though this time to our home, and we end up in the kitchen, talking and laughing, and it's a moment, a weird, wonderful moment, where there's some peace, though I still don't quite want to let go of the hate. I want to own it and hold onto it for now. It's mine, and I need something of my own.

"Can I tell you about a moment I really hated you?" I say, leaning across the counter and wanting to destroy any goodness lingering in the air.

"I would love to hear about that," Gabriel says.

"I should say," I continue, "at the time, I wasn't sure who I hated more, you or Christa."

"Go on."

"It's ultimately a funny story."

"Cool, I'm intrigued, really."

"Okay, here it goes. At the time, I was stuck in this debate, was it Christa I hated, because she did not, would not, could not, go to sleep like a normal person? Which was to say, she did not, would not, could not go to sleep when it was bedtime, instead choosing to be awake, and not willing or able to climb into bed and fall asleep, which even in and of itself wasn't the problem. People have problems falling asleep—adults, children—they get into bed and close their eyes thinking their dreams await, but then open their eyes again and nothing awaits them, just voices, darkness, anxiety, and the thousands of reasons they do not, will not, cannot go to sleep—death, theirs or that of their parents, bullies, nuclear war, boys and on and on, but even when this is happening, they stay the fuck in the bed and count ceiling tiles and shadows and entertain themselves, and yes, Christa was five years old at the time, but that's old enough to take care of that, right? Yes, it is, was, I did, no one checked on me. I did what I had to do. Christa didn't though. She'd come and find me, wandering around the house, asking for snacks, wanting me to hug her and lie with her and read more books and sing more songs—and I just couldn't take it, which is sort of why I wasn't sure who I hated more."

"Yeah, okay, I get that part, go ahead," Gabriel says, wincing, smiling, and me thinking, like I need your permission to continue.

"Anyway, you could take it. You were rarely sober then, or around much, but when you were, you were so patient, stroking her back and reading book after book to her like your mother did with you—never taking a firm stance, never letting you cry it out or fend for yourself. Jesus, when you were little, your mom wouldn't even let you touch the ground in case you might cry, choosing instead to walk around the house for hours, a Martini in one hand and you in the other.

"But is that what Christa needed? More importantly, is that what I needed? How were the two of us ever going to be on the same page if we couldn't agree on sleep? Further, was your inherent good and calm passive-aggressive in their ways? I mean, anything I said, or did then that wasn't good or calm made me sound like an asshole. Was that part of your game, make me look bad so you could look like the conquering hero? Or was I so tired I couldn't tell the difference between decency and obstinacy? So, okay, I hated you too. You wanted to have a baby. I was neutral. But I did it. And then five years later, you're mostly around, but not always, and when you are, I'm the asshole because you will not, cannot be an adult. Well, forget that, and forget you, even in retrospect."

"Did you mention this story is ultimately funny," Gabriel says, "because if I'm being honest, I mostly suck thus far."

"Mostly? I think you're being very kind to yourself, and I admire it. Your male privilege is stunning, truly, but yes, funny, okay. So, the sleep nonsense, and your general drunken state of being aren't even the primary things I was thinking about at that moment. There's a note from the preschool. There's a crisis involving Christa that requires you and me to come in first thing for a meeting. They won't say what the crisis is, but it must be attended to the next morning, and both of us must be present. I have to call your parents because you're not home when I wake up in the morning and I assume you might be with them, sleeping off the night before—your mom was always happy to wake you up for work and make you breakfast and pretend there's nothing remotely odd about her little prince sleeping on the couch in his work clothes and reeking of bourbon, cigarettes, and sex. But you're not there. It's possible you're elsewhere, at a friend's home, or someone else's, but it's also possible you're sleeping in your car in the driveway, which you are, which in this case is helpful. I'm mostly glad you're there, though gladder Christa isn't awake yet to see you like that. I tap on the window of your car, you stir, smile, and roll down the window. You're still wearing your clothes from the day before. You smell like a Jack Daniels' distillery, cigarettes and you know, sex.

I pause here for dramatic effect and Gabriel smiles, which I hope is because he remembers the story and isn't just being a selfish prick.

"'Hey,' you say, as if there's nothing unusual about waking up in your car, 'what's doing?'

"Right there, I could've chastised you, should've chastised you in the same way I wanted to chastise Christa for not staying in bed, but I do not, cannot, will not. It's too tiring.

"'Fuck you, and take a shower, please,' I said. 'We need to go into school with Christa for a meeting. There's a 'crisis,' which must be discussed."

"Nothing more is required. You don't get hungover. You respond well to aggression. You'll do anything for Christa. And so, with that, you're out of the car, a quick kiss on the cheek, into the house, showered, shaved, work clothes on, and you have Christa in your arms as you dance down the stairs and into the kitchen for breakfast.

"I mean, Jesus, you were the worst person ever.

"Anyway, the crisis meeting goes down like this…

"'We're glad you came in.'

"'Christa is delightful, playful, curious, and smart.'

"'We love having her here. Everyone does.'

"'Overall, she's doing great. There's just this one thing we're concerned about.'

"'Maybe we shouldn't have called it a **crisis**. And it's obvious she's clearly loved. We want to stress that. But is everything okay at home?'

"'Okay, well, are you using 'I' phrases and positive reinforcement?'

"'Have you created charts to reward her for good behavior and choices?'

"'Great, so anyway, here's the thing, Christa is an *aggressive hugger.*'

"'Yes, that's it, nothing else, but that's not nothing. She hugs the other children super hard when she sees them, and she gets so excited she sometimes knocks them over.'

"'Yes, aggressive hugging is what we call it.'

"I'm sure I didn't mean to laugh, and I'm sure you probably didn't either, but I did, and you did, and I can't, won't, stop, laughing, and neither will you, and soon we're hugging each other, and laughing together, your head on my shoulder, and mine on your chest, and I'm wiping tears from my cheeks, and it was so not cool, but I must admit, for the moment, I felt better than I had when I went to sleep the night before, and much better then when I woke-up that morning, and that's not nothing either."

"That does have a funny ending," Gabriel says, smiling, with his brown eyes popping. "I really was kind of dick back then. I always loved you best though, you know that. I was acting out. Something I won't do when I'm not drinking."

"I know," I say, "it's fine now, but is it messed up that I want to have a drink with you like old times. Maybe just one?"

Gabriel pauses, he knows the answer is of course it's wrong I asked, and no he can't, there's no way, and I should know that. And I do, but there's part of me that thinks it'll be fun, and I want some fun, and there's part of me that knows it'll destroy him—and I kind of want that too.

"Sure. One can't hurt," he says, not so convincingly.

And so, I pull out the bottle of Jameson's we keep for the occasional visitor, I pour us each a finger, and we clink our glasses together.

GABRIEL

One can't hurt.

Has there ever been anything less true? Also, if there's any real question about who Hannah hates more, I think it's been settled.

Not that I begrudge her the hate—she's come by it honestly.

Still, would she be disappointed in me at this very moment? That's another thing. Hate runs its course—fire hot, then ice cold. It must. One can only maintain that kind of intensity for so long. As the hate cools, it curdles into not caring much, which I suspect is how things will play out with Hannah in the immediate future.

Hannah's also been home for a week. She's doing better. In doing better one finds clarity. And what Hannah will see is without her hate for me, and without Christa to care for together, I don't have much to offer her.

There's also the *other* thing, but first, let's pause on the other thing, because it must keep coming back to this: why does anyone stay together, and if the reasons you stay together stop working or can't be fixed, how does any of it even work?

I'm not sure I have an answer yet, and so there's the other thing—I'm just not ready to talk about it.

Instead, let me say this, my mother would be disappointed in me at this very moment, my father too. And not because of what I'm about to do. Check that. This requires clarification. They wouldn't be disappointed in me for having that first drink with Hannah and not stopping at one drink to hit my mantra, go for a run, and beg to that which is holy to get back on course, and ignore every impulse roiling my suddenly fragile brain—which now wants nothing more than to take my hard-fought sobriety and throw it out the window. My parents would feel bad about that. There would be empathy. They know it's a battle one loses and wins until one finally loses or wins, and this is a setback, and part of the journey.

But it wouldn't disappoint them.

No, what would disappoint them as I sit here contemplating the gin and tonic I'm about to make love to, is how I'm using this loss of mooring as a justification for cheating on Hannah. The fact is, I plan to start sleeping with other people again—women, men, whatever, the alcohol has nothing to do with it, and that part is simple. What isn't simple is why?

Or maybe it is?

I didn't want to have even one drink, and I did everything I could not to do so, not the least of which was ignore how ass life had become.

Still, there was the one drink I had with Hannah. It really was just one, and despite the cognitive dissonance and internal drama that surrounded my slip, I really believed I could have looked past it. I made it a whole week without another one. Then today I lost my job too, and while I knew it would mess with me as much as I knew I wouldn't be able to avoid it, it feels like a sledgehammer.

Why did I lose my job?

Pick a reason.

My position is redundant.

No, wait, it was because the numbers were down.

No, it isn't that. It's because management is going in a different direction, and there's a mandate to streamline.

No, sorry, it's because if one hires a change agent, change must follow, right?

Whatever else it is, my firing is this: they don't need me anymore.

That's what the haircut said, "We don't need you anymore."

Every day for the last week, I went to work, the taste of that one drink was still on my lips and blasting through my brain and I was good—I was fine. I was going to stay in control of it and not go any further around the bend. But when I got into work today, people looked at me like they knew something—the furtive glances, the sad expressions, the mumbled-under-their-breath hellos, and quick exits, and then I saw the note to please come to Stan Stuffy's office first thing. As I walked in and saw the grin on his craggy mug, I knew he was happy about what was about to happen. Which he was as he smiled and said, "We don't need you anymore." I stood there for a moment, and I waited for a look of empathy or humanity, but there was nothing. He turned to his cell phone and started to flick through messages.

He was done with me.

I was done.

As I walked out the door of his office, threw some stuff in a box and headed out into the day, the sun hit me in the face, and I knew I'd never be able to make sense of it.

It's true I was appreciated once, valued, and I worked hard. But it's also true that maybe I could never see the big picture. Maybe I was unable or unwilling to keep learning and adjust, make new opportunities, and I believed that loyalty alone, and doing your job well, was enough. It wasn't. The reality is, beyond not drinking, I never could embrace that we change or die.

If I'm being honest, being fired wasn't what I found confusing. I knew I could never totally grasp my endless limitations. I also knew I needed to be more self-aware—I wasn't—and I wasn't willing to do the work.

How though could the haircut have said to me they don't need me anymore?

There must have been a better way to say that.

It was like a murder and to enjoy it was twisted.

But now for the reality check. Stan Stuffy doesn't need me, and Hannah made it clear she doesn't need me either. This is the real point of her reminiscing about the nursery school story. Sure, it's funny and there's something madcap about it. It's just there's no more nursery school and no Christa—not right now. She isn't responding to my daily texts. Officer John isn't returning my messages and I can't bear to call him. Bob Morton will only care if I come up with more money and if I didn't feel like I was able to before I certainly can't after being fired. Nobody is coming to the Facebook page anymore, and I have no idea what to do, which is like murder upon murder upon…yeah.

When one isn't needed, one at least wants to be wanted and one will find that want anywhere one can. And so here I am a week after that first drink with Hannah, sitting at Neary's and getting ready to drink more, and cheat, because I don't want to die a thousand deaths. Losing everything I've already lost is death enough, and yes, I'm acting like a baby and playing the victim. I'm now pretending I need an excuse to feel wanted, and sleeping with someone other than the person I usually sleep with just might make me feel that. I know this is nonsense and I'd rather not be so predictable with my poor behavior and acting out. It's anger and hurt and the intense desire to let drink do the talking and thinking for me is driving this whole sequence of events. I know I should say, I love Hannah and Christa, and we built something decent, stable, with family meals and reading at bedtime, holidays, ice skating, and bowling, and ballet recitals, laughter, and laundry, school pickups and parent-teacher conferences, and we might yet have that again if I want it bad enough. Of course, now it sounds like I'm trying to convince myself of this, which I suppose I am. But it isn't just about work, or Hannah or Christa—though having these things taken from me is going to warp any clear thinking. It's also about how happiness and stability are also a trap. Is that a rationalization? Of course, it is. It's just the happiness and stability I built and attend to isn't very adventurous either. I'm not adventurous. I choose not to be. I'm focused on being a good father, a husband, a good man, and while there's nothing heroic about doing so, nor should anyone confuse doing what's right with anything remotely heroic, it does require one to be normal and boring. I thought there was going to be something more. At least something extra in addition to such efforts. I would do the work and a reward of some kind would await me. But the hard work, not drinking, and trying to be a better version of myself, has rewarded me with what—nothing. There's nothing profound or weird or beautiful in my life.

There was Hannah.

There was Christa.

There was work.

I really tried to find meaning in those things and for the last three months I really tried to find Christa.

Now I don't know about any of it, and this ultimately is what my parents would hate most: I don't have meaning in my life, and I don't know how to find it.

Did I even deserve what I had when I had it?

I look at the drink sweating in front of me, and the dude sitting next to me, and I feel the familiar ache in my brain—the great longing to feel the gin as it wraps its legs around my tongue, the excitement of the tears that will come as it washes across my mouth, and into my throat, burning and cold, triumphant, only to be followed by someone's calves I've never seen or even imagined before this very moment, pinioned around my waist, my face and what's left of my alcohol soaked brain. I reach for the drink, and as I do, I recognize this is the moment where I consciously destroy whatever is left of me and might have even been saved. It's at this moment I'm most conscious and still have my faculties at play. I can back out of this suicide mission. I can repeat my mantra. I can go home to Hannah. I can take a long run, calm the voices, and remind myself, that I don't need adventure—I built something I'm proud of and it was hard, but I did it. I fixed what needed to be fixed, and came out on the other side, and even if it's temporarily lost, it's not the end. It's something terrible, maybe, but it's not the end. Or doesn't have to be anyway.

"Are you talking to-o-o me," the dude with rockstar hair and nice suit sitting next to me says, as he turns his handsome mug towards mine, words slurred and slushy, eyelids heavy, gripping his drink with both hands as if his life depended on it. "You keep l-l-l-o-o-king at me, I see your lips moving, and I think you're saying something—so now I'm just wondering if you want to fuck or what?"

Why not?

We drain our drinks and we're gone.

HANNAH

"I know something about people being gone and fucking around," I say to Kelly the therapist.

"What's prompting this declaration," she says.

We're outpatient now, and it's not going to last, not for me. I don't have anything to talk about with her anymore. Not that I can't come up with some things for today.

More immediately though, I'm struck for the first time that Kelly is Gabriel's type. The brown hair and the short professional skirts, her calves—he loves calves—her skin.

How did I overlook this before?

"Is everything okay?" Kelly says, smiling awkwardly, and bringing her hands to the top button on her blouse, which she fastens.

Was I looking at her chest?

I'm a monster.

"Yes, everything is great. Gabriel is messing around again," I say, more matter-of-factly than I intend to. Still, it is what it is. He drinks, he cheats, it doesn't mean anything.

"Do you want to talk about that?" Kelly asks.

"Not really. I'm also pretty sure he's lost his job but hasn't told me yet. He's like one of those Japanese guys who dress for work after they've been let go, and since they can't bear to tell their wives, they get ready for the day, leave the house, and sit in a park. That's Gabriel, but he doesn't go to the park, he goes to Neary's. He knows I know he's not working anymore. We just don't acknowledge it."

"You seem nonplussed by this."

"It gets old, plus Gabriel's mother will take care of him. She always does. His father drank and she took care of him—Gabriel drinks, and on and on."

"Okay. Well, you haven't talked much about Christa. How long has she been gone?"

"Three months."

"How does that make you feel?"

"Can we talk about something else?"

"It's your time, but I'm interested in what it feels like to you."

"I planned to talk about something else. A memory. But it's connected. I mean it's all connected though. Everything is, right?"

"Sure, go ahead."

"I was younger than Christa is now, and I don't know what I was dreaming about exactly, though I know it involved the movie *Alien*, and the idea that something was growing in my stomach, mutating, pulsating, morphing into a creature not quite human, and I knew this because I was on a table, metal, slick, cold to the touch, and the room was still—quiet—and there was this gnawing, and my stomach started to tear and my hands went to the tear and I tried to physically prevent it from spreading any further. I was holding the sides together, pleading, fighting, sweating, and then everything was just black. But only for a moment. I was lying in bed. It was an afternoon nap gone horribly awry and as I calmed down, I thought God damn my dad for suggesting *Alien* in the first place. My intent was to laugh it off, and not focus on how I was probably supposed to be at school. I'd left and no one seemed to notice. What I found myself focused on though was the fact that my mother was already home from work—which didn't make sense—and I could go to her, get a hug, some positive mother 'keep your chin up' affirmation, and move on with whatever the day held. As I reached the hall outside her bedroom door, I heard her humming "Afternoon Delight" to herself. I also smelled perfume. As I walked in, she spun around, her flaming hair alive, her smile beamed across the universe. Who was this? Because it was not my mother—not like this, not this glowing, or this vibrating, and so very alive. 'Hey,' I said, skinny little arms in front of me, needing a hug, warmth, 'I'm totally freaked out. I had this terrible dream, and well, hug, please?' 'Sure, honey,' she said before quickly hugging me and stepping back to smooth her flowy batik dress. She didn't want to be there at that moment and play mom. She had some-where else to be which didn't involve me. I didn't know who her plans involved, but I'd seen her with the skeezer dude from next door walking together near the school. She'd been laughing and touching his shoulder, and he was playing with her hair. I knew what I needed to know then, and the exchange at home reinforced it. Good for her, I thought, if she's decided to be happy. My mom paused in front of me, looking frazzled and unsure of herself. It felt like she was wondering what the right thing to do was and I might've said, 'could you stay…?'"

"Might've said?" Kelly says. "But you didn't, which would be a normal thing to do in a situation like that. Why didn't you?"

"I don't know," I say, but I do know. "Okay I should say, I do know. My family wasn't like that and when my mom then said, 'hey, your dad will be home soon,' I just smiled, said 'okay,' and watched her go."

"How did that make you feel?"

"I didn't feel anything. It's like with Gabriel's behavior, even with Christa deciding to go missing, which I say only because I've convinced myself she's safe and working something out. But people need to live their lives, and it's great when they make good choices, and everyone benefits from them. They just usually don't."

"Well, you say everything is connected. Do you feel you could've asked Christa to stay?"

"That's a really good question," I say, and then I get quiet. The answer is obvious, yes, clearly, of course I could've asked her to stay, but I don't say it. I also think maybe I don't need to ditch therapy quite yet.

GABRIEL

How does one live one's life or make good choices? These are good questions, and I've rarely had good answers to them.

By rarely I mean tonight, though after such a long stretch of nights not like this one, this night has become like so many before it, bars and cigarettes and small talk and quick, sweaty, sad sex, lost hours blurring together into a long, desperate, guilt-soaked song. These nights are the norm, again, and I'm captive to them, as well as my worst instincts and impulses.

Whether this is living an actual life is only a question of whether I consider another version feels conceivable to me. I must be able to see that other kind of life, imagine it, remember what it was like. What it looked like, smelled like, how I navigated it. There's a roadmap there and while it's currently just beyond my grasp, it doesn't have to be—not if I choose to see it and conjure it.

But I don't want to.

And I can't, not now, not any longer.

So, whether this is a good choice is no more important to contemplate than whether this is a life. It's the only choice, and now, it'll have to play out until its bitter and inevitable end.

Whether Hannah has thoughts about this remains a mystery to me. I don't ask, and she doesn't offer, and we are where we are. Which is nowhere. Which is why I'm quietly opening the back door to my parents' house and not my own. Hannah doesn't need to see me like this, nor do I want her to. She may not care, she may think it'll pass, or that she'll find me in the street, but whatever the outcome, she doesn't need to see me like this or smell my poor behavior as it wafts off me like smoke over a sewer grate.

My mother won't care. She'll take care of me, and whether she looks askance at the behavior and even if she pulls away emotionally to protect herself—something she's well practiced at—she's accepted this as a responsibility, carried from one generation to the next, ashes to ashes, and such. I grab a blanket from the closet and lay down on the couch. I close my eyes. As I will myself to sleep, a car passes, the headlights wash over me, and I'm taken back to another night on this same couch.

I was watching *The Tonight Show* with my mother. This would have been the 1970s, Johnny Carson was king, and at some point, I fell asleep, and she covered me with a blanket and went off to bed. I was dreaming about Icarus and the Minotaur, which we were reading about in school. How bright the sun must have been when Icarus climbed towards it, the heat on his face so warm, the light moving from startling to blinding. I realized that the heat and light were now enveloping me as well, moving to and fro, dancing, and impossible to pin down, now everywhere at once and getting closer. This wasn't a dream however, it was real, and the light was closer still, forcing its way through the living room window. I felt my senses heighten, even as the dread arose in my throat and gripped my neck. I could hear these mechanical pings and a weird grinding, a crunch and thud, before the lights came to a rest right outside the window. This was followed by a loud and deafening silence, and I thought, this is how an alien abduction starts. The lights in the window were clearly a UFO approaching—the silence a precursor. The dread was now oozing down to my chest, gripping it, twisting it, not letting go. It struck me how jealous my father would be when he learned he had missed this. Visitors from space. It was everything he'd ever wanted. Evidence that it was true. Still, this was proof, and he would have to appreciate that when I told him about what I had experienced the next morning. I started to wonder what would happen to me. How long I would be gone? If time would stop while I was away in the alien's spaceship? What were they looking for? Why did they think I could provide such answers? I got up from the couch, but I couldn't see anything. I could wait for them to come take me. I could also be brave, steadfast, and go to them myself. I walked to the front door and as I touched it, I waited for something to happen, a ripple of heat, an explosion. But there was nothing. I walked out into the night in my pajamas, barefoot, covering my eyes with my hands, shielding them from the glare so I could better see what awaited me. There were no little green men or spaceships though, just my father asleep at the wheel of his car in the driveway, which had come to a grinding halt on top of my bike. The engine was still running, and the lights were on. I leaned in through his window and turned off the lights, killed the engine, and coaxed him out of the car and onto my former spot on the couch. I tucked him in. I ignored the smell of whiskey. I kissed him on his stubbly cheek. I headed to my room and passed my mother on the way. She was standing at the top of the stairs in a bathrobe, arms crossed, mouth tightly clamped shut and wordless.

Wordless.

I fall asleep thinking how perfect the word is for everything going on and not. There's nothing to say and no right words to not say it.

HANNAH

I have no words, but this is because I've entered some kind of fugue state. I'm sitting in the emergency room waiting to learn about what's happening with my father, lost in the memories of all which has come before with him.

The two of us headed out in the middle of the night to Friendly's after watching *Hill Street Blues* to get Fribbles as the pimply-faced teenagers who ran the place were trying to close.

Playing miniature golf at Tiny Taylor Town as we dodged the unceasing waves of mosquitoes who dive-bombed anyone who dared venture out during the depths of the summer heat.

Going to see *The Cheap Detective* one afternoon at the mall where my dad laughed so hard and so often, I was embarrassed at first to be around him and then worried about his sanity.

The long hikes around State Park and up Buttermilk Falls, where we talked about our favorite episodes of, *I Love Lucy*, yet always agreed it was the one involving Ricky and Lucy dancing as she tried to hide the eggs in her shirt.

Having lunch at Neary's and debating how *Ordinary People* could have possibly beat *Raging Bull* for the Oscar, something my father considered a true American tragedy.

Going to the Arena to see the Charley Daniels Band on The Legend of Wooley Swamp tour, my first concert ever, the Harlem

Globetrotters and Curly Neal, the Ringling Bros. and Barnum & Bailey Circus, Gunther Gebel-Williams and his dazzling mane of hair, and Sha Na Na, though neither of us could ever recall why either of us thought the latter was a good idea.

The road trips to Thousand Islands where I encountered spin art for the first time and Hershey Park, which my dad hadn't confirmed was open yet for the season and wasn't…and on and on and on and on.

"Hannah."

"Hannah?"

"Hannah!"

I'm jolted back to my senses by Gabriel who's gently putting his hand on my shoulder from behind and attempting to draw me back from the world of memory and escape.

I don't know where he came from. He wasn't home when the hospital called. My father was out for an early run, he collapsed on the sidewalk, and here we are.

"Hannah, hey, are you with us. The doctor would like to talk to you," he says.

I turn around to see Gabriel and his deep brown eyes, looking at me, gentle and caring. There's also a young doctor staring at me, uncomfortably, but patiently. I stare back at him, his roundish face, and never-been-shaved skin, and try not to think about the fact that my father's health has been entrusted to someone who barely looks older than Christa.

"Hello," the doctor says. "Is your mother here? There are some preliminary results to share, and I'd like to let everyone know at once."

The doctor has long hair parted across the left side of his face that he's constantly brushing away from his eyes, and I don't know whether to speak or pin it back for him.

"No," I say, as I run my palms along my stomach and brush the wrinkles out of my shirt. "There's no mother and there's no one else."

"Okay," the doctor says, brushing the hair out his eyes again.

Before he can speak, there's movement from the other side of the emergency room, a space I hadn't even noticed before this moment. There are other people here, patients and family members, staff hustling back and forth like extras on a movie set—and an endless mélange of pings, beeps, and *whirrrrs* which permeate the room.

I was in my own head, but now I'm not, and I see Tracey is here too. She appears like magic and wow do I feel bad—of course, there's someone else.

"Hey, I'm the fiancé, you can talk to me too," Tracey says breathlessly, touching my shoulder, and reaching out to shake the doctor's hand.

"I'm sorry," I mouth to her.

"Please," she mouths back, as she engulfs me in a hug, burying me in her ample bosom—an embrace I willingly embrace.

The doctor pauses.

I can see he's already exhausted from dealing with us.

Doctors aren't prepared to handle stuff like this. This being families and their confusion about what's happening with their loved ones. How they're desperate to feel less fragile and it's on him to somehow make sense of it. On the other hand, he is trained to find problems and fix people, and since that's what he's trying to do, he'll wait until we seem ready to listen.

"Okay," the doctor says, "we've been running a series of tests—and we need to run some more—and while I don't want you to be alarmed yet, we definitely have some concerns."

"Concerns? What the hell does that mean?" Tracey says, leaping forward, before catching herself when Gabriel gently grabs her arm, something I note with an odd mix of pride and attraction.

The doctor pauses again.

He's probably thinking about how he's not prepared to deal with this kind of nonsense either, anger or fear—raw emotion. At this point, he's not anything more than a messenger with little control over why he's here or why the patient is as he is. But he knows none of us care about those concerns and so he continues.

"Look," the doctor says, directing his attention to me, "there are going to be more tests, and we need to hold your father overnight. There was already something happening with his brain, he banged his head on a tree branch while he was running, and we think it triggered a stroke. It's lucky someone was out walking their dog and found him immediately. If he'd been home by himself, who knows…"

"A stroke…," Tracey says loudly, before closing with a nearly silent, "…uh."

"Shut up," I say, willing myself not to cry.

Everyone uncomfortably looks around at everything but me.

I really need my mom, which should feel so crazy—why now—but sometimes nothing makes as much sense as that.

"So that's it," I say, stiff-lipped. "You have nothing else?"

"That's it for now," the doctor says. "I'm sorry. This is a lot to take in, but please go home, get some sleep. Your father is sedated, and there's nothing more we can do tonight."

At that moment, the doors to the emergency room fly open and the EMT guys come crashing in, one pushing a stretcher, and the other sitting on top of someone and repeatedly pushing on his chest. There's chaos, families scattering, the young doctor running off, and people everywhere. We're standing, then drowning, in the middle of it. I start to re-enter the fugue state I'd been in just moments before. Gabriel grabs me by the shoulders, and as Tracey clears a path, he steers me outside of the hospital and into the cool air. I let it wash over me like a wave and then I'm screaming at the top of my lungs, though not a sound comes out. After that, I feel faint—my legs no longer able to hold up my torso, my arms limp, my eyelids so very heavy.

I'm falling, and it goes on for forever, which is wonderful, and very freeing.

GABRIEL

Hannah is falling, falling, falling.

Tracey and I grab hold of her and ease her to a bench across the parking lot from the entrance to the Emergency Room. She's frozen in amber, with seemingly no inclination to wake up, or return to us, and for a moment, I wonder if this is permanent. If she's the soldier, and if she'll now remain like this—present, and a reminder of our past imperfections, but not moving, for all of time immemorial. Her eyes are wide open, and she seems at peace, but there's nothing calming about seeing her like this. There's the sense that someone can pass between your fingers, between this world and the next, and you can't control it. Still, it's one thing to recognize that you have no control and another to accept it. After a few moments of this, Tracey and I start to lose it a little.

"Wake up, move something, a finger, your head, anything," we scream at Hannah, shaking her by the shoulders and looking for a sign of life.

Hannah snaps back to attention.

Tracey hugs her and I try not to cry—Hannah wouldn't be pleased.

"Everything is cool," Hannah says, "I got a little overwhelmed and faint. I was disassociating maybe, but now I'm cool. Promise."

"You seemed so far away," Tracey says. "It was scary, and you know how much I hate that. Don't pull that shit again, got it?"

"Yes, sorry, I slipped away for a moment. It was peaceful, and I wanted to feel that, and not let go. But it's not cool, I know, and I'm back."

"Good, let me drive you home," Tracey says.

"No, thank you, Gabriel can take care of that, right?" Hannah says.

"Totally, yes, anything, of course," I answer.

"Yeah, sure, are you okay to drive?" Tracey says, firmly, folding her arms across her chest, and giving me the once-over. "You smell like a fucking brewery, and you look like hell."

"I'm fine," I say.

"He's fine," Hannah says.

"Okay, fine," Tracey says as she gives Hannah a hug, "I'll see you here tomorrow then."

Tracey pulls away and looks at me.

"Drive carefully, lover boy, you have precious cargo there," she says, before walking off.

I take Hannah home, I drive carefully, I tuck her into bed, and then I don't know what to do. Having a drink seems obvious, but I don't want one, not right now. I don't want to be numb. I want to feel things—which is weird—it's a perfect time to feel nothing.

I don't question it though. I want it to be a sign. I want it to mean something.

I put on my running shoes.

I haven't run since the last time I did so with Ed—before I started drinking again and before this recent collapse. The run wasn't pleasant, nor was he, but it was necessary, and this feels necessary too.

I go back out into the night.

I feel the first step shudder through my entire body, and for a moment, I'm certain my knees will collapse under the weight of not just my actual weight, but the emotions piling up like a car wreck on my brain.

There is sadness for Hannah, my fears for Ed, my own complicated feelings for my parents, and my inability to make sense of Christa's disembodied presence in our lives. She's here, but not, and maybe not ever again.

There is also the dissonance of being trapped, of things I didn't ask for or create and the commensurate pain and awfulness.

I didn't ask for it.

But of course, I did.

Everything I am, I asked for, and if I built my own walls—that's no one's fault but my own.

I channel my whacked-out energy into taking one step, then another, my tweaky knees, torched lungs, and balky back, ensure I won't find an actual rhythm, not easily, or quickly anyway. But I do get past wanting to hurl on the street and then the less paralyzing aches and pains in my shoulders, neck, hips, and chest slowly dissipate. The horrible thoughts previously gripping my harried, alcohol-saturated brain, slowly dissipate as well, leaving me somewhere bordering on comfortable, out of breath, and shuffling at best, but moving forward—part of this world and another parallel one—where I might once again find a foothold and remember again how to be happy, Zen, and free.

Soon, and with some surprise, though maybe it was my plan the whole time, I'm back at the hospital. It's quiet now as I ease into the emergency room, down the halls, past security, onto the elevator and into Ed's room. He's lying there, lights beeping and whirring around him, his white hair shooting off in every direction, his eyes tightly clamped shut, tubes running to and from his nose and mouth, his lips thin and rubbery. IVs pump clear solutions into his papery arm, a monitor on his index finger, the knuckles looking old, beauty-marked, and gnarled. His skin is washed out and grey, the color of late winter—when the sunlight is sparse, and the mood is depressed. There are also monitors attached to his chest, perfectly proportioned leeches, which follow and track his every tortured, phlegmatic breath. His old man chest is saggy and melting, his pectorals conical and flabby. Patches of chest hair intertwine with one another to form a patchwork of sparse shrubbery across the landscape of his failing body.

Staring at him, incapacitated and small, and not the man I've grown up around and let down, I'm struck less by how terrible it feels, and more about how much I love him—how real and deep it is—even if I've never quite allowed myself to acknowledge it before now. I want to tell him how I feel. I pause. If I can't say anything to him when he's awake and he can hear it, then I shouldn't tell him anything at all. Still, I need to talk, Ed is right here before me, and he can listen, even if he doesn't respond.

"Before whatever happened to you today, Christa went off with Josh to wherever she is, I re-engaged in my drinking and poor behavior, before even my father drank too much, I was little, and it was just me and my mother having breakfast in the kitchen, tucked into the yellow benches that surrounded the table, the wallpaper covered with polka dots. I was eating Cheerios—the spoon repeatedly smacking against the side of the bowl. My mother was eating grapefruit and she winced with every bite. I watched her as I always did, captivated by her dark hair, the way her cheekbones were etched into her face, how her eyes danced when she smiled. I was trying to figure out what made her tick, and she said, 'your grandfather always insisted I eat grapefruit—how there's nothing healthier,' and I thought about how her father also drank and was far from healthy, but my mother was, and I needed her to stay that way. So, I was glad she was eating grapefruit, and when she was done, I asked her if I could plant a grapefruit seed in a planter with some dirt and grow a grapefruit tree of my own. My thinking was maybe if we had an unlimited supply of grapefruit in the house, my mother could stay healthy forever. She was happy to plant the grapefruit seed with me—she was humored by it—though I only realized that later. But we planted a seed, gingerly packed it into the dirt, watered it, and moved the planter onto a small table by a window and under the sun. Then I waited for something to happen and tried not to stare at it. Soon there was a little green bud, and while it didn't seem very promising—it existed, it was something. I kept watering it and watching it, even praying over it, though that didn't involve much more than putting my hands together, moving my lips, and shutting my eyes tight. One morning, there was a tree, of sorts, spindly, but sturdy, with bark and length, and growing towards the sky. It kept growing and needed to be repotted, before being moved from the table onto the floor. For months, then years, the tree kept twisting and turning, and I started to wonder how big it had to be before grapefruit began to grow from it. One day, I said to my mother, 'we're going to have grapefruit soon,' because of course we were, the tree was majestic and wonderfully exotic. She replied, 'sweetie, you didn't think this tree could grow actual grapefruit, did you? We don't live in the right climate for that.' She said this kindly, but it was then I realized I couldn't protect her from anything. Nothing could. No one can protect anyone, not their wives, parents, fathers-in-law, or daughters, much less themselves, from their inevitable decline.

"And so here we are, Ed, no one ever protected you from anything, and I'm sorry about that. You deserve better. Truly."

I lightly touch his arm, and then I start to sob.

I take a moment to steady myself at the edge of his bed so as not to float away, I say my mantra, "I am not empty, I am open," I take a breath and run home.

HANNAH

Kelly the therapist is wearing a Tartan skirt today, and I find myself absorbed in its crisscrossing horizontal and vertical bands, losing myself in the rich combination of red and green. Soon I'm floating above the session, watching myself staring at her skirt and the endless permutations contained therein.

"Hey Hannah," Kelly says, gently. "What do you want to talk about today?"

I drift back into my body.

"Can we talk about my father. He was always there for me, and now you know…," I say, trailing off.

"No, I don't know, but yes, of course, what are you thinking?"

"He's in the hospital. He's had a stroke. I'm not sure if he's going to come out of it."

"Oh gosh, I'm sorry," Kelly says, wiping away a sudden, urgent tear before composing herself in one smooth and effortless motion.

"Yeah, thanks, I'm not sure what to say about it, but I do have a memory I want to share."

"Okay, go ahead," she says.

"There was this one evening when my father was out. He worked a second job at night then. My mother got a phone call. After a flurry of furtive whispers, she hung up, and asked me to come with her. We'd been watching *The Tonight Show*, which my mother and I did a lot. We'd snuggle on the couch, her arm around my shoulders, me curled into her hip, enveloped in a burnt, flowery mix of Charlie perfume and cigarettes—there was always a green and white carton of Kools and a sweaty can of Tab nearby—her long red curls merged with mine, wild and untamed. Most nights whether my father was there or not this is where she and I ended up, on the couch, watching Carson.

"Years before that, when I was in kindergarten, my teacher Ms. Moore asked everyone what time we went to bed. I wasn't sure. I didn't know when The Tonight Show ended. Everyone else said they went to bed at seven, six-thirty, or eight, so I copied them, speaking fast, and low, combining everyone else's bedtime into one time, 'around 6:307:008:00,' I said, before I put my head down, hoping no one would notice.

"'What time did you say, Hannah?' Ms. Moore asked in her soft old lady voice, staring at me kindly from underneath her massive, black-dyed beehive.

"'Around 6:307:008:00,' I repeated low and fast.

"'Hannah is lying,' Pam, a soon to be ex-friend yelled. 'She stays up until like midnight with her mom watching *The Tonight Show*.'

"I wondered if that was what my mother meant when she said you could never trust other girls with your secrets.

"Anyway—I digress—so there I was on the couch with my mother when the phone rang. She jumped up and ran to it, the waft of perfume and cigarettes trailing her across the room. She spoke in hushed tones I couldn't follow beyond, 'now, no' and 'her father isn't home.' That was followed by the request for me to come outside with her—which I did. She directed me to climb into the back seat of this old, green Plymouth Valiant while my mom and the young skeezer neighbor guy talked in the front. I heard her say, 'I want to leave, but without Hannah, no, maybe, I don't know.' My stomach started to hurt, and my mother started smiling and crying at the same time. Soon they kissed, and I thought about my father, which made my stomach hurt more. At some point I fell asleep in the back seat and the next thing I knew my mother was gently shaking me. I woke up to her big smile, her wild curls, and her scooping me up in her arms, then walking me back into the house and laying me on the couch. Soon she was stroking my arms with her fingers and nuzzling my neck—her hair tickling my nose. Then she was crying, and she told me my father would be home soon and I needed to get some sleep. She also said she had to go, and didn't know when I would see her next, but she loved me so much. She needed something different, she said. Something more. Soon the words were blurring together—she was too young, she wanted to see the world, explore things, live, gloriously. She also said she wanted me to be tough, always tough—no tears, no bullshit, no weakness. After she wiped away her own tears, she composed herself, and before my eyes closed again, she waved a little wave, skipped down the front walk where the neighbor guy was leaning against his car, smiling a crazy smile. Then she was done waving, she jumped into his arms, and they were gone."

Kelly is quiet, unmoving, and nods her head a few times, before saying, "uh-huh, okay."

"When I awoke again, my father was sitting next to me drinking coffee, his eyes red and puffy. He was rubbing my back, and when he saw me open my eyes, he smiled, and I was so happy to see him that I took him in my arms and hugged him until it was uncomfortable for both of us. For years after that, I sat by the window wondering when my mom would come home, and I even looked out to the stars wondering if that's where she might be, soaring and swooping, free to become one with the universe, a constellation all her own. But she didn't come home. My dad, however, was always there. When I got my period, he ran to CVS for tampons in the middle of the night. When I got this bad perm and needed barrettes if I was going to make it to school the next day. When I got bullied or had the flu. He was there for me. When I couldn't sleep, or liked someone, he was reliable, sturdy, there, always—and now there's this, and I wasn't able to be there for him or protect him. What kind of person does that make me?"

"It's not the child's job to protect the parent," Kelly says, "which doesn't mean it isn't hard and doesn't mean you haven't been there for him in the past and can't be there for him now when he needs you."

"Okay, I guess, but it's killing me. I hate it and it's so confusing," I say.

"That's because you're human."

"Yeah, well, I never wanted to be human."

I didn't.

Not ever.

Not being human is being able to rise above the clutter and noise.

Not being human is to exist beyond normal feelings.

Not being human is not counting on anyone and being able to take care of yourself.

I believed I was able to embrace these things, but maybe I'm wrong, or worse, maybe I'm human.

Huh.

GABRIEL

I think it has something to do with love, finding it, nurturing it, appreciating it. I haven't done a good enough job with Hannah, I didn't think about it nearly enough with Ed, and with Christa, I tried so hard, but I don't know if it made a difference.

I don't even know if I truly know what love is, but I can find out.

"What is love?" I say to my mother.

My mother takes a pull from my one-hitter, coughs, then laughs, her eyes tearing.

She's getting high for the first time today and being treated for breast cancer.

You would think that Ed's stroke would be enough. That the universe would choose to distribute parental health issues more equitably, but the universe doesn't care. More than that, my mom's treatment isn't a new thing. Should I already know this? I would say so. Might she have told me before today? Again, I would say so. But she didn't. She prefers to tell me now when it's clear to me something is going on. Which it is. She's too tired. Too slow to respond to questions. Her always flawless skin is papery and brittle. Things aren't right, and here we are. She's feeling too sick to walk, and I have suggested the two of us get high, and getting high makes me think about love, it always has…what love is, tastes like, whether I can feel it—in my heart, my brain, my hands, solid, something I can grip and mold, hold and manipulate.

I ask my mother what love is, because if anyone knows she will.

Maybe I'm getting ahead of myself though.

I'm taking a walk through the park with my mother.

This has become our ritual ever since Christa went missing nearly four months ago. Every Thursday morning, I pick her up at 7:30 am and we walk. Sometimes we talk, and sometimes we don't. But it doesn't matter, we commune with nature. We let the sun splash over our faces and the dew pool on our shoes, and the bad things, grief, loss, anger, regret, wash away, cleansing us—if only for a brief time. We connect and where so many things may not be truly good, this is good. It's peaceful. It's a return to the womb as it were. It's also become important to us, and we choose to accept it for what it is.

I'm thankful this opportunity has presented itself to me. I never counted on it happening or even hoped for it. But here it is, and I can only hope that Christa and I will enter a similar plane someday. A place beyond the pain and confusion that has rippled across this time in our life and will surely ripple well beyond it.

My mother and I meet regardless of what's going on, though before the diagnosis, and the chemo, there wasn't much going on.

Hannah is home again, but not really—she's up early and out of the house for work and therapy.

Christa isn't here and I try not to think about how things would be if they were normal and like they were before.

Though I still do.

In this scenario—the normal one—Christa will wake up for school, I might make her breakfast, and a lunch she won't eat. I might talk to her, or not. Christa's unlike me in that way. She doesn't awaken with energy and words—ready to tackle what awaits her. It's hit or miss with her, something my mother will never quite understand. Some people need time to exit sleep—their head, their dreams, and fears—and enter the day. It's an effort for people like them. It's a project.

Could that be why Christa's gone? Because even though I know this about her, and even though she's more like Hannah in this regard—reserved, more in her head, needing distance and space—neither Hannah nor I can totally accept it. We must imbibe her, experience her, and control her—be involved in her every motion and cellular change.

Isn't that what I'm still doing now?

Am I not hoping to somehow control something uncontrollable by endlessly thinking about her, trying to guess what she's doing with her days and wondering how she's functioning in the broader world? If Christa was here, I'd constantly be trying to figure out how she was interacting with her peers, teachers, even the air itself.

That's too much for anyone to manage, right?

The idea of being away from me, us, must feel better to her than being with us.

Christa created some distance and Josh makes that possible. He's her escape pod. Plus, he isn't invading her space. He's there, but not too there, and he isn't me.

This possibility must be fine with me.

However, what if it isn't fine with Christa? She's chosen to go away and has no connection to us. But what if Christa feels she's made the wrong decision, wishes she didn't leave and is worried she can't just come back. Not easily anyway. That doing so involves admitting to herself leaving was a mistake. A disproportionate reaction to something which can be talked about and doesn't require actual distance, just boundaries and better communication.

Not that Hannah and I are always good at talking. Or is it listening?

Then again, maybe I'm wrong. I'm wrong about a lot of things.

Maybe Christa's working as barista or waitress, writing poetry, cleaning hotel rooms, waking up to the same sun that Hannah and

I are, breathing, living, making a life with Josh that doesn't include us. She's happy and has no regrets. Each day is filled with little spikes of joy, untethered from me, us, and our soul-sucking needs.

Not that I know anything.

Christa's not here and she's not in contact. I don't know what the story is, I can't know, and it's unbearable.

Then there's me, I'm here, but not anywhere really. I don't work. I can look for work, but I don't. Instead, I do the laundry, have some drinks, change light bulbs, do the laundry, wash the dishes, make little repairs, make them again, fold the laundry, paint doors and walls and ceilings, admire my work, paint some more, drink some more. I pretend to look at job boards, but I know it's not going to lead to anything, and not merely because the jobs themselves blur together into one amorphous job I can't and won't be able to get as I stare at my laptop through my fuzzy, gin- and weed-soaked vision. It's that I'm not fit for work anymore—and it didn't take any time at all. I know I can still take orders and deliver for those who employ me. But to sit somewhere every day, wondering when it's going to end? No, that'll not work. It isn't my normal. I'm not that guy, and not unlike the Christa of my imagination, I'm untethered from what I knew and what I was, and I can't imagine ever being that guy again.

The point is, Christa doesn't bound into the house after school and doesn't tell me about her day, and at some other point, Hannah doesn't come home while I'm already making her dinner—something fresh, healthy, not frozen, not processed or defrosted—she deserves better as she gets better. It's not exactly pleasant between us, and there isn't any sort of happiness, or placidity. So, with Christa not coming home for dinner, much less going off to her room after dinner and television, and Hannah grabbing food and going to her home office to do some work or skipping dinner entirely to go to the gym to work out, I'm alone, and every night I drift out to a bar and whatever the night brings—only to start again the next day.

My parents are another thing. Sometimes I see them and sometimes I don't. It's tricky with them—especially when they're together. Growing up, they didn't raise their voices, nor fail to care for me, make sure I was supported, or love me. Their love was qualified, however, to some extent, by my father's drinking and the attention it required, but more so by their focus on each other. It was wholly absorbing and insular. There was them, and there was them and me. I was the third wheel, welcome, but mostly tolerated and not a priority. They never said it. It just was. The way they looked at each other, their intense interest in how each was doing and feeling—happy, sad, angry, anxious—and what they were thinking or reading about—politics, sports, art. Or how their day had been, the ignominies—the slights at work, being cut off on the highway or supermarket—and appreciations—nature, light, their dreams—travel to Japan, hiking in Alaska. They also focused on their needs—physical, spiritual, emotional. All that and managing my father until he sobered up, followed by them moving forward with the new and improved version of him, which meant the two of them talking all the time, and about everything, and at the expense of everyone else. To witness that level of absorption is to know awe, and that's how I felt about their relationship. But even knowing awe doesn't negate the need to search for something of your own, love, and attention from anyone—and in any way. It's a means to dull the pain and it's who I am. It's so cliché, and yet to be cliché, doesn't something have to have at least some basis in truth?

I would say so, and so here we are, my mother and I, doing our Thursday thing. When one adds chemo, fatigue, and nausea to the mix, my mother needs me, finally, and I need to be needed so badly right now—even if I didn't think I needed her as well. But I do. We need our mothers, always and forever. They're home and safety and stability in an impossible to understand world they brought us into. So, there it is, and here we are walking, sometimes talking, together, and getting high, because she feels sick, and she doesn't want to. And I talk about love when I get high, and so there's that too, sickness and love intertwined—a Freudian romcom as written by Nora Ephron starring my mother and me.

"What is love?" I ask.

My mother takes a pull from my one-hitter and starts to cough and tear and laugh before she can even formulate an answer.

"What's love?" she says when the coughing and laughter finally stops. She looks pale and old, her skin nearly translucent under the daylight beaming down from overhead, but she's still plugging away. "It's not what you think it is."

"What does that mean?"

"It means that one must love oneself before they can ever love someone else, and you don't love yourself. You drink, you get high, you sleep around, you don't work. Someone who loves themself doesn't act like that, and if you can't work that nonsense out, and frankly, that's the easy stuff, then you can't love anything, or anyone."

"Why beat around the bush?"

"Sweetie," she says, stopping for a moment to catch her breath, before facing me and cupping my face with her hands. "You asked, and I love you, but your behavior's ridiculous, embarrassing. Love's hard and you don't want to do hard."

"Being a father and a husband isn't hard?"

"Of course, it is," she replies, "but you asked about love, not doing the right thing. You're supposed to willingly choose to be a father and a husband over most everything else. If you didn't, you'd be a jerk, and while we may have failed you as parents, I know we didn't raise a jerk. No one is going to reward you for doing what you're supposed to do, and anyway, that's not working on how to know love."

"It's been so hard with you and dad as models," I say, which is something I want to believe. "How can anyone be like the two of you?"

"What does that mean to you?" my mother asks.

"It means you only ever had eyes for each other—the way you looked at one another. That you put taking care of him ahead of caring for yourself. When he got sober, he devoted himself to you. It was like a movie or something."

"Honey, you idealize a situation which had a lot of moving parts by smoothing down the rough edges, ignoring the struggles, your father's behavior and how I needed to hide from myself to survive. You even ignore how by my staying with him through those early years of drinking and indecency, I chose him over you. How in some ways, I abandoned you."

"But you were always there, for both of us." I protest knowing she's right, but not wanting to accept it.

"True, but at what expense? And not for me, but for you, and even for your father. I wouldn't let him go and maybe that's what he really wanted and needed. So yes, now we're here, after a lot of hard work, but at what cost?"

I never think about the work it takes to understand love or keep it in my life and like so many things I don't understand, I'm not sure I ever try to figure it out.

"Choose to do the work or not, just commit to your choice and be done with it," my mother says, kissing me on the cheek before starting to walk again.

I don't know what to do with this advice. Tomorrow, who knows, today, not so much. Instead, we walk, not talk, and I choose to focus on the impossibility of everything.

HANNAH

If everything is impossible, then you can try anything, right?

I want to ask Kelly about this. It seems like I'm going to have to start doing things differently, taking chances, blowing things up.

Otherwise, I may just fade away to nothing.

I don't say this.

I do, however, take a moment to soak up her lovely argyle skirt, with its pearl and purple hues, ignore whatever she asked me moments before and start to talk about a boy I once knew.

"He lived next door. He wasn't cute or especially nice. But there were days where there was nowhere else to go and nothing else to do and I couldn't stare at the ceiling tiles in my house for even one more minute. So, I would go over to his house, and I didn't do much beyond watch television and count his ceiling tiles as opposed to mine. And most of the time it was fine—I wasn't alone. One day he said he was trying out for the hockey team, he needed to practice, and he asked if I could play goalie? Yes, of course, I said, a little too excitedly. It didn't matter that I knew so little about how to do what he was asking. It was something to do. There was also something sexual to it. I'm not sure I had that language yet, or could identify the feeling, but it was scintillating, private, physical. It seemed kind of hot. We went into his garage, and he gave me a stick and some gloves, and he lined me up on one side. I'd never been in his garage before. There were some pictures on the wall of his dad in a baseball uniform. He was broad and handsome—young, vibrant, raw—which was also hot. The boy saw me looking at the photos. He said his dad had been a big deal in Triple-A ball, never made it to The Show, but was this close pitcher once. Now he was an insurance salesman. The boy acted so bored with the whole thing, but it seemed like a big deal to me. My father was never anything. Not that I'd ever really been around the boy's father, and I had no idea what he thought about playing professional baseball. His father was nice to me though, and not weird, which was also nice, and that's what I was thinking as the plastic balls started blasting off the boy's stick—one shot after another, smooth, and fast. Sometimes I blocked them, but much of the time I didn't, the balls flying off the walls, the windows. Soon things started to rattle. The entire house seemed at risk of being uprooted from the ground below it, and the boy was so focused, trying so hard, his eyes narrowed, his plump lips pursed—and I was taken with that, and him, and while I should've been more focused on stopping more shots, I began to focus on those lips and his mouth, and what it might be like to kiss him. Soon I was no longer aware of how loud it had become, nor how his father, who was quite big and suddenly in the garage, was shaking the boy, his slender shoulders lost in his father's enormous hands, telling him to quiet down, before storming off. The boy laid his stick on the ground and silently walked away without saying anything. I went home and right after that the boy's father left the family, and the boy and his mother moved away to be near her family. One night, I asked my father if the father left the boy and his mom because we were so loud playing hockey in the garage, and he said, 'No, honey, people don't leave for reasons like that,' and I said, 'So why do they leave,' and after pausing, he said, 'I don't really know,' and I believed him, but only kind of."

"Okay, so I asked you how you and Gabriel are doing," Kelly says.

She did?

She did, and while I mostly ignored her, I must've sort of been paying attention. Why else would the boy and his parents' separation pop into my head?

"Right, sorry," I reply. "I guess I got to thinking about why people stay together when they do and if it even makes a difference whether you stay together if it's just the two of you?"

"Is that how it feels?" she asks.

"It's how it is. Gabriel and I loved each other once. There was Christa. We had that. I didn't want it at first, but once we had her, I really wanted to protect what we created, and I also really wanted to hold onto him. I had to for her. But for me too. I didn't want to love anyone else, and I didn't want to lose anyone else. Now I'm not sure any of it matters to me anymore."

"What does matter to you?" Kelly asks.

"I want to float away and see where I go. I always try to hold on so tight to everything and everyone. Where has it gotten me?"

"Only you know that. Do you think you sound or feel like your mother right now?"

Of course, I do, but if therapy teaches us anything, it's we can't escape our parents' shadows. If we're willing to do the work, maybe we can be better versions of them, but not much more than that—and I'm done with it.

I really don't know what matters anymore, but it's not coming here.

GABRIEL

Is it possible nothing matters anymore? This hadn't occurred to me. Not consciously anyway.

I don't picture a life without Hannah in it.

Why would I?

But maybe the life I take for granted is done with me?

I don't picture a life without Christa in it either and I don't want to. Not that I don't want her to be happy if that's how she wants it.

I don't search for her.

Not physically.

Where would I go at this point?

I don't look at the Facebook page. Doing so is unbearable.

I won't call Officer John. Why would Hannah or I contact him? He's a reminder of how little any of this makes sense.

As for Bob Morton, that's more money, which feels pointless. Whether this feeling is rooted in truth, or my sense of inadequacy remains to be determined.

It's four months now, and I don't know what else I can do besides send my daily text message. That text is sacred, a ritual, and the only thing which prevents me from fully melting into the earth.

Instead, I sit on the couch, the lights low, and I watch a rerun of *Everybody Loves Raymond*. Raymond is hoping to get laid, but it's not happening. No reason really, but that's why it's funny, right? There's never really a reason. Marriage can't be explained. Not when it's good and not when it's bad. People say they can make sense of it, but they can't. I sit around some more, and another episode of *Everybody Loves Raymond* comes on. Raymond is hoping to get laid again, but it's not happening. No reason really. I'm drinking a lot, which might be a problem, but it doesn't strike me as the actual problem. The actual problem seems to be I'm drinking alone.

Which is a red flag.

The solution?

Don't drink alone.

I down my drink.

I put on my shoes.

I wash my face.

Ed tells me to wash my face when I want to refocus and conquer the world. He says in *The Hustler*, Jackie Gleason who plays the aging legend Minnesota Fats stops to wash his face during the high-stakes match with Paul Newman's character Fast Eddie Felsen—the young hotshot who's challenging his supremacy. It's what allows him to recapture his equilibrium and cool. I suppose if one must choose, one will choose to be Fast Eddie Felsen, and by extension Paul Newman, over Minnesota Fats, or Jackie Gleason, in nearly any scenario. But this doesn't mean the scene doesn't have meaning. Or one shouldn't wash one's face when one is looking to conquer the world. It's just, goddamnit, Paul Newman has a beautiful mug, and there's no real debate whether he's the coolest. He is. Full stop. Of course, Ed also says Fast Eddie Felsen claims no one creates their own luck, and Ed agrees—he says he doesn't believe in luck. For Ed, it's about hard work and preparation. Me, I'm not sold. Luck is luck is luck and it's best to embrace no one has any control over anything, whether its marriage, work, or drinking.

I leave the house and start to walk.

I drift past the errant dog-walkers and people coming from the gym, the suits, and the endless banks that seem to pop up everywhere now.

I find myself at Neary's.

This was my place before I stopped drinking, and relapsed. It felt so good back then. Though to be transparent, the late nights could be rough. Not hungover rough either. That wasn't a thing for me. I didn't get hungover. Nor was it a need to rally and face the day kind of rough. I could always rally. What was rough was the rage I felt towards Hannah: why wasn't she more like my mother had been towards my dad—full of affection and attention and a desperate need to make sure I was the best version of myself?

Why wasn't it so much easier?

This one time Hannah and I had been walking somewhere, and we reached one of the bridges that connects downtown to the neighborhood I grew up in. It started to get misty, and as we approached the mist, a couple emerged from its depths, holding hands, and staring into one another's eyes. They were lost in a world of their own making. As I watched them walk by, I realized they were my parents, too caught up in each other to care about the weather or even notice their only child standing in the shadows. That image was burned into my head. That's what love looked like, could look like, ought to look like. It was how I felt about Hannah. But could she say the same? She couldn't. I never thought so, and I never understood it. Why didn't she want me more? More accurately, why didn't she seem to want me as much as I wanted her? I couldn't make sense of it. I had too many feelings—sadness, confusion, anger, longing—and as much as I could shrug them off when I wasn't drinking, they felt volcanic when I was—pinging about my brain with nowhere to go until the alcohol wore off—one day fading into the next.

I was trapped by my rage and my impotence, and it couldn't be managed or controlled. It was so much easier back then to not come home or come in late when no one had to see it. I couldn't stand the memory of it when I stopped drinking. Feeling like that, hating her so much, loving her so much, and knowing I would never leave her or feel any differently regardless of what happened in our lives. Not with the emotion I felt so tightly intertwined with our relationship—and not with Christa in the mix. Then there was the incident with Christa, which I couldn't make sense of when it happened either. With time—and with the clarity I was imbued with when sober—I came to understand how some part of my rage was about Hannah and her unwillingness to let me go. She wouldn't allow me to just float away, and I hated her for that. I couldn't see it until I stopped drinking, however.

Now what, I'm drinking again, and what do I feel?

There's no rage.

I don't feel a thing.

There's nothing.

I'm dead, we're dead, everything is dead, and this feels preferable to a stew of emotions that can't—won't—be controlled.

The first drink goes down smoothly, beautifully.

It's oxygen.

Why was it that I stopped doing this in the first place?

It was for Hannah and Christa, and for me.

After two more drinks, I'm happy, and I should be, I deserve it. I'm not thinking about what tomorrow will look like or how any of this affects anyone but me. I'm on autopilot and I have no control. None of us do.

Huh.

I see Hannah across the room.

Her hair, aloft and aflame, a kinetic life force, all its own.

Her big smile.

She seems happy.

She turns, looks in my direction, and waves to someone behind me.

As she walks past me, I realize it's not her, just someone who looks like her, someone I want to be her.

I down my fourth drink, maybe fifth, my head starts to spin.

I can't focus.

I step away from the bar and go outside.

The crisp air is a jolt to my muddled thoughts, clearing my head.

I look up and out across the universe, the stars dancing above and beckoning, and in this moment, there's also a moment of clarity—an insight of sorts: we're not alone, I'm not alone, and I'm more than this, I can go home, I can run, I can be whole, and I can be better.

I suck down a cigarette, but I can't move, and when the door to Neary's opens, the moment of clarity dissipates with the cigarette smoke—and I walk back in.

I head to the bar and sit next to a woman who could be thirty or fifty. It's not that she looks bad, but she's drunk, and she's tired, and she doesn't care.

She's perfect.

"Hey," I say.

"Hey to you," she says, breathy.

Then she smiles.

Stick a fork in this one.

"How about a drink?" I ask.

"Got one," she says, grandly sweeping her hand across the bar and pointing to the glass in front of her.

"True, but you have two hands, why waste one?"

"Sold!"

I order drinks and decide cheesy will work fine.

"If someone told you that you had a killer body, would you hold it against them?" I say, turning towards her, shoulders squared, leaning in, the space closing between us.

"Of course," she says. "Why are we still here?"

Soon the two of us are smoking a joint and stumbling towards her house.

"You got a problem with cats?" she says. "Because I'm an old cat lady."

"No," I say, "is there anyone who doesn't love pussy?"

She laughs, which is good, but I'm starting to wonder if this is something I want to do.

Am I so dead I'm willing to sleep with a sad, drunken cat lady?

I think back to a time when I was sober and having lunch with Christa. It was at some point between the sex talk and her disappearance. She knew I spent much of her childhood at Neary's, drinking, hiding from her, chasing people not her mother. She also knew Hannah was at peace with my behavior. At the time I wasn't that guy anymore. There was no drinking, hiding, or sexual liaisons. I was done with it, and I didn't expect her to bring it up. We were just sitting there. Back then I would go to Neary's to hang out, and breathe it in, to test myself, and stay strong, something Christa said she admired. She also said sometimes it was fun to sit there in silence with me as I got Zen, became Yoda and something other than. That day though, the not-talking must have gotten to her, and the thoughts must have been slamming around her head. She blurted out, "Why did you cheat on, Mom? Why? What the fuck, seriously? What?" And for a moment, I went to correct her language—something about being a proper young woman, or whatever it is dads say. But I didn't. Instead, I rubbed my eyes, and said I never really dated when I was younger, that I was never with anyone but Hannah, and suddenly, inexplicably, these beautiful women, even men, were available to me, interested, and throwing themselves at me. "What was I supposed to do?" I knew how sad and pathetic I sounded, but it's what I had. I didn't apologize to her. It didn't seem necessary in that situation. At first Christa was quiet and I assumed she had nothing to say. It was as if she'd traveled to a parallel space, away from me, her feelings, the truth. But then I saw movement behind her eyes, and anger, which I recognized. I waited for her to say, "Don't sleep with other people. What's hard about that?" But she didn't. She was stuck on something she didn't understand or know how to articulate. She had no way to make sense of her feelings and she decided it was pointless to try.

I felt sick looking at her, knowing it was how she really felt about me, but worse not being strong enough to say something to close the gap between us.

And I feel sick now looking at myself. I'm out of control, everything I'm doing is pointless and I know that too.

I just don't know what to do about it.

Though maybe I do.

I could stop myself, redirect my energy, get refocused on being sober, decent, finding Christa whether she wants to be found or not.

But I won't, not right now.

I'm on a path, and I need to see it through.

It's infuriating, and I hate myself, my weakness, but we're at the cat lady's home, and I must go in, and with all due respect to the cat lady—cats are not the problem. Everywhere I look or turn are buckets and drawers filled with random ephemera, towers of stuff, neat, collected, and looming about the maw—both guardian and jailer.

Do you need Garfield calendars dating back to 1978?

Because she has that covered.

How about plastic Lucha Libre wrestling figures in a range of garish colors?

Those are here too.

Comet cleaning products, bungee cords, bottles of Tang, or cases of New Coke?

It's here.

Organized, alphabetized, and color-coded.

There are cats too.

She didn't lie about the cats.

So many cats, and they're leaping among the endless crates only to disappear behind endless shelves.

I pause for a moment to take it in.

I need to get out.

I must get out.

"There are so many sales," she says.

I don't respond, I know there are sales, of course, but this, this is crazy making—she knows that, right?

"Let's go," she says, "my room is back here."

When I get there, at least a dozen cats are on the top of her bed. Uh.

She shoos the cats off and hands me a bottle of tequila sitting on her nightstand.

"One more drink?" she says.

I take the bottle, lean my head back, and down an enormous swig, drinking so much, so fast it starts to stream down my cheeks—a burst of alcohol tears. When I look up, she's lying in her bed with nothing on, and when we're done, I can't even look at her, not even as she curls into me and kisses my neck.

I light a cigarette.

"Yuck, stop, you can't smoke in here," she says in a little girl voice dripping with disgust.

I look at the drawers and shelves and the cats running around the room. I can't smoke—here? I then look at her and I want to be cool and relaxed. I also want to be nice. She's done nothing. She's who she is, and she hasn't tried to hide it or pretend otherwise. But I'm who I am, filled with self-loathing, and it has nowhere to go.

"There's no smoking in this pathetic squalor of a life," I say. "Are you serious?"

It's the meanest thing I've ever said.

Also, this whole idea that I'm dead inside, and beyond rage, that's wrong. I've been lying to myself and anyone who cares to listen. If anyone still cares.

"You need to leave," the cat lady says, covering up.

I leave, and I don't know what Raymond would do at such a time, but I hope he would know it's time to stop drinking, because like me, he knows this isn't going to work anymore.

HANNAH

"It's not working anymore," I say to Tracey, an array of empty shot glasses and beer bottles between us.

"What's 'it?'" Tracey replies.

"Me and Gabriel. Even at his worst, I never really thought about why we stayed together. There was so much history, and I didn't care about his behavior—and Christa—nothing was more important to me than her feeling stable and safe. But now, I don't know, what's the point?"

"You love him, right, and there are your vows. Until death do us part. It means something," says Tracey, who, let's note, may call herself my father's fiancé, but has never been married.

"Do you believe any of that?"

"I! Believe! In! Love!" she says, jumping up and dramatically thrusting her drink high into the air, before watching the foam spill into her cleavage and sitting down with a thud.

We're trying not to think about my father or what's going to happen to him, not when none of the outcomes look good.

He dies.

He lives, but in a home.

He never quite speaks again.

These are not options, they're death sentences—slow, horrible, inevitable—and we must wait to see what happens. Which is unbearable and much too painful to think about. So, we drink a lot, and talk about Gabriel, and in this way, we don't have to talk or even think about my dad.

"You know I've never really been with anyone else, right?" I say, "and to be clear, I mean, I've never had sex with anyone else."

"Whaaaaaaaaaaaaaaaaaaaaaaaaat…yeah, I guess I knew that. We're talking *actual intercourse*, right, though really, huh?" Tracey says.

"I was always too scared about getting pregnant—about getting hurt. Gabriel was right there, and he seemed like enough. I didn't never not do anything with anyone else. But it wasn't much, and no, not intercourse, which sounds so Victorian, may I interest you in intercourse, sir. And now, it's like what was I thinking?"

"You know I love you so m-u-u-u-u-ch," Tracey slurs, pounding another shot, "and not like a mother, well, not like your mother, more like an older sister—not much older, mind you, but I never understood what you were thinking, and I never felt I could give you unsolicited advice about sex and love. It didn't seem right. Though I did hope to lead by example."

"You failed," I say, breaking into a smile.

"Yeah, I did," she says, and then she starts to cry.

"No, no, sweetie, no," I say, moving to her side of the table and sitting next to her. "I was joking. You didn't fail, you were the best, and there was good with Gabriel, and for a long time. And look, it was always going to be hard to top our first time anyway."

With that comment, I start to drift away, trying to take in the memory whole.

"Tell me about it, I would love that," Tracey says, putting her head on my shoulder.

"Okay, it requires us to go back to the Challenger launch and Christa McAuliffe and the assembly we had at school to watch it, and how glorious it was going be to see her aloft and free of the obligations that kept her tethered to Earth. But first, there was homeroom, and when I got there that day, the only thing I could think about was whether everyone knew something had happened between Gabriel and me the night before. It was the day after the first time we hooked up, which was awkward, and weird. We'd also had our first fight, but it was nice too, and I wanted to know whether I looked different in some way or whether it was clear to everyone something had happened between me and someone else. I had to look different, you know, and they had to know, right—how couldn't they? And I thought, were they looking at me funny? Yes, they were. Of course, they were, and they didn't have to say anything for me to know it was true. That said, I also recognized that based on any Kelly Preston movie ever made…"

"I love Kelly Preston," Tracey says, briefly looking up. "She was so pretty and classy, who cares if she was living a lie."

"I know you love her, sweetie," I say. "I saw *For Love of the Game* with you…"

"Ah, Kevin Costner, God he's still so handsome. I'd leave your father without a moment's notice for him. I would bang him on request, in an alley, a car, a bathroom, it doesn't matter."

"I know, you tell me that all the time."

Tracey looks up and kisses me on the cheek. Given the circumstances, she's way more of a mom than I ever could've asked for. Which I say with respect to Carolyn, who I need to figure out how to talk to when I'm not in the hospital and despite how I'm feeling about her son.

"Okay, back to my deflowering…," I say.

"Yes! Deflowering—totally," Tracey says.

"So, based on any Kelly Preston movie I'd ever seen," I continue, "I knew no one would truly know anything about what I may or may not have done, much less care, if I hadn't had sex with someone. There's no impact on the teen time-space continuum without having had actual intercourse, and from that perspective, I wasn't sure what Gabriel, and I did would count as something anyone could bring themselves to care about. Also, didn't people only stare at you as you made your awkward descent down the stairs from a bedroom in someone's house during a blowout party when that someone's parents were out of town and the music came to a jarring stop when you least wanted to be seen? And doesn't an unrequited love interest of some kind need to have been lurking nearby as well, crushed by what they believed had transpired, their final weeks of high school doomed to an endless cycle of Kenny Loggins' songs and desperate, achy longing? Yes, that's exactly how those things happened, so really, things would be totally fine, which to be honest was a disappointment in some ways."

"You know a lot more about these things than I do," Tracey says.

"Yes, I do, thank you, and there's more to come, promise."

"Like sex?"

"Indeed!" I reply, slamming one of the random tequila shots still on the table.

It goes down like fire, and as I start to tear, I think, I'm not Gabriel, and I'm going to regret this tomorrow.

"Get to it then," Tracey says.

"Yes, I'm on it. I was just standing there waiting for something, anything, to happen, but life was not the movies, and when all that happened was Mr. Grabby coming in behind me and slapping me on the ass, I took my usual seat off to side by myself, and decided to refocus on the launch, space, and the possibilities of it all. Soon we were being shuffled off to the gym for the assembly, and we were sitting there in the bleachers, and I saw Gabriel off to the side, and I was so happy to see him. I gave him a quick, little wave, and then I pointed down to the floor where they were wheeling in the enormous television they only brought in for events like presidential inaugurations and gave Gabriel the thumbs up as they turned it on. There was this sense of dynamic energy as they prepared us for takeoff, and the idea that any time, man—and in this case, woman—headed off into space, it was something epic. How this is what separated us from animals—innovation, curiosity, and the urge to explore the outer limits of what we thought we understood. And then there's Christa McAuliffe in her mom, teacher, civilian glory and I loved her so much, and I wanted to stop fantasizing about how she would come back to earth and as she was celebrated across the country she would come to our school, and this very auditorium, and when we made eye contact, she would beckon me to come down to the gym floor and give me a hug. Because yeah, that was a fantasy, I got it, and the actual launch was reality, and it was happening, and there was the buildup as we listened to the countdown and the reverberations across the Challenger and the room, energy, and excitement combined and contorted. Then there was lift off, and I couldn't breathe, and there was a moment where I was certain the Challenger would pierce the sky itself, rip the fabric of space and explode into some other galaxy full of darkness, but for a billion stars showing them the way. Then maybe twenty seconds later, there was a plume of smoke that didn't seem right. I squeezed my eyes shut, wishing whatever seemed to be happening to stop happening, even if that meant time itself must stop, but nothing stopped. Not the smoke. Not time. Not even the pounding in my chest, which threatened to burst forth across the bleachers. We watched in horror for ten more seconds—twenty, thirty, a minute passed—the smoke grew puffier and twistier, ten more seconds, then the Challenger disintegrated and fell back to the earth. My brain shut down. All I could hear was 'Christa' echoing across the echo chamber that was my brain. No one could live through that, not even Christa, especially Christa. She was dead. She wouldn't be coming to school. We wouldn't be making eye contact. She wouldn't be hugging me. There was no more Christa, and the sky was aflame for the wrong reasons…"

"Oh honey, I forgot where this was going and how much you loved her, I'm sorry… though, if I can be honest, this is kind of a buzzkill," Tracey murmurs.

I choose to ignore her, I'm on a roll.

"For a moment I wondered if I would ever be able to move again. If I would be able to leave my seat. Or if I would merely take root, merged with the bleachers as we became one—and I remained in the very spot until the bleachers, me, everything, were but dust and memories. It seemed possible and real as the great silence in the room engulfed us and wrapped itself around me in an embrace that threatened to pull me under the sea when I was barely treading water as it was. I was sinking. No longer at risk of taking root or turning into dust, just a watery freefall, and headed to the bottom of something vast and unknowable. But the moment passed and the collective shock—and trauma—was let loose. It started with tears, and it was followed by screams. I couldn't bear to be around that kind of pain. It freed me to move again, to liberate myself from the morass, and I started to run, picking my way through the other students, their red faces and tears and sweaty hair soon behind me as I pushed through the gymnasium doors, running and heading down the hall to I-did-not-know-where…and then I heard, 'Hannah!' and I didn't know if I heard my name in the recesses of my own head or from the sky somewhere above, but it stopped me in my tracks. I turned, expecting to see some ghostly version of myself, the me of some future self that would tell me it was going to be okay, that the pain and shock of having witnessed this tragedy would fade with time, and things would make sense again. But when I turned, it was Gabriel, standing there, and there was nothing weird about seeing him then—of course, he would be where I needed him to be. The universe may have been folded in on itself, but there was this beautiful boy standing before me, and he was there for me, and he loved me, he had always loved me, and he always would. And I didn't need any boy, or anybody, to make me feel okay, save me, or be my hero. I was hero enough for myself. But there he was anyway, and he was glowing, and that's what love, and yes, the trauma did then—it magnified even the smallest details. Everything was alive and breathing and organic and dynamic. Love was also a magnet whose pull knew no bounds, and we were soon running towards each other like some terrible teen romance. The war-scarred lovers long on the make reunited a million miles from everything we'd known and been, coming together again—every molecule of our beings molded, bent, and warped into one as time momentarily contracted, history froze, and the earth briefly stopped orbiting. Next, we were kissing, consuming one another, right there in school. No one was around. There were no distractions. No family or friends. No concerns. Just us, lips together, and apart, hands everywhere, and just as I visualized it would be. Which meant, the only question before us, was whether we were going to sneak into a maintenance closet, then, there, and consummate a moment, which couldn't possibly ever be replicated quite like it again, or would we wonder what might've been for the rest of our lives? It wasn't much of a choice. Life felt like it could end at any time, and somewhere behind that closed door, jeans crumpled, underwear twisted, and limbs tangled, sweaty and sad and happy and weird, love and loss oozed into one euphoric moment, everything changed…and here we are."

"That was awesome," Tracey says, popping right up. "I lost my virginity in the back of a pick-up truck with our gym teacher. He smelled like Old Grandad, Camel cigarettes and Bengay."

I ignore her and I wonder if what I described is anything like what Christa is experiencing. A euphoric love supreme. A creation of the timing, passion, youth, loss, hate, and beauty which accompanies true escape. I wouldn't begrudge her that and yes, I'm always thinking about her—even now.

"I need you to know," I say, "I haven't forgotten about Christa. I text her every night before I go to bed. It's my thing."

"It reminds me of Kaddish," Tracey says.

"What's that?"

"The Jewish prayer for the dead."

"Really? It makes you think about the dead?"

"No, it's not like that. The text is like your daily ritual, and it's reflective of how much you love and miss her."

"I do, and I hope she's fine and she's in love, even if I must manage my rage and fear about not truly knowing if she's in love or safe or anything."

"I know."

"More selfishly though, if Christa is happy, and I want her to be, I'm a little jealous too. I don't know if I've ever quite felt like I did after that first time again. Not that the sex itself was great. It got much better. But the first time was unreal. It was chemical and cosmic. It was fire. Now I've still only been with one person, and I may never again feel what I felt that first time."

"Forget Gabriel! Jesus. Go find someone else. I mean, isn't that the real point of you telling me this story? There was a moment—a horrible, tragic, amazing moment—which indelibly marked you, and you've been chasing the feeling ever since?"

"I guess, okay, yeah, but who, how, do I just go out and find someone, anyone? I don't think so."

"What about Officer John? He was hot when you were in high school, and he still looks damn good. He's also kind of a safe choice. A known known and that's fine. It's easier."

"That seems too weird."

"Yeah, I know, but doesn't everything feel that way now?"

GABRIEL

Is everything weird now? Yes, yes, it is.

"My name is Gabriel T——," I say, looking out across the room.

"Hello, Gabriel," the room says back.

I've come to an AA meeting. I didn't feel like I had to do this before. Going cold turkey worked. This time feels different, like I don't have too many chances left to get it right.

"I have a drinking problem. I beat it for a while, but you know beating it for a while just means it'll beat you back when it gets the chance—"

I hear some "amens," and even see a high five or two in the back.

"My story begins at sixteen when I was invited to a party at the end of sophomore year. I'd never had a drink before. But there I was, and there was this girl, not my wife Hannah, who, to be clear, was the only person I've ever wanted to be with. But there was no Hannah yet, we were friends, whatever, but no—there was a connection, yes, and desire, on my part, but nothing profound or romantic. So, I was at this party, and I didn't really know anyone beside John, the host, a one-time superstar basketball player, who I'd ended up in study hall with, and who even though he was cool, and even though he got laid, and was good-looking, was also into comic books. We talked about the X-Men, and we'd go on and on about who could take who in a fight, though we both agreed, the facts were the facts, and no one was going to take out Dark Phoenix if she didn't want to be taken out. In that sense, it wasn't even worth arguing about, which didn't mean it wasn't worth discussing. We would also discuss what it would be like to sleep with her. Dark Phoenix was not just invincible, she was crazy hot and had these incredible boobs and long red hair. John could at least speak from some kind of experience. He hadn't slept with any mutants that I knew of—okay, that's a joke—but he'd banged a lot of chicks, which, I was envious of, and I hadn't…but I digress.

"So, 'Moving in Stereo' was playing, and I was wandering around John's backyard. My Stan Smiths oozed into the wet lawn with every step, and I wasn't sure what I'd been thinking when I had decided to come to the party. No one there was going to be talking about Dark Phoenix. No one there was going to be talking to me period.

"'Hey,' I heard.

"The voice sounded familiar. I looked around, swiveling my head this way and that. It was John's girlfriend Maggie. Like John, she was also a junior, and an actual girl who wasn't Hannah. She wasn't someone I could ever expect to talk to and yet she was talking to me. It was me, right? I looked around, there was no one else there, so yes, it was me—okay.

"'He-e-e-e-y,' I said, tentatively.

"I still didn't quite believe Maggie was talking to me.

"'Can I get you a drink?' she asked as she laughed her amazing laugh, and I tried not to stare too long at her green eyes or the freckles on her nose, though freckles, that was a thing for me. I also tried not to draw attention to how wobbly she was, which was obvious to me, and in being obvious to me, it could quickly become obvious to her.

"'A drink would be great,' I said.

"I ignored the fact that I'd never had a drink before then, or how my father had a drinking problem. It wasn't something we ever discussed at home, but I knew. This though, was an opportunity to talk to a girl that wasn't Hannah, an exercise in social interaction, and something that might make me better at luring Hannah into my web, which so far had not gone well. She grabbed my hand and led me through the crowd. She was smiling the whole time and ignoring the snickering and grins as I tried to ignore her kinky blonde hair, which swayed just inches from my face, and her cutoff jean shorts, as the frayed threads swung to and fro across the back of her legs and bottom of her butt. We got to the keg, and she tilted the cup, filled it up, and handed it to me. She crossed her arms across her chest and the Wham! wife beater she was wearing and mouthed, 'go!' So, I did. I lifted the cup to my mouth and started to drink. The beer was icy cold and bitter. As it hit the back of my throat, little tears started to form in the corners of my eyes. I hated it and I pounded it. I had to. It was for her.

"One beer became two, then three, then I was dancing with Maggie to 'Tonight She Comes,' and I was happy. It was wonderful and I was laughing, and Maggie was laughing because I was so hilarious and cute, and then she was crying because John was upstairs having sex with some girl named Sonya, or Tonya. I didn't know what she was saying, but I had another beer, and another, and I hugged Maggie because she seemed sad and she put her head on my shoulder and started dancing really slow and I tried not to put my hands on her ass, or anywhere, but there weren't too many places for them to go, and she took my hand and led me away from the party and off behind the garage and she sat me down, and she was still dancing, just really slow now, eyes closed, her head bobbing as she moved back and forth, and then she slid off her shorts and her underwear was covered in polka dots and she was still dancing and I was happy I'd grabbed a beer on the way. I was nervous and excited, and I'd never even kissed someone before and now this was whatever this was, and soon I heard 'Just What I Needed' drifting in from the party and I was drinking my beer, and I started having problems keeping my eyes open. I shook my head and I tried to focus as Maggie danced towards me, her thumbs tucked into her polka-dot panties, and I shook my head again to keep focused, but I was drifting away, and Maggie was getting blurry. I started to dream about Hannah and when I woke up, it was morning, there was no Maggie, my clothes were damp from the dew, and the sun was coming up. I got on my feet, walked to 7-Eleven, and microwaved a burrito to eat for the rest of the walk home. After that, I didn't have the chance to kiss anyone else until Hannah. Not that I really wanted to kiss anyone else. I started having lots of chances to drink though, and once it started—it didn't stop for a long time. But you know that part of the story, right? Thank you."

There are some more "amens." I feel relieved. I did something I had to do, and I feel good about myself. Proud even. It's the first time in a while. I take a seat and after the meeting, a guy walks up to me. He has weary eyes and a kind smile, and he reaches out to clasp my hand.

"Hey man, thanks for sharing," he says. "I know how hard it is and I admire you for coming in and doing the work. You may not know how this works though. It's not really like you see on television or in the movies. You can't just show up and hijack the meetings with your monologues. You need to listen too, be patient, and find a sponsor, you know?"

I don't know. This is the first time I've tried this. But I don't say that. What I do say, is "sure of course," and as he walks away, I think, if I'm not welcome here, it's cool—I'll do it myself.

HANNAH

I work at a local landscaping company, and it's easy to describe how it works. For a long time, it was mostly office-manager type stuff. I ordered paper when it was low. I made coffee when I got in. I paid the bills. I ensured the office was clean and professional-looking in case potential clients came by. When I started, there was a group of men who comprised the team that worked out of our location, and who needed taking care of. Men always need to be taken care of.

Like me, those men never left.

There's Jim. He's sort of bald, doesn't talk much, goes about his business with a small, tight smile, and stays focused on doing whatever little it takes to get his job done and get home.

There's Bill. He has a wiry build and always kind of vibrates. He helps manage his family farm, never removes his baseball cap, and runs on black coffee and a low-level mania.

Then there's Jerry, another former athlete gone to pot, who's putting in his time as he slides along on his fading charisma, and who, despite his huge gut, is not bad looking when he laughs.

They mow lawns, rake leaves, pull weeds, and occasionally get creative with trimming hedges. They ensure things get done smoothly out in the field, while I make sure everything runs smoothly at the office. It's a lot like being a mom, and I know the mom thing.

There's also Albert who was once one of them and is now the boss. If he sweats, loses his cool or gets upset about anything, you'll never know based on his moment-to-moment demeanor. He's super-mellow and as likely to smile as frown. He gets done what must be done. He tells me what he needs. He keeps it light.

"Did I ever tell I about the time my wife and I went to Jamaica? I mean look, I smoked some dope back in high school in the seventies, okay I smoked a lot of dope—it was the seventies— but by that trip, I was married, I was working here, raising kids, and not smoking a thing. It was our twenty-fifth wedding anniversary, we hadn't taken many vacations, and we went to Jamaica, which was nice—tropical drinks and sand, jerk chicken, whatever. One evening my wife was taking a nap, I wandered out to the beach and some dude with dreadlocks asked me if I want to get high—I thought, this is vacation and it's been a while, why not? It'll be fun, right? He handed me this enormous Bob Marley joint he was smoking, and I took a long hit and when I woke up hours later—still on the beach, I had no shoes and no wallet and how was I going to explain that to my wife?" Albert says, before breaking into laughter.

This is good, this job, this place. It's not hard. I feel appreciated. Happy. It works. Plus, I've gotten more responsibility over time, which is nice too. I've never lacked for confidence, and there was just a lot of shit not getting done properly—so at some point I took over the human-resources-type stuff, classes on OSHA requirements, best practices around hiring. The office grew, and my role kept growing. Soon there were more people to hire, and then more after that. Hiring became my thing and I enjoyed it. Giving people a chance, explaining how insurance and retirement plans work, helping them build a life. I mean it when I say that— for so long, this was enough for me. There was tending to Gabriel's nonsense, battling with Christa, having lunch with my dad at Neary's, and coming to the office. It was low stress, there was stuff to do, I took care of people. It was good.

But today, after being away in the hospital, and even though everyone is welcoming—even Jim, who forces himself to hug me—and the work is still the work, and it's safe and stable, I start to wonder if I might slowly lose my mind repeating the same dumb tasks again and again and again—while also staring at the same beige walls and listening to the same people tell the same bad jokes. What's the point of this? Any of this? In one form or another, I've lost my daughter, father, and husband, and now I'm going to do this, every day, why? It's like being trapped in some never-ending loop that stops and starts and stops and starts again in the same place even as the things that might require me to play it safe are no longer a presence in my life.

Suddenly I'm spinning.

I can't breathe.

Panic crawls along my chest, my neck, my head.

I close my eyes.

I place my forehead on the top of my desk.

I wait for the coolness to wrap itself around my brain.

I rub my temples with my index fingers, the small circular motions lulling me into another place, another headspace.

I look back up, stare at the beige walls and beige carpet, and I think about Tracey's last words to me at Neary's. Not her very last words—those were, "I'm going to throw up. Please move my hair out of my face," but her last, almost cogent words, "Go bang Officer John. What's the worst that can happen?"

Officer John.

What's the worst that can happen?

What do I even know about him?

Nothing.

Maybe that's good, though maybe I can do some research as well.

He'll be on Facebook. Everyone's on Facebook, and people hook up with old love interests and unrequited high-school flames there every day. Families implode and people move across the country leaving children fatherless and motherless because of Facebook. It's why Facebook exists, so we can troll our pasts, immerse ourselves in nostalgia, and try to save our present selves by recapturing something of our youth by sleeping with someone we once knew.

Well, unless that's urban myth—which would be disappointing.

Anyway, even if I reach out, it doesn't mean Officer John will be interested.

It would have to seem weird to him as well, right?

There's the hospitalized father and the drunk husband, and there are younger, less challenging women everywhere.

Those things and Christa....

I know she's okay.

Well, I've chosen to accept she is.

I have.

And then, even if John's interested, it doesn't mean I have to do something about it.

Which is what it comes down to, right? I don't have to do anything.

It just doesn't have to work like that.

I go to Facebook and look him up.

There's a shirtless shot.

Also, weird.

There's the slight paunch. That I knew of, but also, ink, a lot of it. That's unexpected.

Not much else to go on though.

There are numerous pictures of him hugging fake blondes with fake breasts.

Otherwise, he drinks, goes fishing, rides snowmobiles, and ultimately, the only real question is whether I would sleep with someone who posts pro-NRA memes?

I might.

I craft a message, nothing too forward, just "Hello, it's Hannah. This is weird. How are you doing?" I hit send and I wait. I pretend to work, although what I really do is stare at the inbox and wait for a response of any kind. When one finally arrives, I must admit I smile, and maybe even pump my fist a little, something I've never done in my life. Then I read the message, "Yeah, this is weird, but it's cool, do you want to meet up or something?"

Yeah, I do, and it's on.

GABRIEL

WHAT THIS IS NOT, is on…Hannah doesn't even recognize me at first. There's a look of familiarity, fleeting, more like she's thinking we have maybe once met at a party. I represent some slice of history. Here and gone. A part of her brain and her memories that had been tucked away, possibly never to be seen again. Maybe that's true, and not merely because memory is so tricky, but because we're all on some kind of plane spanning generations and centuries, and not so much born to live and die, but to be forever reborn in new shapes, with new identities, traveling across time and space, and attempting to bend something so much bigger than we are to our will. Hannah may not even know me as her husband. Maybe that's a construct I created. A relationship which is part of a world I built in my head to manage the confusion and fear that come with being alive in the first place. Which is to say, maybe we met in some parallel world, of my making, or someone else's. I'm a person she interacted with in some other time and place, no more, no less.

And why can't this make as much sense as anything else?

Why can't there have once been a party where we briefly merged only to unmerge again? Picture it. The party was on a sprawling estate with manicured lawns, pear trees, and a maze crafted from towering bushes. It was somewhere off in the middle of endless fields and woods, with cars and revelers coming and going for days, tall and short, fat, and skinny, white, black, brown, and yellow, beautiful suits, pinstriped, and charcoal-gray, swanky dresses—cinched at the waist, backs exposed. The costumes—feather boas, masks, flowy maroon capes, and ink black top hats. The atmosphere had been louche and oozy. Spirits flowed and splashed on sleeves and floors, sticky to the touch, cigarettes appeared to float in the air, ashy parapets extended from bejeweled hands, mounds of opium, ingested on puffy white couches surrounded by shimmering velvet curtains. The white smoke wafted from room to room, its sweet maple syrup smelled pungent and sharp. It wrapped itself around the partygoers in a vaporous hug as they danced and screwed and slept and hugged and lounged, bending, and laughing, eyes scrunched and mouths pinched, draped across one another in an endless sway and swoon.

How I got to this party was a mystery, and magical. One moment, I was here or there, and the next I was being swept into a ballroom, drink in hand, hair swept back, shirt crisp, a broad smile indented across my face. It must have been destiny or fate, because there she was, Hannah, red hair afire, her laughter rapturous and cascading—and I was drawn to her on a cloud, which danced and spiraled bigger than the universe. A moment of connection. A brief kiss. A hug. A dance. Merged, then not, afloat again, smiles and ashes and smoke, carried me away to the next thing and the thing after that, only to be back again, and wandering the fields, looking for her, seeking her out, around every turn, behind every wall, peering, glancing, gazing, staring, scrutinizing, everything, everywhere, trying to find her, but failing, because Hannah was a ghost, and that party never was.

I awake.

I stare at the ceiling and grip the twisted sheets of my bed.

Hannah lies next to me, her red hair splayed across the pillow in a puddle of flame, twisted in the sheets herself.

It's still dark outside.

I lace up my running shoes and head out into the morning,

the dew saturating my shoes, soaking my brow and T-shirt. Not drinking is a battle, which I know too well, but I in no way anticipated the weird fever dreams that would haunt my sleep this time around. They draw on the random slivers of my life, unpacking them, and riddling them with confusion as they morph into something twistier and far more like a funhouse mirror than I could ever conjure during my waking hours.

Of course, Christa wasn't missing the last time I stopped drinking.

I might've once been filled with a rage long since tempered, but I never felt like this—a naked vessel enveloped in an ache and grief that clings to my brain, unceasing, and warping my every thought and movement. Yet, despite the trippy voyage that sleep has become, and the long, white-knuckled sweat that marks my days, I'm going to hold it together.

I'll do so today, tomorrow, and every day.

I'll get up early and run if that's required.

I'll focus on one step and then the next, step by step by step.

I'll keep myself focused and distracted, centered and safe, and in the moment.

I'll be fine.

When I'm not fine, I'll deal with it by going to talk to Ed.

Going to meetings won't be a thing for me. I'm not sure I can't hijack wherever I am or be there for anyone, but those closest to me.

That's next-level stuff, and I'm not capable of that, not now.

I need to talk though, I know that, and Ed is always willing to listen. That he can't respond and may never be able to again is horrible and sad, but perfect for my needs.

What I won't do is hide bottles of gin in the garage and I'll not stop by the liquor store just because I can.

I'll not run into a bar for a quick drink that becomes two, five, ten, every afternoon and evening.

I'll always go straight home.

I'll be fine.

I'll be engaged, present and listen if Hannah wants to tell me about her day.

I'll ignore the endless layer of sweat on my upper lip and brow and the desire to run away, not just to go for a run, but to disappear.

I'll do this for them, for me.

I'll repeat it again and again, day after day.

I'll be fine.

HANNAH

Gabriel isn't drinking again, and this is good. I believe it'll stick, and he'll be fine. I want him to be fine, but it doesn't matter to me anymore. It's not that I don't want him to be healthy or happy. He deserves to be as happy as anyone else, but I'm not sure it's for me to worry about. Christa isn't home, and that's not okay, and will never be okay, but we'll retain our belief that she's fine, and Josh is kind. I sometimes wonder if I should care more about how Josh is doing. This would require me to care more about Josh than his parents seem to. Josh's parents made it clear from the start they felt he had moved along, and they were fine with it. In not caring about Josh, it meant they didn't care about Christa and if they can't generate any energy to find him or care about him, then I can't either. What I can do is focus on this construct of near positivity Gabriel and I have embraced. In this construct Christa is fine, she must be, and in believing this, Gabriel and I can persevere and adapt, and we'll do so for as long is required to survive Christa's disappearance. This belief is a silent compact we've made, but otherwise, none of this has anything to do with how I feel about or react to Gabriel anymore.

I once learned how to move around Gabriel's indiscretions, his moods, and his inconsistencies. I enjoyed the good stuff, the humor and affection, the intensity of his being there when he was there. I needed him, we needed him, and I was willing to take any version of him we could get. I don't need him to survive or thrive, though, none of it—not anymore. He doesn't work, nor even pretend he ever will again. His job went away, his confidence went with it, and he's stopped trying to make it work. He doesn't drink or sleep with other people, though I never really cared about the latter. I cared that he lied so much and made me feel so crazy. The sex with other people—not so much. He didn't love them. He was drunk, and he was acting out. He always came home to me and how can I care about any of that after twenty years of marriage? I've spent my whole adult life with this person and if we're more like siblings now, and if he now spends an inordinate amount of time puttering around the house fixing and re-fixing things, so be that too. It's okay, it really is, and yes, I'm trying to convince myself of this. That's fine, denial is a powerful tool and there's no reason to disregard something that mostly works for me.

Still, even if this is true, there are still more important truths I must embrace. They're visceral, they're inescapable, and I must be able to admit they're viable too—that they can exist outside of my head. I must say them out loud so they can get the oxygen necessary to take form. If I can do that, they'll become real—and they'll take flight.

So here it goes.

I can't fix Gabriel.

That's not hard. I know this, it's a truth, but again, it's about being purposeful when I say it. It also means when Gabriel says everything's fine, I can't ask him if everything's truly fine. If he really followed-up on some job lead when I know he didn't. If he's worried, he needs a drink, or whether going for a run might help. It means fighting the inclination to ask the things I want to ask and willing myself not to worry about them. It also means waiting for him to tell me things. Or if I ask about something, anything, and he chooses to not tell me anything of any substance, accepting it, because that's the way it is, and none of its real anyway. Nothing is happening. He's not happening. I'm cool with it. Which isn't to say that I plan to discuss any of this with Gabriel. It'll be what it is, and if he notices, I'll say something, if not, not. So, there's that, and maybe I'm not saying it out loud, as much as willing myself to embrace it.

The other truth isn't that.

It must be embraced and spoken to an audience of one. Gabriel is done sleeping around, he's not drinking, he's chastened, and things are as fine as anyone can ask them to be, and so now it's my turn to mess things up, without really messing them up. Gabriel can handle it, or he'll have to, and Christa won't know about it, because she isn't here, and so that's that, and the time is now.

It must happen now.

And so it is that I walk up to Gabriel as he's sitting on the couch. The sun's just going down, and the shadows are dancing across his face. I steel myself and I strike a pose that reflects some kind of agency.

"I plan to sleep with Officer John," I say. "It's my turn, and if you have feelings about that, you need to keep them to yourself."

The words hover between us and linger. We then watch them take shape, before turning to dust and floating away.

I linger for a moment as well, but Gabriel knows there's nothing he can say or do and chooses instead to nod and assume a serene equanimity as the evening sun slowly engulfs him.

GABRIEL

Is there truly nothing I can say or do?

About some things, yes, but others, at least I can own up to them, expose those moments to the universe, and try to make sense of my behavior over the years.

At least this is what I'm thinking as I drift from my run to the hospital and Ed's room.

"I wonder whether telling you this memory in reverse will allow me to see not only where things went wrong, but how I could have prevented them from being a memory in the first place. If I were to do that, it would look something like this...

"Everyone was crying, everyone being me, Hannah and Christa, beautiful Christa with Hannah's red hair and my grandmother's smile. But it wasn't just crying, that's important, because more than wanting to understand—I want to be honest, tell the truth, be judged, and make amends. So, it wasn't just crying. Hannah and Christa were sitting on the floor by the wall in the kitchen and Hannah was holding her, they were shaking, their red hair merging into a wild ball of flame. On the wall behind them, the remains of my beer meandered towards the floor, the suds scattershot and drying. The bottle itself was on the ground, still spinning, though slower, soon to come to a halt. The bottle was on the floor and doing its spinning thing because moments before

I had backhanded it out of frustration, it had launched from the table at light speed, and it had missed Christa's amazing six-year-old head by inches.

"Why did I backhand it, why not?

"No, that's not an answer. That's nonsense. It's evasion. And it's no answer.

"I can look back now and blame the pressures of work and marriage and taking care of a small child and the responsibilities that come with parenthood, plus the loss of freedom and self. Or I can take a step back. I'm going in reverse, right?

"I'd gotten home from work. But before that, I had stopped at Neary's with the team. I'd three, no, four drinks, seven at the most. Alyssa from high school was there. She reminded me of the time we were at the skating rink when we were kids and she made fun of me. She was acting cute, though it should be said, she was still cute and maybe I confused looking cute with acting cute when, in fact, she was just trying to get a rise out of me. She was home visiting her parents. She worked back then at some magazine in some city, single, no kids or attachments. We'd once almost kissed in high school, on a couch at a party, which party, I don't know—it doesn't matter. There was a party. Officer John, still shooting guard John, was there, and Hannah had wandered off, and there was so much alcohol, and people doing bong hits. Alyssa and I were on the couch. Alyssa who was always too good for our town and way too good for me.

"But there we were back in high school and on this couch, and she was talking about the skating rink that time too, and she was teasing me, being playful, and maybe I was the best option among so many poor ones, but she said something dopey and drunken like, "and what's it like to kiss a guy who read *Are You There, God? It's Me, Margaret* anyway?" She was joking, but she was also edging closer to me. Her breath was on my face, and it smelled like cinnamon. I pulled back, and I said, 'no, I can't, you and Hannah are friends, and this isn't cool,' and it wasn't cool, though they weren't really friends, and Hannah and I weren't together, and at that point, might never be. I truly had no idea if Hannah and I might ever be anything, and so what was the big deal if I kissed Alyssa? But it was a big deal. I would never want to hurt Hannah, much less mess things up before they've even started, and I pulled back, and Alyssa gave me this look of pity and moved along.

"And so, on that night after work, and all those years later, she was teasing me about that as well, mocking me for being scared to kiss her, and yes, she was drunk, her judgment compromised, but she really seemed to find it humorous that I wouldn't kiss her at that party. That I'd a chance, and I'd chosen to blow it because I was loyal to the mere idea of someone. She also reminded me how I'd been a 'fucking pussy,' her words, and scared to get caught. It was true. I had been a pussy. I wanted to kiss her on the couch that night. I wanted to sleep with her. But I didn't, and I'd made the right decision.

"But had I?

"Did it matter?

"There's the rub, right?

"What's one kiss or whatever when you knew you were in something for the long run?

"I didn't know, and why did I care what Alyssa thought after so many years?

"But that's also the rub—and being male too. I didn't want to feel weak, emasculated, and I didn't want to be teased, not when so much was already so hard with Hannah and Christa, and I had so much anger. It was pathetic of me. I knew that. I just didn't care. So, I left the bar where I stopped after work, and had three, maybe four, maybe ten drinks, and ran into Alyssa, who was maybe trying to be cute, but was busting my balls too. I wanted to have sex with her, and I did that back then when Christa was little, slept with anyone I could, and I probably could've slept with Alyssa that night, but I also didn't want to try and then find out she didn't want to. I couldn't bear the humiliation if I was wrong. I walked home instead, and as I did, I was stewing in my thoughts, and not sober. Or maybe I was. The feeling of anger and weakness as disorienting as any number of drinks. I got to the front door, and I paused on the porch to collect my thoughts. I could already hear Christa crying about something, and I had to steel myself to even walk into the house. But I did, and I walked straight to the refrigerator, and I grabbed a bottle of beer. My head was pounding, and as I put the bottle down on the table, I thought a hug might be nice, a nuzzle, some baby neck, maybe lose myself in Christa's hair. Just take it in. But Hannah said something about whether I really needed another drink, and Christa repeated it, and it could've been cute, but it wasn't cute. Nothing was cute that night. It was just another thing, and another thing and another thing. I wanted to punch something, but there was nothing to punch. Instead, I swung my hand in frustration as I tried to make some kind of point that only I understood. It's possible I wanted to hit the beer bottle sitting there and wanted to act dramatically. But maybe I didn't. It might've been an accident. It doesn't matter. I hit it, and then I had to watch in slow motion as the beer bottle flew by Christa's precious head and bounced off the wall behind her. Beer and suds everywhere as Christa fell off her chair and crawled to the wall, and Hannah was crying and scared, and I was freaked out—no longer drunk and after that moment no longer drunk again for a long time. It was the first time I stopped drinking and it held for so long. But then, with Christa missing, well, it just wasn't long enough."

Ed doesn't respond. He never does, he can't, but I feel better.

I've released the toxins and can go out to fight the good fight for another day.

I touch Ed's arm as the lights beep and whirr, and then drift out to where I came from, one step followed by another.

HANNAH

I'M NOT FREAKED OUT or angry. Nor am I drunk or weighing what's cute or not cute. I'm pragmatic and focused as I walk out the front door and head to Officer John's place to see what it will or won't be, and that's exactly how the thing with Officer John starts.

I mean, that's technically how it starts—it really starts like this: I raise my fist to knock on his door, and before the *rat-tat-tat* of knuckle on wood can happen, the door swings open.

"Hannah, baby," Officer John says, smiling at me, as he drips into the doorframe, and pauses to slurp me in from head to toe. "You hungry?"

Seeing Officer John like this causes a lot of cognitive dissonance.

There's the guy with the perfect hair, pressed uniform, and spotless shoes, who once ruled the basketball court, and is now an oddly intimate part of my life due to Christa missing. That guy is distant, but professional and retains enough of his youthful glory and confidence to feel as untouchable as he believes himself to be.

This guy is something else. This guy is a shirtless, totally inked dude named John in his not-perfectly-coiffed professional glory. His name curls along his still tensile right forearm, "John," in expansive Gothic letters. "So that they can identify the body," he tells me. Gracing his left forearm is "Mom," cliché and wonderful, wrapped in a heart with an arrow protruding from both ends. Mermaids and anchors cover John's shoulders and biceps. An expansive set of dragon wings are spread across his shoulder blades as red, yellow, and purples flames creep up the back of his neck, stopping short of where his collar falls. Jesus hangs prone and dying for our sins on his chest. And an endless array of vines, flowers, dragon tails, barbed wire, chains, railroad tracks, flames, thunder, Koi fish and women's legs swirl, intertwine, and festoon every spare inch of the leftover skin, merging into an explosive cacophony of seizure-inducing, yet mesmerizing, colors. I find myself completely lost in—separated by time and space from his doorway—and floating somewhere off above.

"Hey, Hannah, you with us?" I hear John say, from some galaxy far, far away.

"Yes," I say as I snap back to attention and his bemused gaze. "What are you serving?"

"Smelt," John replies. "I caught it this morning."

Officer John steps back and sweeps his arm in a grand gesture of welcome as I walk into his tiny one-bedroom apartment. The air is dead and stultifying. A mix of pot smoke, fried smelt, body odor, and the lingering toxins of a recent sex act that follow John's trajectory across the room like a vapor trail, creating a pungent, and wholly noxious reek, which will surely linger on my clothes, and in my nose for the rest of the day. The curtains are closed, leaving a dusky haze and cave vibe throughout the room, which is missing only some glistening stalactites in the corners to round out the effect. The floor and cinderblock shelves are covered with an array of Hobbit pipes, medieval axes, Japanese swords, biker magazines, Chinese language newspapers, and record albums. On one door is a poster of Frank Zappa, naked, hirsute, and hunched over on a toilet. I assume this is the bathroom, though I never intend to find out. There is also a ratty futon, the color of spoiled cheese, and covered in cigarette burns, ash smears, vomit spray, soy sauce, and what appear to be drops of dried blood—a pattern that might otherwise be labeled white trash Pollock.

The door to the bedroom lies ajar, and there's a nude woman lying on John's bed. Her long legs, bottle-blonde hair, and dark roots splayed across the soiled sheets. I briefly absorb the woman's curves and full breasts and try to ignore comparing them to my much less curvy hips and way flatter chest.

"Get rid of her," I say. "And please change those sheets."

"Yeah?" John says.

"Yeah."

"Done."

GABRIEL

Is everything done, because right now it sure feels like it?

Of course, hospital time isn't normal time. Things go extra slow. Time as we know it, isn't even a thing here. To be clear, things happen on a schedule, the time-of-day matters, but you don't experience time in the same way. It's sluggish, an old creek, inching along, turgid, and exhausted, and what else can you do, but nod in agreement with the weird ebbs and flows—when you aren't in fact nodding off. And so it is that I'm sitting here staring at Ed, high, eyes half-open, my mom dozing next to me. We started our walk, and we hit my bat—I know, sobriety—but I consider getting high with her to be a public service, not to mention I've conveniently embraced harm reduction. Either way, my mom is too tired to continue walking after we smoke. She wants to see Ed though, and I can't see Ed enough. He's become my anchor. Plus, Hannah's not really visiting him. No real explanation, she can't deal with it, and maybe that's okay. She took care of Ed for years, and now there's not much to do. But he should have visitors, I need him, and it's fine, though today, I can't quite keep my eyes open, and Ed rarely opens his.

Sitting here as I am, I contemplate whether I should do Ed the favor of smothering him, but I could never do that, and I pray no one ever asks me to—I don't have it in me.

So, I nod, and as I tilt into the morass my mind wanders to, I meander into a fantasy about Christa's life as it may exist in some parallel space. In this version, she's still run away with Josh, because I don't really see a version where that can't happen, but unlike Hannah's mother who never checked in with her, Christa sends us postcards.

One is postmarked from somewhere in Ohio has a Buckeyes logo and simply states, "Doing fine."

Another from Florida has a cartoon alligator on it and reads, "Thinking of you. Please don't worry."

A third one is from out west, Oregon or Washington—it doesn't matter—has a welcome sign on it and says, "Seeing the world!"

They're written in Christa's teenager scrawl, flowery and buoyant, the "Os" presented as smiley faces, little hearts over the "Is," immature, and not fully formed.

In this fantasy, she and Josh haven't come back, but she writes often enough that I decide not to worry about her any more than I normally would. Which is important. To mostly know where someone is and what they're doing doesn't mean you can't worry about them. In this version of things, however, Christa's truly on an adventure. She's seeing the world, experiencing things I haven't, and learning to take care of herself. I know this because of the postcards. They make it almost okay, and most important—they allow me to not be scared for her safety.

Instead, I picture her and Josh being the things I wish for Hannah and me to be.

They're transparent with one another.

They're content with each other.

They don't bury their feelings and seek outside pleasures or escape.

They plan for their future together, while establishing individual identities separate from their union. They know what they want and need for themselves—and from one another.

They know they can come home to us with open arms and know they can leave when they're ready to—no guilt or concern.

Further, Hannah and I are healthy—or healthy enough—and the anger we carry towards each other and the world is mostly worked through and worked out.

Still, even in this alternate scenario I'm not quite at peace with the role Hannah has played in Christa's departure. Hannah feels she practically raised herself and it's true. She also believes she doesn't need anything and so has killed the part of herself that might need anything from anyone to keep going. The problem is that in killing it that part of herself, she can't always understand how others might need things and sometimes people act out when they don't feel seen or heard. It's the kind of thing a teenager might do, and the kind of thing Christa did. I can understand why Christa and Hanna are as they are with each other, but I've had to kill part of myself as well to get through this—the part of me that wants to think about nothing else but Christa. So, I don't think about things such watching Christa dance in the living room to the Beatles, seeing *Beauty and the Beast* and the sense of awe and joy she felt, making pancakes on Sunday morning as Hannah slept or the endless memories that are otherwise so easily accessed.

I also don't let the thoughts which tell me to hate Hannah for letting this happen creep in or take hold either. There are just as many scenarios where I am at fault. I fight with Christa too. I talk too much. I pick at things. I don't validate feelings. It's no challenge to suck at parenting. No one owns that sickness. Plus, who am I to pass judgment on Hannah anyway for one night, when I wasn't home for the fight? I missed so much of what was happening and failed them so many times. I haven't been the man or father I was supposed to be, and it would be ridiculous for me to pretend otherwise. How I've even become the man I am at present is something I will unpack to my final breath. But if there's hate for Hannah, or resentment, or whatever it is I feel now when I'm not drinking, I must let it go. We're playing the long game, and we're in it, together, regardless of the short-term decisions either of us makes that don't benefit any of us.

And yet, after five months of Christa missing, I'm allowed to fantasize about the day she walks back in the door, and when that happens, what are we supposed to say? Her beautiful face—Hannah's face—is gaunt and hollow. She's taller and lankier. Her red hair is long and tangled. Her clothes are dirty and creased by the miles. Her smell is ripe, too much outdoors and not enough soap. She's older now, weary, and it takes everything I have not to melt away in front of her. But then Christa pours herself a cup of coffee, hugs us both, smiles her big smile and for a moment, everything breaks inside of me, planets collide and realign, space folds into itself, new universes are born, and when Christa goes off to take a shower and sleep, no explanations or apologies, Hannah and I fall to the floor, hugging and cracked, but colliding and realigning, too.

It's beautiful, glorious, and right, and maybe it doesn't have to be a fantasy.

That's not to say I have any more of a belief that Christa's coming home than I did when I walked into the hospital today. It's just I want to believe in something. I can't believe in myself, not yet, or Ed, which is heartbreaking. Not Hannah either, or us—not right now. Nor my mom, because who knows, and my dad, no, forget that.

There's only Christa.

I need to concentrate on her, again, un-kill what I've killed, and make it right.

HANNAH

MAKING THINGS RIGHT, BELIEF, and fantasy, that's funny to me as I lie here naked, a light sheen of sweat covering my exposed skin, the cool air of the hotel's air conditioner leaving me chilled, little hairs popping on my thighs and belly—me caught up in the repetition pattern of an affair.

The sex is great.

The sex is great because it's illicit.

The sex is great even though the state of illicitness is false because Gabriel knows something is going on, if not when or where.

The sex is great because it feels wrong, sneaky, inappropriate, and amoral, illicit.

The sex is great, so let's stress the sex is great, while acknowledging it must be—it's the way affairs work.

The sex is great because everything is new and different.

The sex is great because it's physical, not gentle, or respectful, tender, or the act of two people in love, or looking for love, and wanting to be sensitive to the rules around that.

The sex is great because it's just sex, it's nothing more or less than sex, and there's a real argument for just sex for sex's sake.

The sex is great because we're having it in cheap hotels out by the highway, so it feels dirty, though again, we don't need to be secretive—I'm just never having sex in John's apartment again.

The sex is great because the sex is great the first time there is sex despite how nasty John's apartment is and the ripple coursing up the back of my legs and into my brain, is an explosion which refuses to fade.

The sex is great because we don't acknowledge the elephant in the room: John didn't find Christa, didn't try very hard to do so and doesn't want to think about it—I want to hold onto my belief that she's safe, and only think about that—and so the sex is great because of and despite such things.

The sex is great, but will the sex not be great at some point, when the urgency fades, and it's not so new? Yes, but do I need to worry about that now? No, I don't. I don't want a relationship. I want sex which is great.

I trace the tattoo of the angel's wings across John's back with my finger, and I feel him shudder and stir. He rolls back over to face me and smiles his John smile. He slides his hand down between my legs, and everything is wet and ready.

"How did this never happen in high school?" John asks.

I try not to concentrate on his hand, the ripple already building between my thighs, or my almost complete disinterest in talking at that moment.

"Are you joking? You don't remember the time something almost happened?"

"What? No," he says, still smiling and doubling down on his attention to my vagina, the friction increasing, the ripple building.

"In the kitchen, at that party after I kind of chased after you?"

"Was I drunk?"

"Yes, definitely."

"Was I a dirtbag?"

"Almost, kind of."

"Sorry," he says, pulling his hand away from me, leaning back, looking at me, appearing almost anguished. "I wasn't cool back then and I feel sick about it. I also don't remember a lot of it, especially after I got kicked off the team. Did you ever try again?"

"No, I didn't really do those things—it was a moment, it was unpleasant, it kind of passed, and nothing like that happened again until Gabriel."

"So, nothing with no one, ever? Bullshit. I don't believe it."

"Okay, I have, like one story," I say, "but it's dumb."

"Let me be the judge of that," he says, kissing my neck and slowly grinding up and down on my hip.

God.

"All right, dirtbag," I say. "There was this one time before Gabriel and I were a thing, and you and I almost, sort of, had a thing."

"Okay, hit me," he says, breathing heavily in my ear.

"Okay, so, I wasn't involved with Gabriel yet. We were just friends, and it was like the end of sophomore year, and I didn't know if it was ever going to be more than that, and I didn't really go to parties, but I wanted some kind of human connection beyond the completely non-physical contact I had with my dad and Gabriel. But that involved taking initiative, and taking initiative required alcohol, because I wasn't going to make that happen sober. So, one time, I heard about this party near my house, and I went, by myself, and I made a beeline for the keg, and I slammed one beer, then another, and it was so fast and so cold, my eyes began to tear up, but it was okay—I wanted the results. I also wanted, needed, to be in control, and I surveyed the room looking for someone who was not too big, or too good-looking. I also didn't want anyone my age, or anyone who looked especially confident. I was seeking a young dude, willing and happy to be directed, a mathlete, or if it had to be an athlete, someone who sat the bench. At first, I didn't see anyone like that anywhere, but then I saw this boy I'd seen at school. A ninth grader. He played varsity basketball, and he had this soft looking skin and these striking blue eyes buried beneath this mop of blonde hair. I took him by the hand, and he shivered when we touched. I put my finger to my lips super-cool and led him through the crowd, up the stairs and into a bedroom. I lay down on the pile coats, and I pulled him on top of me, kissing his neck, his face, moving his hands to my breasts, what there was at least, and then between my legs, not letting him undo my pants. At first, he was fumbling, his elbows and knees clanging into me, but then there was some rhythm and heat from him moving and sliding. I closed my eyes. I rolled on top of him and started to feel warm. Soon I wasn't even in the room, I was floating above it, and away from it, and then I was back, flushed, drained, happy, and I pushed myself off the boy and got ready to leave. He looked at me desperate, wanting me, wanting more, so I leaned over, and start rubbing his hard-on, jerking him off through his jeans. There was a shudder, a small smile and complacence. Then I headed home."

"That's hot," John says, looking flushed himself. "Jesus, seriously, you did that. I'm stunned, I'm horny and I find it hard to believe you never did anything like that again."

"Yeah, no, the thing with you wasn't cool, and then there was Gabriel, and I don't think I quite realized it then, but he was safe, and I waited for it, him, to click for me."

"But no one, nothing—when he fucks around on you so much?" he says.

I guess everyone knows about that.

"Yeah," I say, sitting up, looking at him, "it isn't my thing, and Christa, you know."

Christa.

There it is.

The elephant in the room.

I roll over onto my back, and John does the same.

We both stare at the ceiling, no ripple, no great sex, instead just feeling lost and dirty, and not in a good way.

GABRIEL

Is there ever a time when we do not feel lost?

We are our memories, pain, and habits, and we're destined to wallow in and repeat them, unless we can become unstuck, and find a way out.

I'm trying to do that now, not drinking and taking care of myself. I suppose Hannah thinks she's taking care of herself and maybe she is—addressing something she feels she missed. I don't know, we're in different orbits right now, living different lives, and that's okay, we'll find our way back to each other, back to something. That's how it works.

One must have purpose as well though, and a focus on something bigger than oneself. Hannah doesn't have that, and she'll need to learn that for herself.

That's how it works.

I do have a purpose again—a renewed focus, and not just being sober, but a focus on Christa. I don't want to believe my focus on her ever wavered. It's just I know it did. There's my daily text, but that's been it, and I hate myself for that.

I also almost hate myself for using Ed as I've been. It seemed smart at first, but he's lost to this world and has no choice in serving as my magical vessel of goodness and unconditional listening. He always wanted to help though, and this helps, period, hard stop, and I want to believe he'll be okay with it.

"I'm thinking about Christa," I say, "and I'm thinking about purpose and how when I was drinking, I faltered, and I didn't do enough to bring her back. You tried to tell me, and I wouldn't listen, but I'm listening now, and I'm reminded of a memory I want to share with you. It's also a path forward; I'm sure of it. Anyway, Christa, Hannah, and I drove through Amish country when Christa was younger. We stopped at a tiny storefront museum called Train City, USA which advertised itself as possessing the largest model train set in the world. Hannah and I thought it was cool, but that was it, cool, nothing Earth shattering or life changing. But for Christa, it was akin to a pilgrimage—as if she'd travelled to Lourdes or the Western Wall. The whole ride home she talked about how she'd found a purpose. How she was going to build a model of our neighborhood. How she wanted to understand the details and minutiae of what makes things work. She got into this dialog with us, with herself, about how she needed to touch things for them to be real and this she could touch with both her hands and her brain at once. She spent the rest of the trip sketching out what it would look like, pages of ideas, specs, and measurements, the materials she would need. Watching her work on it was mesmerizing—moving—and I promised her we could work on it when we got home. But we didn't. I got busy with work or life or whatever stuff we get busy with, and Christa gathered the sketches, placed them in a file and put them on the bookshelf above her desk. She became a teenager. She left. She's missing. I'm not saying that's why she left, but it's not nothing. I started to think though, what if I could build the model for her— might it become a kind of beacon? I know it doesn't make sense. It's magical thinking, dream nonsense, but I found there was no returning to a world where I didn't do this.

"I went into her room a couple of days ago—I've stopped in there two to three times a week since I stopped drinking again to take in the quiet—and I was struck by how static it was. The room has gone untouched since she left, and it felt unnerving. This time I moved her bookshelf and desk into the spare room, and I began to build the model Christa envisioned. What's been so inspiring is that it's real, and it's tangible, and like Christa I realized the power of having something I can touch. I started by crafting a replica of the mountain behind our home from Styrofoam I bought at Ace Hardware. I shaped and molded it until it climbed toward the ceiling, and then I added paint, layer upon layer of browns, reds, and greens. I blended them together, followed by dirt, mud, grass, rocks, and twigs from the backyard. I built our home too. I got the color right. The dimensions. I furnished it. I bought two Jean Grey figurines to represent Hannah and Christa, their red hair afire, and I got a Wolverine figurine for myself. I know, I'm no Wolverine, but still.

"From there, I removed the sketches from the file they were in—their paper dry and wrinkled, yellowed at the edges, but legible. I reviewed her ideas for the rest of the neighborhood and I'm moving on to those next. After that, I don't know where it's going to go, not yet, but I'll figure it out. The important thing is I've found purpose again, and Christa is front and center, and whatever happens, happens.

"It would be great to have your help with this. It would've been great to have come to you more when you were here, but doing so made me feel weak, and I'm sorry for that and for the choices I made."

Ed doesn't respond.

I head home and get back to work.

HANNAH

The important thing is that my father is lying in bed. He's face up and staring at the ceiling. His breath is low and his skin gray, but for some pink that remains flushed across his cheeks. The rims of his eyes are red and teary. He's dying. He's been dying, but this is different. They say his organs are shutting down. He's stopped trying to live, and I assume this is a conscious decision. He's done doing this life, or at least doing it this way. I try to give him cold water from a pitcher, gently jabbing the straw at his wrinkled mouth, silently pleading with him to take a sip, but that isn't going to happen, and I know it isn't going to happen—he hasn't sipped anything in weeks. I'm doing this for me, and I know this, and I want it because I need something to remind me of what he's really like—not the empty vessel lying before me. I also need to control something, anything, because everything's out of control, and this is what we do when things are out of control—we grab onto whatever we can. I can't do anything for him though, not anymore. He's slipping away, right here in front of me, and he's not coming back. This is the end game and I'm so sad about it. I may stop breathing as well if I don't remind myself to keep doing so.

As I pull the straw away from his lips, I focus for a moment on how full they are, and unlike so little else I associate with him, how female they look. Those aren't my lips. My lips are thinner, with the kind of slight bulge on the upper lip that occurs when one squeezes a water balloon from both ends. I know mine are my mother's lips, or from her side of the family anyway. Not that there were many pictures of them. Even now I wonder which of my features are my mother's and which are my father's. The hair is hers—of course. The legs, long and tumbling forth from my short torso, could be hers, but are probably his. The eyes are his. The almond shape, the light brown color, including the way my left eyelid almost droops, but not quite, thank God. My neck, which is almost regal if you look at it from the right angle, is his as well. My hands are an odd mix. They're big, too big, neanderthal—that's him. Yet still lean, the fingers spindly, and hers. All of which is great for rolling joints.

I'm crying.

When did this happen?

It's so slight, I almost don't notice it, but it's getting stronger, and embarrassing, and for a moment I think, I can't let Christa see me like this. I can't look weak in front of her. My mother doesn't allow that and while it's one of many elements of her legacy I would rather not copy or model, I can't help myself.

I press my hands to my face and wipe away the tears.

"Let's take a break," I say, looking at Christa as if she's here, because I need that too: Christa home, with me, holding my hand.

I can't do this, or anything, without her.

In this moment, and in this fantasy, I text Christa again and again about my father, morning, afternoon, and night, not just before bed as I normally do, and she and Josh come home despite their desire not to—preferring to stay away and revel in their happiness.

Or maybe in my fantasy they come back because it's fear and embarrassment which has kept them away as long as it did. They aren't happy, they're scared, and angry, and this is the excuse they need to end the whole charade.

This isn't clear yet.

But it doesn't matter, Christa's here, she's good and I'm happy about it.

Christa and my father never quite had a relationship.

She found him creepy and sad.

I accepted it, and I didn't push her to make a connection with him despite her feelings.

Luckily, this is a fantasy, where none of that applies.

That said, I still can't mess this up.

I can't ask her too many questions.

I can't provoke her.

I can't be me.

"Is this what it looks like?" Christa asks.

"What," I say, looking at her beautiful skin, wanting to stroke it, but holding back.

"The end?"

"One version of it."

"What do you mean?"

I look at her again, Gabriel's cheekbones stare back at me, and my mother's big, searching eyes.

Uh.

"Nothing honey," I say. "That's sadness speaking."

"So, what, were you thinking of someone else?"

"My mother, maybe, I'm not sure, she didn't leave like this."

"She just left, right," Christa replies, grabbing my hand. "It must have been terrible."

I try to ignore the reality that my father's lying there before us and this is the kind of intimacy that emerges around the dying—the comfort of saying whatever you want, however you want, because you somehow decide they can't hear you anymore. But what if they can? Can we know what's going on with their brains, and their spirit, or what's being absorbed as they prepare for the journey towards what comes next? I don't believe in life after death. Death is death, we're here, and then we're not. We hope we live a good life, full of joy and love. We hope we make an impact, leaving some kind of legacy behind. Then we must let go, some sooner than others, but at some point, we must let go. There's no choice. My father deserves better than leaving like this. Maybe most of us do. But he really does. And so, what do I owe him now as he lies here? Should I be silent and reverent? I hope not. I want to keep talking.

"It was terrible when my mother left," I say to Christa, "but then it wasn't, time passed, and your grandfather was here, available, present. Then you came along, and everything was okay, or as okay as things can be."

"And dad?" Christa says.

Right, Gabriel, of course, where's my head.

"Yes, of course, dad, too—he was right here as well."

"But not always."

"No sweetie, not always."

With that Christa is gone.

I thought staying with Gabriel was a sign of strength, not being my mother, whatever. But Christa is gone, and who knows what she learned from me, or what anyone needs to make sense of anything.

There's movement behind me, a hand on my shoulder, and hot, sad breath on the back of neck. I don't have to look. I know who it is.

"I'm here," Gabriel says.

I reach back and cup the back of his head with my hand, and he lowers his forehead onto my shoulder and wraps his arms around my waist.

I allow myself to cry, and I do so long and hard, and until there are no more tears.

GABRIEL

There's a new normal.

Before the tears, the embrace, and my first contact with Hannah after who knows how long, I'm sitting in the back of Ed's room, watching Hannah mourn, and trying to make peace with something not peaceful.

But this, here, now, Ed's room—this isn't normal. There's fear and sadness, pulsing and alive, like a muscle, or an abscess. I'm never scared or sad when I drink. I don't feel much of anything, and I like it so much, but now, not drinking, I feel everything, which is wonderful when it involves something wonderful, or even something less than wonderful, and merely pleasurable, such as laughing at a television show. That's a gift, and something only not drinking allows to occur. Fear and sadness are tough though, and I've been unable to embrace the powerlessness that comes with those feelings. The crippling sense everything is cracked, I'm falling down a hole, and there's no escape.

I hate it.

Hannah needs me though, and she needs me not drinking. Though what she really needs is a hug, and a shoulder—not a hero or a drunk. Not someone who can fix things, nor someone who prefers to run away. She needs someone who can stand up, walk across a room, lean their forehead onto her back and wrap their arms around her waist, so she can cry and cry until there are no more tears.

So that's what I do.

For a moment we're something else, somewhere else, we're the old normal—the one where we walk home together, figure each other out, live in a world we've created where everything is new and fresh, and the possibilities remain unlimited.

I want to hold onto the possibility of this, but Hannah slips away from me, wipes the tears from her face with the back of her hands, straightens and stares at me for a moment. I'm transfixed. She's the girl from the ice-skating rink. She looks at me and she gets me. Then she reaches up and strokes my cheek with her hand.

My brain explodes.

I close my eyes and take in her touch.

When I open my eyes, she's gone, and I'm alone.

There's a new normal.

HANNAH

Gabriel's touch meant nothing to me, which should be distinguished from it having meaning. His coming to my father's room meant something. I needed it, and I loved him for it. But I didn't feel anything—no connection, no emotion, no desire. We're past that, or we are for now. And so even though there are funeral arrangements to make, and Tracey and I will need to drink way too much, I want to be touched, and I want to feel something. So, I call John, which is how I find myself transported from the hospital to a hotel room where we lie half-dressed, kissing, and about to do something I really need to do.

"Hey," John says, pulling away, "do you have any more stories? You must have something for me."

I really don't want to talk. Talking is not why I'm here. I also don't want to tell him stories about my sad life. That's not what this is about.

"No, I don't think so—not now," I say, reaching for his neck, wanting to pull him closer.

Talking didn't end well last time we were together. How can't he care about that? Even Gabriel would have the sense to remember how things went down when we were previously together and do anything not to repeat it.

"C'mon, baby, nothing? Your stories are hot," he says.

He's filled with longing and desire, and that could be attractive, but it's not. He's killing what's left of why this means anything to me and now, with this, he's not very appealing and may never be again. He could be anyone now, and this isn't John's fault. He is who is and has been, but I'm not sure I can ever look at him again.

I roll over on my back and pull the sheet up to my chin, I don't want to be more exposed than I've been or am about to be.

"Okay, you want a story, fine, here's one I haven't thought about in ages," I say.

"Now we're talking," he says, getting up on one elbow, his desperate sex vibe blasting across the bed.

"I went to the Y. It wasn't my idea. Why would I go to the Y? My dad had suggested it, because why not? It was cold outside, and there was a pool inside. It was a goof. And I could survive a free swim when there was quite literally nothing else to do. I walked into the locker room, and there were children screaming and running around, haggard-looking moms, wet towels and steam, everything oozing slime, the noxious scent of chlorine permeating every corner. All I could think was—don't go anywhere barefoot, don't sit, don't touch anything. It was a cesspool of crud and nastiness. I eased out of my clothes, and I tried not to look at my thirteen-year-old body in the mirror. I didn't have hips or breasts. I hated it, and I moved as quickly through the locker room as I possibly could. As I ran out of the locker room, and into the quiet hall leading to the pool, this man stepped out of the men's locker room across from me. He was older, saggy, his chin dropping to his chest, his breasts bigger than mine—twisted outward and conical. He was short too, shorter than me, and holding a towel at his waist. I'd never seen him before, but I knew he was a creep, and I averted my eyes away from his terribly purple nipples, his wiry shoulder hair, and his runny eyes. 'Hello,' he said, as he stepped in front of me, his maw agape and rapacious, his incisors sharp, threatening. Or maybe they weren't, maybe I was just imagining how scary he seemed. The hall was so narrow and poorly lit, quiet, empty, and

I was wishing my dad might inexplicably be around to deal with this for me. 'You're Hannah, aren't you?' he said gleefully. 'Your mother went to a summer camp I worked at a long time ago. She was beautiful, her hair was fire, and you look just like her.' His eyes got dreamy as he shared this. I didn't know what I could trust as true. Nor did I understand how he was suddenly standing so close to me. He was, right? He dropped his hand from his waist while thrusting it forward, forcing me to shake hands with him, and as he did his towel shifted. He was wearing an ill-fitting, navy-blue Speedo, his penis pulled out to the side, gray and shriveled, an alien worm, nearly translucent—the blue veins elevated and throbbing. At first, I couldn't tear my eyes away from it, but when I could, I pushed past him, and as I did, I felt his hands brush my ass, his touch deposited there like a burn. I dove into the pool and stayed underwater so long the lifeguard had to jump in to check on me."

I look at John. His eyes are glistening, and he's smiling.

"You happy?" I ask.

"Uh, yeah…so you want to fuck now or what?" he asks, leaning towards me.

It kills me how much I misread him.

Though I suppose I didn't.

It's not his fault.

GABRIEL

How might we assign fault?

I'm thinking about this as my mother and I go for our walk. Ed's funeral has come to pass, and now amazingly, the world goes on like nothing happened. People are going to work and posting family photos to Facebook, the Starbucks are open, and the Earth is rotating just as it was before Ed died.

Whose fault is that?

No one's, I guess. It's what life is, ever moving forward, and not susceptible to the needs or wants of any person.

But what about the personal? How might we assign fault in our own relationships? And maybe more specifically, how might I do so? Moving forward means seeking self-awareness, owning one's mistakes, making amends. I can't escape that, and I don't want to.

For example, I could've been a better son-in-law to Ed. I loved him and respected him. I wished him only happiness. But was I there for him, present, available? I'm not sure that was my job, nor would he be alive now regardless, but could I have been a more perfected version of myself for him? I could've, and that haunts me. Christa? Yes, no question, again, it's also about being present—too much, too little—Hannah and I may never know what was needed with Christa, because that too is how the world works. Hannah is easier. I wasn't present, and I certainly wasn't perfect. It may yet prove to be something we can fix, but not now, and not yet. My father, and I'm thinking about him, a lot. How can't I? Unlike Ed, he's alive, but we're not going to be more than we are, two people who say hello, and why this is, isn't something I'm supposed to understand. I'm just supposed to accept it. What about my mother? She was always present for me, and somewhat perfected, yet I never created a space for her and Christa. I felt guilty about Christa feeling wigged out by Ed, and I didn't do what I should have felt obligated to do. It's so complicated, but the relationship with my mother is also the relationship I'm doing best in, even if the bar is so low with every other relationship, it doesn't take much.

My mother passes me the joint.

She's going to live, and I have a chance with her for things to end well, healthy, if not happy, and as she would say, happiness is a lot to ask for when content should suffice.

I think about what I put Hannah through over the years, and I wonder if it was similar for my mother. My father drank for so long and wasn't home so often. I didn't know what he was up to, and I never tried to figure it out. I never saw her cry or whisper furtively into the phone to her friends though about things that must've involved my father. There were nights when he wasn't there, when we would stay up late watching television, eating ice cream, laughing, but we didn't talk. My mom just didn't do that. But she was there, and she was strong, always. She was also patient, and consistent and I admired it—even as a kid. It couldn't have been easy. None of it is.

"Thanks, mom," I say, finally taking a long drag on the joint and passing it back to her.

"For what?" she says.

This is not her kind of thing, whatever it's going to be.

"For being present," I say. "It couldn't have been easy, and you wouldn't have been at fault for not being available to me. But you were."

"Do you know the story of Medea?" she asks, seemingly apropos of nothing.

"The Greek myth," I reply. "She killed her kids or some such nonsense, right?"

"Yes, 'she killed her kids or some such nonsense,'" she says, rolling her eyes. "Medea's husband abandons her, and she kills their children as an act of revenge."

"I'm not sure I knew that part of the story. That's kind of messed up."

"It is '*kind of messed up*' as you so eloquently put it, but she's been abandoned, and while it's revenge for that—it's more as well. Medea needs her husband to notice her, pay attention, and she knows it's the only way she can get him to do so."

"Okay, why are we talking about this?"

"It's just, one wonders what it would be like to kill one's child at times. Back then, back when your father was drinking and not home, wasn't paying attention to me, and you were still little, I thought about that. Killing you. Not actually doing so, but…it's not like he ever wanted to be a father—sorry, you must realize that by now. Later after he was done drinking, he was present—your words, about me—it's just when he wasn't, when you were a child, I thought about how he would have to pay attention to me after he came home to find I'd murdered you."

She takes another drag from the joint and looks at me.

She says this like it's a matter of fact, which it is for her. For her, everything is a matter of fact.

"How does knowing that make you feel?" she asks.

How does it make me feel? That my father never wanted to be a father? I guess I know that. Not that I know what to do with the realization in this moment. But her wanting to kill me? I get it. I know what it's like to not be heard or seen, though more importantly, I know what it's like to not hear or see the person right in front of you. To be so wholly absorbed in your own ridiculousness the person in front of you might think they need to do something drastic to get any kind of reaction.

So, I get it, I really do, and after I get the joint back, I tell her so.

HANNAH

How does my affair with John make me feel? It began as a blur of sex and bong hits and late nights and early mornings, sore body parts, thighs, lower back, triceps, my jaw, raw skin, emotions, orgasms, twisted sheets and back seats and hotels and empty offices. I was enthralled with the act, if not actually with him. John was a vehicle, a launching pad—a source of revenge and cum. He's not Gabriel, or married life, or being the mom of a missing kid.

Also, and this is important, being with him was never about feeling crazy like I did for so long with Gabriel.

I knew he was cheating on me—hooking up with other people in bars and parks and alleys, my house, skuzzy motels—and yet he could still look me in the eye and deny it, causing me to pause every time and ask myself if this was the time he was telling the truth in his measured tones and his pleading eyes—stroking my arm and standing there taking my verbal assaults and my resolute desire to just know the truth. Which he would calmly insist I knew, because there was nothing not to know, and I was so wrong for thinking otherwise. Did he ever call me crazy? Not in so many words, that would have been disruptive, visceral, twisting things in directions he didn't want my head to go—logical places born of his incessant redirection, obfuscations, and otherwise stupefying explanations about where he might have been versus where I was sure he was or where

I might have seen him. But had I seen him? Gabriel would look at me bewildered. How could I think he'd been doing any of those things in any of those places? That wasn't his car, or even his face. I was confused, it happens, work and Christa, and history—he understood. It's just I was wrong—he would remind me he'd learned his lesson. He couldn't bear to hurt me anymore, or lie to me, and he hadn't—he swore to it. But he did lie to me, and he didn't, which is to say he was always lying—that's how it works. It's beyond lying. It's a completely fabricated alternate truth. So, did he ever call me crazy? No, not literally. He just made me feel crazy, like I didn't know anything about anything, and couldn't judge what I thought I knew, or who I was, any of it. It wasn't real. I wasn't real, not the I, I knew, the one I had lived with—the one I could trust, the caretaker and mother, and responsible employee. I couldn't be trusted by *me*; I couldn't trust myself. Because that's how it works too.

Does it matter that Gabriel is done with it again, or this time it was brief, and I don't really care? Only in that I get to feel like I'm crazy a lot less often and I don't have to expend energy on the insanity that comes with it: looking through his pockets, checking his phone, leaving work to see where he is, playing detective, reduced to being a stalker, not a wife. But does that mean I'm not crazy? I'm not so sure. In exacting my revenge on him and taking my turn, I have become at least briefly wedded to my desire to have sex—to chase it, get it, live, and breathe it, and cum as often as I'm able. And this does leave me a little unhinged, punch-drunk anyway. I'm woozy from thinking about it. Quite literally drained from the experience of it.

At first, I didn't want to stop. I couldn't stop thinking about it, and how available it was to me—how and when I wanted it. I had hit a sex lottery. But I always knew it wasn't a real thing. It wasn't a relationship. It was a reclamation project. I also knew this feeling was based as much on the idea of it as the actual act itself. I wasn't myself. I wasn't respecting the rules, or marriage, or the thin veneer that separates adults from teenagers, and so of course, it was going to be amazing, until it wasn't. I honestly believed I understood that. That I was tracking it, and it would change. It would have to change. Stop. John would suddenly not look right or smell right. I wouldn't feel clean one day. Or be able to get clean. Maybe I wouldn't be able to achieve an orgasm. Doubt would enter my mind. There would be awkward elbows and banging teeth. Maybe we would just stop to talk about something, and I would be, like, *what am I thinking?*

And so there is this moment, or moments, where I stretch whatever, it is beyond anything I want it to be. John becomes nothing more than masturbation, and I don't need John or any dude for that. So, is it any one thing? Or is it everything? A series of conversations that suck. Sex that is suddenly so less than. Or is it just a complete lack of interest in doing whatever it takes to do this. I don't really know. I just know I'm done and I'm going back to my normal life.

GABRIEL

SOMETIMES MY NORMAL LIFE goes like this.

"What's up, motherfucker," Officer John slurs.

And other times like this.

"Take me as I am, unless you're still too much of pussy," Alyssa says.

Though before that, let me back up for a moment.

To remind myself how I'm seeking a newfound sense of balance, truth, and sobriety I go to Neary's. I order a sandwich and a drink, a glass of seltzer, and I sit there. I let the atmosphere and associations wash over me in little, jagged waves. There are the smells—the stale beer reek circulating throughout the room, the flop sweat and perfume, the ever-lingering burn from cigarette smoke—the way it infiltrates every open space and article of clothing it can cling onto. There are also the sounds, the clink and clatter of glasses mashing into one another, the laughter and cheer, low murmurings, whispered conversations—conspiratorial and hushed, cell phone rings and text pings, the beeps, and whistles from the corroded Pac-Man machine, the bump and *thw-a-a-a-ack* of the cue ball completing its journey. There is the feel of it—the gummy touch of the faux-wood table, the condensation sliding off the glass and pooling below, the bodies passing through space before me, all that skin, glowing and alive, moving, breathing, occasionally making contact, a bump and pulsation, and bouncing off one another before ricocheting in new directions, onto new contacts. There is the way the glass molds itself to my hand—how it's meant to be there, fulfilling its destiny, solid and brushing my lips like a tender kiss—before the burn hits my tongue, throat, stomach, and head, and I explode into the universe, reborn again and again and again.

I remember it all.

I also feel it in my skin, which still crawls with excitement and anticipation at the mere thought of it, but now, I practice sitting with the feeling and condition myself to not want any of it anymore. Not the drink, or the smells, the explosions, or sex—feeling nothing, being nothing. Instead, I focus on being a body in the world, a shell, gliding from one moment to the next, muscle and skin and bones, requiring only the bare minimum: Hannah in my life, whatever that takes, and Christa, somehow, again. It's about balance, about nothing being over stimulating, and not requiring the slippery slope of pleasure or arousal. I'm an Aesthete. An appreciator of beauty for the mere sake of it. There'll be nothing more, even if there'll always be more. I'm this, settled, here, now, testing myself by not testing myself. This is a generally uneventful experiment, it's about regulation—and I'm good, I'm good, I'm good.

I'm also in my spot, near the back of the bar, taking in the energy, the skin, the smells, and touch, and more than good, I'm focused, centered, and being perfected.

"Waddup, motherfucker?" Officer John says, his speech slurred.

Ah, man.

"Not much Officer John. What's up with you?"

Officer John looks like hell, gaunt, strung out, wasted. I try not to picture him on top of Hannah. That was a thing, her thing, she had to take care of herself, and it's none of my business. I also know it doesn't have anything to do with Christa—the elephant in the room. Officer John knows nothing about her or Josh, and he isn't going to figure anything out. It's my job now. Still, I can be cool if he needs me to be.

"I'm not going to ask for your forgiveness," Officer John says, thudding into the chair across me. "That's not my thing,"

"It's cool," I say. "Seriously, we're good here."

"You fuck a man's wife, and he says, 'it's cool.' What's wrong with you?" Officer John says, slamming his hand onto the table, my drink rattling, the pool of condensation below it, spraying my shirt.

Officer John wants a forgiveness that's not required, but why not grant it and be done with it?

"You're forgiven, brother," I say.

"Fuck you, man," Officer John replies, leaping up and on the verge of tears. "Aren't you going to hit me or something?"

I stand up and I walk around the table towards him. He steps back, and I keep walking, hands up, and then as I lean in, he flinches, and I hug him.

Officer John starts to cry, first small sobs, then bigger, fatter tears that wet my shirt.

"I miss her," he says.

"Me too, and I'm sorry about that," I tell him, and this is the truth—possibly the greatest truth I'll say all day.

I'm still in my spot, nursing my seltzer, the late afternoon light slicing through the window, the slight tang of Officer John's scent lingering on my shirt and cheek. I need to leave, and not because I have anywhere to be, though I should pretend I do, but because while I'm lingering, and enjoying just one more moment of silence, and the kind of peace I could always find in a bar, there are things to do—Christa things.

"Take me as I am, unless you're still too much of pussy," Alyssa says.

This isn't the first thing she says to me, but it's where we are now.

Alyssa's home. There's no big city job, no grand evenings and small apartments, messed-up relationships with shallow jerk-off dudes who want her to be younger, more innocent, and into sports or finance or whatever, while still willing to engage in anal sex and make them breakfast in the morning. I know this because she lets me know it in a torrent as she quaffs a series of vodka gimlets, possibly the first ever ones made in Neary's. She's home because her father has cancer, and like her mother before him, there's no cure. He's going to die soon, and there's no one else to be there for him. That's the amazing thing about this age, we're forced to watch our parents deteriorate, piece by piece, and we get to decide if we're going to be the ones who care for them. For Hannah, it was technically an easy choice, even if the time was brief, and she faltered along the way. I haven't really had to make any such decisions yet. My mother follows her own path, and I'm happy to follow her. As for my father, we'll see how that goes.

For Alyssa, it's something else. Her father wasn't kind. He was filled with anger and frustration. There was a need for perfection and success from his children he couldn't achieve. Instead, he sat on the couch at night drinking his vodka gimlets and nursed endless grievances that slowly calcified into a roiling mass of hate, which resulted in everyone moving through the house knowing that every affront he suffered at their hands—an uncapped tube of toothpaste or wasted food—might lead to an explosion. Alyssa's certain her mother's death from cancer was the result of the toxic environment she, her long-damaged brother and mother had to endure living under the same roof with him. But Alyssa came home—despite this—she decided to care for her father. Her brother wouldn't, couldn't, and as she said when she first sat down, she's the "hero-child." That being a phrase she learned during a brief stint in therapy she abandoned after hearing the phrase "emotionally absent" one too many times.

Do I feel empathy for her now that I know about her terrible childhood and understand Alyssa is relegated to a life of striving at all costs as a means for somehow connecting with her father's own unfulfilled dreams? That the alcohol and the distance, the fear of explosions and violence—things I've tried to combat for the sake of Hannah and Christa—are her experiences as well? And that she won't achieve any true closure—a phrase I assume her therapist must have used at some point—because she won't be willing to embrace it?

I do.

I feel sick for her in the way that being exposed to her toxicity is upsetting to me now. We all want to feel good, it's selfish, but it's human and real. In our more selfless moments, we hope others can feel good too, and when we can, we want to help. And so it is that I sit here, and I embrace Alyssa's angry, crackling energy, and seek to absorb it and draw it away from her—an attempt to offer a moment's respite.

One might ask if this isn't selfish too, some kind of God complex? The attempt to sit here and consume the world's pain, merely an effort to pretend it's a test of myself and my fissures, when it's truly an exercise in feeling superior as I deign to hug the bedraggled screwer of wives and absorb the drunken spew from the hater of fathers from atop my Aesthete's throne? Of course, it is. I'm flawed and needy and seeking validation from somewhere with my life on hold.

I know this and I try to embrace that too.

"Take me as I am, unless you're still too much of pussy," Alyssa says.

That offer, however, is one I'm not ready for, nor interested in. Alyssa wants to feel something, anything, and she thinks I can help. The old drunken me would have accepted the challenge. I might've even felt an obligation. I can't anymore. It can't be that way.

"I'm too much of pussy," I say, thinking she'll feel better if I defile myself.

This is the second great truth of the day.

"That I already knew," she says.

Alyssa walks away in disgust, and I'm left alone, needing to get home, and wondering how a day like this happens, repetition patterns and tests, reminders of who we are, and how the universe works. It happens when we're centered, and we accept we're part of something larger. This is my job now, being present, well, that and caring for Hannah, and if lucky, Christa, if, when, needed— no bitterness, no anger, no nothing.

HANNAH

I haven't been present, and I'm not sure I've cared about anyone but myself lately. In relation to Gabriel, I'm fine with that, my father, not so much, and Christa, I'd rather not even speculate. Which is also to say, in terms of Gabriel, I have no idea what he's been up to, and it's fine, I never wanted to be his keeper, and I've been happy not to be.

When Gabriel asks me to come up to Christa's room with him, I honestly don't know what to say, I'm not even sure I remember the last time we spoke.

I'm also not sure what to expect.

So, when he opens the door to her room, let's me walk in before him, and turns on the light, I'm both stunned, and taken aback. I've been clueless about his activities, but this, what's facing me—all it does is cause me worry.

Still, I force myself to smile a little smile, and walk over to the massive platform laid out across Christa's room, touching the trees, looking at the details of the neighborhood, the mountain behind our house, which seems to go on forever as it climbs towards the ceiling, the house itself, our street, the streets it connects to, my eyes darting to and fro, absorbing it, moving around, leaning in, before looking back to our house again, and lingering there, taking in the great attention paid to every brick and shingle, including the room we're in at this very moment, and the small figurine standing at the bedroom window, which, with her dazzling red hair could be me, or my mother, but it's Christa. It must be—right?

I don't know what Gabriel expects from me, or even what this is exactly, but it's moving, and devastating, and what else can I say or do, but say and do what's expected of me.

"Wow, this is awesome," I say, because that seems most supportive, and because it's true, even if it's weird, obsessive, and upsetting.

"Really? Cool," he says. "It needs a lot of work. Do you want to help me finish it?"

"Are you serious...?" I start to say, and at first, I'm not sure where I'm going with this. He's obviously serious. Instead, I finish my sentence with, "...I know you are, and yes, anything."

Gabriel looks relieved and for a moment, I think he's going to faint.

"Do you want to see the best part?" he asks.

"There's more?"

I know it's possible, likely, that I sound like I'm mocking him, but he can choose to ignore this if he wants.

"Yeah, there is, go lie in Christa's bed and close your eyes."

"Some people will do anything to get a girl in bed, won't they?" I say, caught up in the moment as I lie down on top of the bed, propping myself up on my elbows and patting the space next to me.

At this point, Gabriel zones out, reminding me of me.

"Hey man, are you coming over here or what?" I ask.

That doesn't seem to be enough of a prompt. He's not moving, instead he's sort of smiling, sort of lost in something.

"What's up? Do you think I'm going to bite you?"

That seems to work.

"Right, sorry," he says, climbing into bed next to me. "Close your eyes, please."

Gabriel kills the lights and leans over to turn on the rotating lamp positioned next to the platform. As I shut my eyes, I'm amazed at how far apart two people can be on a bed so very small. It could be miles. A Grand Canyon worth of space, and a chasm not to be crossed on this day—if ever again.

"Okay," he says, "now, slowly open your eyes."

I'm engulfed by a universe, illuminated and beautiful, as it rotates across the walls, the ceiling, and both of us. Gabriel has cut out a galaxy's worth of constellations, planets and shooting stars into the lampshade, creating a universe of our own, and as we lie there taking in the endless space, right there, just beyond our reach, I start to cry.

"What?" he says, and what else can one say at a time such as this.

"It's beautiful," I say, abruptly intertwining my fingers in his, mini explosions going off in my brain as I slowly melt into myself. "Why?"

He breathes in, and out, and then wiping away tears of his own, he starts to talk.

"I thought about how much I've failed you and Christa, but how there've been good times as well, and love, and I also thought about that time we went and saw that train set in Amish country, and how mesmerized Christa was, and how much we felt like a family that day, and how much she wanted to build something like this, but I let her down, and I thought, why can't I build something like that now. Maybe it could be a beacon or something, or a map of some kind for Christa to find her way home. Maybe she's just lost. We all get lost, but if this spoke to her, beckoned her, maybe she would come back. Who knows what that would mean, but I want to believe it could happen, and we can connect with things so much bigger than us—with powers we can't conceive and access to the stars and beyond. And if it's even somewhat possible, it must be worth it, right?"

All I can think of is there's hope and there's nothing, and if you can't try to embrace hope, what's the point of anything?

"Right, okay," I try to say in a convincing fashion. "Of course, that's possible, and if you need my help to finish it, okay, happy too. Let's go."

With that, I hug him as hard as I can. He hugs me back, and before we get started, we both lie there, under the stars, where anything does seem possible.

GABRIEL

"SOME PEOPLE WILL DO anything to get a girl in bed, won't they?" Hannah says, lying down on top of Christa's bed, propping herself up on her elbows and patting the space next to her.

I'm not really paying attention to her. I'm stuck on the idea that anything is possible, or at least, we must believe it is so.

I believe it, and I'm reminded again of how beautiful Hannah is as she lies there in Christa's bed, and how I may never be able to love anyone else, ever, regardless of whether she and I ever truly find some way back together or not.

I pause.

I picture kissing her, and there's a charge in doing so, electric, a spark of some kind, static rippling across my lips, and shooting into my brain and down my spine, briefly paralyzing me, my arms going numb, equilibrium lost, we're bonded together now and forever—and I find myself briefly transported to an alternative version of us where things didn't get so broken, and we're not so damaged, and how the kiss takes place in alternate past, one that leads to dates at the drive-in and late nights at Denny's, holding hands as we walk across bridges in the mist, attend formals, where I wear my Converse high-tops because I'm certain doing so is cool, and Hannah lets it go because it's cute, we're cute, and everything is wonderful and as it should be; and at some undetermined, and somewhat inexplicable, point, there is sex, though despite how often I think about it, with Hannah, and Nastassja Kinski, Paulina Porizkova and Farrah Fawcett too, sometimes all at the same time, it's somewhat impossible to imagine what it would be like—where it would happen, and how it could possibly come to transpire in the first place, but it does somehow, and it's weird and wet and desperate and sweaty and not without confusion and awkward pauses, the finding and losing and finding again of rhythm, but by then, it's not just about sex, but the building of something, the two of us, picking colleges together, or at least, colleges close enough where we can see one another on the weekends and occasionally during the week, sneaking around, drinking coffee and smoking cigarettes, drinking Miller Lite ponies, hanging out in the library, and having sex on our dorm room floors, our beds, the bathroom, wherever, however; and maybe we go abroad together, living in London or Barcelona, places I've only read about, walking the streets, imbibing on the history, their smell and taste, and then backpacking through Europe, sometimes not showering for days as we move from one train to the next and town to town, getting high, eating on the cheap, on the move, young and free, and maybe one or both of us kisses other people at some point, wondering if this is right, feeling scared we have committed to something so powerful too soon, but that only makes us want to commit more, there's no one else for either of us, so there's that, and that's done; and then there's work, maybe back home, though it could be anywhere— why not? I'm going to become an engineer, and somehow work on rocket ships and Hannah, will, can be, anything, a scientist too, but maybe an interior designer, or something in advertising, an artist, work that's creative and inspires her; and there'll be a small house, and a dog, Roy, and children at some point, yes in this version there are two children, a boy and a girl. He'll be named Bart, and she'll be Christa—she would have existed in any world— and everything feels right. They'll play Little League or dance, or both, and we'll read comic books and go on family trips, driving for days to visit obscure oddities such as Nebraska's biggest ball of twine or castles made of chocolate; and Bart and Christa will grow up to be smart and good, they'll have their struggles, Bart will blow out his knee playing high school football and watch his scholarship opportunities evaporate, but then find photography during his recovery, skip college entirely, and follow his talents around the world, never quite settling down, or finding love, which makes us nervous for him, but he'll be adventurous and happy, and productive and at peace; and Christa will get to college and struggle with binge-drinking, and she'll have to come home for a semester when her grades are so low she isn't welcomed back, but she too will find some direction, and like me, find her way into engineering at the local community college, and then build on that, college and graduate school, living in some big city, getting married, and becoming so successful building and designing amazing things that her husband—or wife—cares for their children as they build a life; and every so often, everyone is home at the same time, and there's such joy and grandchildren too, and I don't drink or mess around, and never did—it never felt necessary or wanted, and Hannah and I are cool, and this despite Hannah's cancer scares, and the car accident that leaves me wary to drive, the knee replacements, and the grind that accompanies the love that is marriage, the times I do not, cannot, will not talk, because why, I don't even always know, I just don't, or we'll go to bed mad, because people do, they have to; and there'll be anger over money, and arguments about parenting, because yes, we should be on the same page, but we're not always. Still, we keep going and going, writing wills, and buying burial plots, Hannah's flaming hair turned grey, and mine well gone; all the while living a life, not as grand as I may have dreamed about, but not this one either. Most important, we're together, which is a lot, and which is the point, and all I really could have ever wanted with her; and then I pass in the night, peacefully, in my sleep, my heart done doing the work, and Hannah goes just a little longer, living with Christa, and then passing herself, the cancer coming back, but so near the end and so absolutely complete in its invasion that it's quick and painless, thankfully; and so there the two of us are, dust and particles and one with the universe, but together, in space, stars forming our own constellation, Hannah and I, and I and Hannah, because that's what we are, and where we are, everywhere and nowhere, the universe continuing to evolve and grind itself, ever-forward, day by day and inch by inch, now and forever.

"Hey man, are you coming over here or what?" Hannah asks, snapping me out of my reverie.

I smile, but I can't quite move yet, I don't want to lose the feeling of what that parallel path might've looked like, what we could've been and still might be—different decisions, different opportunities, more attention to our needs—and all the possibilities contained therein.

"What's up?" she says. "Do you think I'm going to bite you?"

That works, and the moment passes, because this is now, and this is this story, and we need to live it, and see it through to the end.

"Right, sorry," I say, climbing into bed next to her. "Close your eyes please."

I kill the lights and lean over to turn on the rotating lamp positioned next to the platform, as Hannah closes her eyes.

"Okay," I say, "now, slowly open your eyes."

When she opens her eyes, she's engulfed by a universe, illuminated and beautiful, as it rotates across the walls, the ceiling, and both of us. I've cut out a galaxy's worth of constellations, planets and shooting stars into the lampshade, creating a universe of our own, and as we lie there for a moment, taking it in, the endless space, right there, just beyond our reach, I start to cry.

"What?" Hannah says.

"I want to feel hopeful."

"Then do so."

"Okay."

After that, we get to work.

HANNAH

We get to work, that's what people do. They find a way to come together, to create understanding, to make peace.

And so it is, that as night becomes morning, I think about Christa and the day she left six months ago. There didn't have to be a fight. Or more accurately it didn't have to go so far. I could've chosen to tune out her nonsense. I could've chosen to ignore her eyeroll. I could've chosen to talk less, much less, way less. I could in fact have not said anything about anything, because it's all so ephemeral and stupid in the grand scheme of things.

I know that now, I knew it as soon as it happened.

I just couldn't know it when I needed to know it.

It doesn't work like that, knowing, not always anyway—and not when we most need it to.

And so, it also is, at some point, Gabriel and I are done with Christa's beacon, and we go downstairs, and we make coffee, and we stare at each other, tired, and red-eyed, cups in hand, unspeaking, and as we do this, Christa walks in, and what are we supposed to say?

Her beautiful face is gaunt, hollow.

She's taller and lankier.

Her red hair is long and tangled.

Her clothes are dirty, creased by the miles and her smell is ripe—too much outdoors, not enough soap.

She's older now too and weary.

It takes everything I have not to disintegrate in front of her, here and gone, smoke.

Christa pours herself a cup of coffee, hugs us both, smiles her big smile, and goes off to take a shower and sleep—no explanations, or apologies.

For a moment, everything breaks inside of Gabriel and me, planets collide and realign, space folds into itself, new universes are born, and they die, only to be born again, but then it comes back together, and we fall to the floor, hugging and breathlessly awaiting the next chapter.

ACKNOWLEDGEMENTS

There is no *The Missing* without those who brought me into the world, my mother and father, Judy and Mike Tanzer, long my greatest supporters and inspirations.

I couldn't do what I do, and how I want to do it without the fierce love my wife Debbie has blessed me with, nor the expansive and sometimes fraught range of emotions I didn't know I had access to until the boys, my boys, Myles and Noah came into my life.

The Missing is what it is because I'm lucky enough to know Joanna Topor MacKenzie and Leland Cheuk, and have endlessly benefited from their vision, as well as all the literary and editing superlatives I can muster.

I also want to thank my blurbers Giano Cromley, Leesa Cross-Smith, Christine Sneed, and Chris L. Terry, the most gorgeous of humans, both in terms of their wordplay and stunning looks.

Finally, it's been a number of years since my last work came out and I want to thank the countless friends I've talked to and hung with during that time—you've kept me focused, sane, and hustling. I hope you know who you are, though if there's any confusion, I'll be sure to let you know—post-haste.

ABOUT THE AUTHOR

Ben Tanzer's acclaimed work includes the short story collection *Upstate*, the science fiction novel *Orphans* and the essay collections *Lost in Space* and *Be Cool*. He's a *storySouth* and Pushcart nominee; a finalist for the Annual National Indie Excellence and Eric Hoffer Book Awards; a winner of the Devil's Kitchen Literary Festival Nonfiction Prose Award and a Midwest Book Award; has received an Honorable Mention at the Chicago Writers Association Book Awards, Traditional Non-Fiction and a Bronze Medal from the Independent Publisher Book Awards. Ben has also written for *Hemispheres*, *Punk Planet*, *Clamor*, *Men's Health* and *The Arrow from AARP*. He lives in Chicago with his family.

7.1BOOKS